Dead Crude

Danny Verity, PI #2

Chris Blackwater

Catisfield Books

ISBN (paperback): 978-1-7393050-2-4
ISBN (ePUB): 978-1-7393050-3-1

A CIP catalogue record for this book is available from the British Library.

Chris Blackwater | www.chrisblackwater.co.uk

May 2024

Cover design by Caroline C Cole | www.citystonepublishing.com

To my parents, who instilled in me a lifelong love of reading

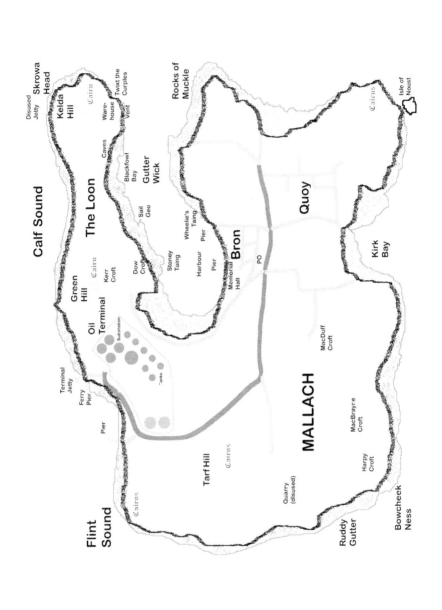

Crude oil from offshore installations is often "spiked" with natural gas to allow it to be pumped ashore. This is known as live crude. Lighter gasses are removed at the oil terminal to produce a thick, viscous dead crude for storage and transportation.

DISMEMBERING A CARCASS WAS backbreaking work. And yet, the killing itself was surprisingly easy. A bolt to the head. A sharp knife to the throat. Quick and painless.

This butchery business was in her blood. Her father used to slaughter all his own livestock. Nancy had helped him since she was a bairn. Now it all went to the abattoir in Kirkwall. Progress had made her weak.

This was a different kind of slaughter. Unplanned and unprepared. There weren't even any proper tools in the barn. A stun gun, a rusty saw, and her bloody shearing knife. Her father's old hatchet was hanging in the kitchen, tarnished now, but still razor-sharp. She considered going back, but dawn was nigh. Her neighbours would wake soon for the morning milking. They were not the sort to ask questions, but they would be curious. And curiosity kills.

More hacking and chopping. At least it kept the black thoughts at bay. The fear of being found out. Overwhelming, sickening waves of guilt. Such senseless emotions. She had no reason for remorse. This was justified. Righteous, even.

There were more pressing matters. Disassembly and disposal. Plenty of hiding places on the island, but things never stayed hidden for long. Soon enough, someone would come looking. Detectives with drones and sniffer dogs and fingertip searches.

What if there was nothing to find? Maybe there was a way. A story her grandpa had told her. About an old crofter who keeled over while working

1

on his land. His whole body consumed. Just the thought of it made her stomach heave.

A faint glow seeped through the solitary skylight. Daybreak. Muffled squeals from the barn. Hungry mouths to feed. Back to the butchery, then. Needs must when the devil drives.

Chapter One

DANNY HAD FORGOTTEN HOW much he hated Aberdeen. The flight up from Leeds was almost as bad as the last storm-tossed trip. In desperate need of a beer, he dropped off his bags at the soulless airport hotel and took a bus into town.

On a rare bright and sunny day, the city was lovely to behold. All that gleaming granite and fresh sea air. Today, the dreary grey buildings merged with grey stone paving and a steady drizzle from grey skies washed any remaining colour from the scene.

He'd arranged to meet Gemma Gauld, his onetime colleague, at Riggers Bar on Union Street. Danny headed inside and sat by a half-open window, sipping a tepid pint of IPA. The table was tacky with last night's beer slops. The reek of stale cigarette smoke drifted in from the overflowing ashtrays in the alleyway outside. There had to be better pubs in Aberdeen. He was wondering if Gemma wanted to keep their get-together as short as possible.

To pass the time, he took out his new private investigator's licence and stared at it lovingly. It was only a piece of plastic the size of a credit card, and the ID photo made him look more like a convicted criminal than a detective.

For someone with Danny's experience, basic training had been a doddle. A few new regulations and acronyms to remember. The rest was meat and drink to a former military policeman. His previous jobs paid better, but they lacked the romance of being a private eye. He was looking forward to telling Gemma all about it.

It took him a while to realise that she was standing right behind him, shaking her mousy mane in disbelief. She leaned over and examined the card. The face she pulled suggested she was less than impressed.

'Daniel Verity, Private Investigator? Ah wouldnae give you a job looking for ma lost sock, yer wee chancer.'

'Thanks for the vote of confidence, Gem. Nice to see you too.'

'I'm sure it is. I hope yer didn't come all this way hoping for a quickie, cos you're out of luck, Danny-boy. I'm no that desperate.'

He and Gemma had only spent a fortnight together on the Cuillin Alpha oil platform and barely spoken since. Despite that, he thought he knew her better than some of his lifelong friends. They had history. They'd survived sabotage and attempted murder. The events that brought them together were far from pleasant, but he was still looking forward to the reunion. He wasn't sure she felt the same.

'Don't flatter yourself, Gem. I'm here on business. Part of an ongoing investigation. Two investigations, maybe.'

'Missing cats, by any chance?'

His first and only paid commission, so far, had involved a missing cat. He wasn't about to tell Gemma. He'd found the cat alright. It had climbed into an electrical substation and shorted out the entire street. His new career was already looking like a messy business.

'No cats. Insurance fraud. There's a shipping company claiming they had equipment stolen while it was waiting to go offshore. The loss assessor thinks they're lying. I can't tell you their name for obvious reasons. They do have plenty of previous.'

'Neptune Shipping.'

'How did you know?'

'They're not the only ones, right enough, but they've been at it the longest. Everyone knows about them. I don't need a private dick to tell me that. Nothing's ever been proved, mind. You're wasting your time and their money. Those Neptune boys are crafty. Too smart for the likes of you.'

'It's a good thing I'm not getting paid on results then. They hired me on a day rate.'

'Oh well, crack on. Write a few reports. You'll be good at reports. So long as you're behind a desk, the world's a safer place.'

'Yeah, thanks. Any more suggestions?'

'Aye. You could talk to Jockie Muirhead. Ma da's old drinking buddy. He'll be hanging about The Angel, blootered as usual. Used to work for Neptune until they laid him off. He'll tell you a few stories for the price of a scotch. Off the record, of course. No one's going to stand up in court and bad-mouth those bastards. You watch yourself, Danny-boy.'

'Why? Are they violent?'

'Not as a rule. But they might be if they catch you snooping around. Jockie won't cross them. He'd never get a job on another boat. Those sailor boys stick together.'

'Well, thanks for the tip. You doing anything later?'

'Aye. But not with you. I'm away offshore tomorrow. Tonight, I've a date with Mr Christian Grey and a bottle of Pinot. If you're still around in two weeks, you can buy me a pint, maybe.'

'I might be in Orkney.'

'What the hell for?'

'Missing person enquiry. A young guy. Works at Mallach oil terminal. His family are worried about him.'

'I'd go missing if I lived on Mallach. They say that Orkney tried to give it back to the Norwegians. They wouldn't take it. I don't blame them. Godforsaken, windswept shite-hole.'

Danny thought that was a bit rich coming from someone who was born and bred in Aberdeen. He said goodbye to Gemma and gave her a peck on the cheek. She returned the favour with a friendly, eye-watering jab to the sternum. Still clutching at his ribs, he staggered down Ship Row, looking for an unholy Angel.

Chapter Two

THE ANGEL USED TO be a Baptist church, according to Gemma. Danny had already passed several ex-chapels that had been transformed into bars. Either the God-fearing people of Aberdeen were in thrall to demon drink, or they'd decided to relocate the houses of the Lord to a more salubrious area.

After crisscrossing the maze of lanes around the Merchant Quarter, Danny eventually found the entrance in a dank alley close to Regent's Quay. At the door to the bar, the aroma of rotting fish and seaweed from the docks met the smell of stale beer and the great unwashed. Inside, it was dark and dirty, with only two or three paying customers perched on the repurposed pews. The Angel might have once been a church, but now it looked more like a doss house. God had definitely forsaken this establishment.

Jockie Muirhead was propping up the bar at the far end of the building, where the altar must have been. He looked like he was intent on drinking himself to a solitary grave. Danny bought him a Glenfiddich. It seemed the thing a private eye should do. Another few units of alcohol shouldn't make much difference to this guy's life expectancy.

'What d'ya want, pal? Ma bowfin wife send you? I'm skint. She's nae getting another penny outta me, the scabby auld sow.'

'I'd like to talk to you about Neptune Shipping. A friend told me you might give me some background. I'm investigating an alleged case of insurance fraud.'

Jockie glanced around the bar, glaring suspiciously at the two old-timers smoking in the doorway.

'Aye, that sounds like Neptune, alright. You taping this?'

Danny opened his jacket to show he wasn't wearing a wire. That was what detectives always did in old films and Jockie seemed satisfied. He obviously didn't appreciate that technology had moved on in the twenty-first century. The smartphone in Danny's breast pocket was recording every word. It might not be admissible as evidence, but it was a handy backup. His memory was lousy and his handwriting even worse.

'Ya better keep ma name out of this, else you'll end up floating in the dock wi' the other jobbies, ken.'

If that was meant to be a threat, it lacked conviction. Even though Jockie was a big guy, he'd have to sober up before he'd be in any state to throw Danny over the harbour wall. That didn't look like happening anytime soon. He was more likely to end up in another kind of dock.

'How long since you finished working for Neptune?'

'Two years, or thereabouts. Said I was unreliable. Unreliable? The only thing you can rely on those bastards for is to cheat you blind.'

'How do they stay in business, then?'

'They're dirt cheap. Yer oil companies always take the lowest price if they can. Then they go piss the profits up the wall. See the money they waste? That's the real crime, I'm telling you. Sure, a few wee firms are fiddling and frigging themselves an extra grand. That's nothing compared to the cash the big boys flush down the cludgie.'

Danny had to agree, but he wasn't being paid to investigate the entire UK oil industry. Wasting the earth's resources wasn't a crime. Not yet, anyway. If that ever changed, he was more than happy to arrest the lot of them.

'Neptune are claiming some equipment was stolen from their depot. Big, heavy pallets. Thieves with a forklift and a low-loader, maybe. Sound familiar?'

'Do you insurance boys never talk to each other? Neptune have pulled that caper every couple of years since Adam struck oil. They change insurers mair often than I change ma shirt.'

That was no doubt true. The armpits of Jockie's once-white shirt had more rings than a giant redwood. The reek of stale sweat was hard to stomach.

'There's no record of any pay-outs being refused.'

'Aye, well, it's never been proved, has it? Friends in low places, like all these sliddery firms. They outsource the thieving, then sell the kit on at a knockdown price.'

'I don't suppose you'd care to share any names?'

'I have a terrible memory for names. Must be the drink. Names can be bad for your health.'

'How about places? Where do they store the recovered goods? They can't just pop them back into a warehouse in Dyce. Someone would spot them, surely?'

'They load it all on a boat. If they have a buyer, it goes straight offshore. Once they sold a dozen crates of knocked-off flanges to the same platform they'd had been shipping to in the first place. New labels, new paperwork. No one was any the wiser. Even got a thank-you letter from the operator for hauling them out of the shite again.'

'And if they don't have a buyer?'

'The boat goes way up to Shetland or Orkney and leaves the gear there until they find a taker. Plenty of places to hide dodgy goods and hardly any folk around to ask questions.'

'Orkney? That's interesting. Any particular island?'

'It wouldn't be Orkney Mainland. There's a wee polis station in Kirkwall, mind. Somewhere out of the way. Mallach maybe. That's just a guess, ken.'

'Mallach? The oil terminal?'

'Aye. If they have pals on the inside, they could use the deep-water jetty for offloading the cargo. They keep themselves to themselves on Mallach.

Well known for it. Miserable bastards. I always hated the place. Won't even sell you a wee drink. Supposed to be a dry island. That doesn't stop the locals knocking it back like it's going out of fashion.'

Danny bought him another scotch. Just a cheap blend this time. Jockie was past caring. By the time Danny reached the door, the glass was empty and Jockie was trying to attract the barman's attention.

He hoped the old boy hadn't noticed his reaction. His missing person worked at the oil terminal on Mallach. Two incidents linked to the same tiny island? It could be a coincidence or just a drunkard's wild guess.

Before travelling north, Danny had watched a series of documentaries about Orkney. The scenery looked stunning, and the wildlife was spectacular. He was keen to pay a visit, despite Gemma's one-star review. First, he had to persuade someone to pay for the trip. It was hard to see what the two cases had in common, but there *had* to be something. He was determined to find it.

Chapter
Three

'Hi, Joey. I think I've got a lead on those missing crates.'

Joey McAndrew, Danny's contact at Highlander Loss Adjustors, sounded shocked. Not shocked enough to pay for a flight to Kirkwall, though. Eventually, he coughed up for the cheaper six-hour ferry trip. He even offered to pay for a meal if Danny's stomach was up to it.

Danny was relieved. He didn't want to go asking for more money from Ross MacLeod's already distressed family. Not until he had something concrete to show for his efforts.

By some miracle, the North Sea was calm for once. Calm enough for him to indulge in a chip supper and a pint of IPA. According to the adjective-rich menu, the fish was locally caught or at least locally defrosted. It tasted pretty good wherever it came from. The beer had that oily aftertaste that everything onboard ship inevitably absorbs. It didn't take him long to empty his glass all the same.

Unless he wanted to head down to the mini cinema and be subjected to a rerun of *Braveheart*, there was nothing else to do. Mel Gibson had a lot to answer for. It was bad enough having the Scots whining over ancient history. Having the Aussies join in was beyond the pale.

Instead, he wandered out on deck. There was a lot of sea between mainland Scotland and the Orkney Archipelago. They sailed past Fraserburg and he watched the harbour slowly disappearing into the haze. Danny thought he could just about make out Wick on the far horizon. Not an island in sight. Still four hours to go and nothing but rolling, spray-streaked waves and the occasional wheeling gull.

Plenty of time to plan what he was going to do once he got to his destination. Unfortunately, he had little to go on. A couple of online news reports and a half-hour conversation on the phone with the missing man's parents. That was about it.

Mrs MacLeod spent most of the time sobbing and telling him what a good lad her Ross was. How he never went off anywhere without telling her. He had a brief chat with Ross' father. The man's accent was almost incomprehensible over a distorted phone line. Hopefully, face-to-face communication might be easier.

All he knew for sure was that Ross MacLeod had left work early last Wednesday morning. He was a security guard, employed by Orcadia Oil, operators of the Mallach oil terminal. Ross had been on the night shift all the previous week. He never came home.

His mother seemed to think something had been bothering him lately. Something dodgy going on at the terminal, she said. The police came and took a statement. There was nothing to indicate foul play. The family had made an appeal on local TV, but so far, no response.

Hard to imagine what they were going through. Losing a child had to be the worst feeling possible. Especially not knowing whether they'd still be alive.

Of course, plenty of young men and women go missing every year. Some of them turn up again. Some just disappear. They end up living rough on big city streets, often as not. Some want to start a new life. They pack up their troubles in their kit bag and walk away. Some don't leave of their own accord. They're killed, kidnapped, enslaved. That was a tiny minority, thank God.

Still, from what he knew so far, Ross didn't sound like someone who'd wander off and leave his family in despair. If the MacLeods knew their son as well as they thought they did, he had to have a good reason for leaving in a hurry. Maybe he was running from trouble, or he'd been taken by force. Either way, time was of the essence.

Danny didn't have the resources to mount an effective search. His best chance was to gather as much evidence as possible. Then he had to hope it was enough to convince the police that Ross was in serious trouble and hadn't just wandered off. Something illegal going on at work or nearer to home. Maybe he saw something he shouldn't have. Said the wrong thing to the wrong person.

The ferry pulled slowly into Kirkwall harbour. On first impressions, it looked like a fine place to spend a few days. There was a distinct fishy smell on the air, but the sun gleaming on the imposing harbourside buildings gave it a warm, welcoming appearance. His B&B was close by, though considerably less grand. An end of terrace house with three small bedrooms, two of which were let out to guests. Danny introduced himself, dumped his bags, and headed back to the quay.

The little inter-island ferry was getting ready to depart, and he scrambled on board with a few minutes to spare. According to the timetable, Mallach was a little over an hour away. The sea state was just rough enough to make the crossing uncomfortable, but not bad enough for him to part company with his fish-and-chips lunch.

As they rounded the headland, Danny caught his first sight of the oil terminal: a sprawling steel city, dominating Mallach's northern shoreline. Beyond was a watercolour backdrop of bare hills rolling down to the distant sea cliffs.

An island of two halves and only one of him. All he had to do was talk to its inhabitants, search high and low for Ross, and break into a secure oil installation. At the same time, he was supposed to be looking for stolen property and tracking down some violent fraudsters.

It sounded like he was going to need some help. His only likely accomplice was off sunning herself on an oil platform for the next two weeks. Unless he got lucky, this was going to be a long trip.

Chapter Four

THE MACLEODS LIVED IN a small, whitewashed stone cottage on the edge of Bron, Mallach's largest village. He was invited into the living room where the family, mum Eileen, dad Donald, and sister Morag, squashed themselves onto a single sofa. The parents looked anxious and seventeen-year-old Morag was visibly distraught. Morag was of an agricultural build, much like her parents. Under better circumstances, she might have been quite pretty, but her lank hair was unbrushed, and her face was pale and tear blotched.

Danny was worried the sofa would collapse under their combined weight and offered to vacate the only other chair. Mrs MacLeod would have nothing of it.

'But you've come all this way to help us, Danny. How's your tea? Would you like a peedie bun? If you need the lavvy, it's just off the hall.'

Danny sipped his milky tea, munched on his raspberry bun and assured her he'd used the spartan facilities on the ferry.

'The island's been ever so kind. Even folk we never spoke to before. Making posters and scouring the hills. Raising money. We'd never have afforded to get you up here otherwise, would we, Don?'

'Aye. Yer some kind of expert on the oil industry, so they say. That bad business on the Cuillin Alpha. Sabotage and all that. And now yer a private investigator. Yer don't stick at a job fer long, do yer?'

'Now then, Don. Give the boy a chance.'

Danny handed the man his shiny new Private Investigator's licence. Don examined it with suspicion.

'Aye, well. Help us find our Ross. Whatever happened to our lad. We just want tae know. That's all we ask. The polis ken naethin, that fer sure. It's like they dunna care neither. Mebbiz, you can do better, eh?'

'I'll try my very best. But I'd appreciate any help you can give me. Contacts, especially. His boss. Work friends. Colleagues. Anyone he didn't get on with, maybe?'

'Aye well, we've made a list for yer.'

The list comprised four scribbled pages of A4. At first, Danny thought it was written in Gaelic. Then he recognised the odd word amongst the indecipherable scrawl. He wished he'd brought his reading glasses.

'Morag wrote it down for yer. Miss Gordon says she has the best hand-writing in class.'

Danny wouldn't like to have seen her classmates' calligraphy skills.

'That's great. I thought teenagers typed everything these days?'

Morag gave him a shy smile.

'Oh aye, I made a spreadsheet first, right enough. Ah was going to email to yer. Ma said it wasn't safe, though. Someone might intercept it, like.'

Someone had been watching too many spy films. Danny took the paper copy and promised to burn it after he'd memorised it. Then he slipped his card complete with his email address to Morag under cover of taking another raspberry bun.

'So this is his boss? Iain Grant?'

Mrs Macleod took the paper from him and stared at it over the top of her glasses.

'Aye. No. Mr Grant is the big man. He's the terminal manager. Kevan Knox is the security boss.'

'Right. Sorry.' Danny peered over her shoulder at Knox's job descrip-tion. It still looked like "scroty hoss" to him. 'How well did Ross get on with Knox?'

'Good. In the beginning, aye. But lately, I'm no so sure.'

'Did Ross tell anyone about his concerns? Grant maybe?'

'He never said. Could be.'

'And do you know anything more about Knox? Any rumours? Anything suspicious?'

'He's nae fae Mallach, ken.'

The fact that Knox was born on a different island, at least five miles away, seemed enough reason for Donald Macleod to distrust him. His wife seemed more forgiving of strangers.

'His sister's son stays here. And he's worked at the terminal as long as I can remember.'

Danny cast his eye over the list again. Most of them lived off the island as far as he could tell from the scrawled handwriting and the weird-sounding place names.

'Did Ross not have any friends on Mallach?'

'Not so many, Danny. A lot of the young lads and lasses move away once they leave school. Here it's all farming and fishing. A few come back, but not many.'

'What about the oil terminal? Ross got a job there. How about his friends?'

'Aye, there used to be a scheme for taking on local youngsters and training them up. That's long gone. It's cheaper to get folk fae mainland Scotland. Them as already know the job.'

'How are they meant tae get experience, if there's nae training, I ask yer? This outfit that runs the terminal now, they're just after a quick buck. They've nae care for Mallach, or anywhere else, mind. Money-grabbing, bastards.'

'Don! Language, please. We have a visitor.'

Muttering under his breath, Mr MacLeod apologised.

'OK, so you think Ross was upset about something going on at work? Could the stress have got to him? Maybe he needed to get away to clear his head. I mean, young men often won't tell their parents about their feelings. What about you, Morag? Did he say anything to you?'

She glanced across at her parents and took a deep breath before speaking.

'Not about work, exactly. There was a girl he was keen on, though. He met her at the terminal, but I'm not sure she works there. Her name's Marissa. He made me promise not to say anything. He said you might not like him seeing an Asian.'

'I've naethin against Asians,' Mr MacLeod said, avoiding her gaze. 'She's no one of them Islams, is she?'

'Dunno. He never said. Her parents are from Malaysia, but they live in London now.'

'London? Lord save us. Whar in their right mind would move from Malaysia to London? Nought but heathens and deviants doon there.'

'Marissa is a nice name. I expect she's a good Christian girl, Don.'

'I doubt that if she's fae London.'

Danny could see why Ross might keep his relationships secret, but he wasn't convinced it had much to do with his disappearance. All the same, it would be worth checking that she was still working at the terminal. They could have run off to Gretna or, even worse, to pagan London.

'I don't see her on the list anywhere.'

'Aye. No. I don't even ken her full name. I expect her email is on his laptop, though.'

'Do you know his password?'

'Of course. But I can't say it out loud. It's a bad word spelt with symbols and numbers.'

After a lengthy discussion, the MacLeods agreed to let Danny have a look at the laptop and even take it away with him for a day or two.

'Don't worry,' Morag said. 'His private stuff is on a memory stick. I haven't managed to find the password for that yet.'

'Private stuff?' wondered Mrs Macleod.

'Maybe he was keeping a diary,' suggested Danny tactfully.

'Oh, aye. I kept a diary when I was a girl. I would have wanted no one to see it, true enough.'

And she really wouldn't want to see her son's porn stash. Or all those videos of inappropriate, drunken behaviour that teenage boys tended to accumulate. Morag could keep a hold of the memory stick for now. If he came across any indication of foul play, then someone would have to go through it. He was happy to leave that job to the police.

First of all, he needed to gain access to the terminal. He was supposed to be the industry expert, but you couldn't wander into a secure oil installation with just the wave of a private investigator's card. Maybe Marissa could help. If she really was Ross' girlfriend, she might be persuaded to get him inside.

'Do you have somewhere to stay, Danny? We could put him up in the front room, couldn't we, Don? Or there's a holiday let in the village. It's not much to look at, but Mrs McAllister keeps it spotless.'

'It's OK, Mrs Macleod. I'm booked into a B&B in Kirkwall. It's better if I stay off the island for now. I'll be in touch as soon as I have anything to report.'

As he left, the MacLeods shook his hand. Morag gave him a rib-crushing hug and burst into tears. They were relying on him. He wasn't sure if he could cope with that weight of responsibility, but they had nowhere else to turn. Danny was determined to find their son, but he had a feeling that this search was not destined for a happy ending.

Chapter Five

THE FERRY WASN'T DUE for an hour. Before heading back to the pier, Danny decided to take a quick look around Bron, the only village of any note on the island. In truth, an hour was plenty to see everything Bron offered.

A row of neat stone-built fisherman's cottages sat along the main road, which curved around the bay. More houses were strung along a couple of narrow lanes leading away from the sea. At the crossroads was a war memorial, the inscription shrouded by lichen. Here were all of Bron's village amenities: one church, one school, one shop. No pub, of course.

On the edge of the village was the Memorial Hall. It was a prefab concrete building out of keeping with the rest of Bron. Danny wondered if it had a bar. The lights were off and no one was home, sadly. Beyond the hall was a small muddy beach. Nets, buoys, and lobster pots lay strewn above a high tide line of seaweed and empty shells.

Probably quite picturesque on a sunny day, but Orkney was even less likely to experience good weather than Aberdeen. Small grey clouds scudded in from the sea on a biting icy wind. Danny turned away and went in search of Mallach's one and only holiday cottage. Mrs McAllister, the owner, was a retired headteacher. She wore a tweed skirt and kept her steel-grey hair in a tight bun. Even without his investigative skills, he could have guessed her profession.

'This used to be a storehouse for the Harbourmaster. Highlands and Islands gave us a grant to do it up. They want to encourage tourists to come to the outer islands.'

Danny wasn't convinced the cottage would encourage anyone to come to Mallach. It looked more like a glorified bothy than a desirable holiday residence. He had the impression that, without the protection of the adjacent houses, it would be swept up by the next storm and dumped in the harbour.

'Well, it's certainly got a lot of character,' Danny remarked. So did Hannibal Lecter. Character was overrated. 'Do you get many visitors?'

'Not so many, but we have our regulars. Mostly birdwatchers and naturalists. We had a couple of naturists once. I think they misread the advert. They didn't stay long.'

'So, is it free for the next few weeks?'

'Aye. Are you with the RSPB? You get a discount.'

He didn't want to lie to her. Despite her genial manner, elderly teachers were notoriously good at detecting lies.

'It's not for me. I have a friend who's very keen on wildlife. She'd love it here.'

Gemma would hate it. She would hate him for even suggesting it. But he needed someone to talk to the islanders. He could hardly understand what they were saying most of the time. It didn't look like he could persuade an islander to be his mole. Despite the endorsement of the MacLeods, an English private investigator was unlikely to get much help from the locals. Gemma wasn't your ideal secret agent, but she enjoyed talking and people liked talking to her.

If he hadn't found Ross by the time Gemma demobbed from the Cuillin Alpha, she was his best and only option. The problem was getting her to spend her two weeks' downtime in an outhouse on a remote windswept island. Breaking into a secure oil terminal was going to be a doddle by comparison.

Mrs McAllister had offered to give him a lift to the pier, but the only vehicle he'd seen by the cottage was an antiquated motorbike. Danny decided he'd rather walk. Fortunately, the rain held off as he made his way along the narrow country lane. There was no traffic apart from one old guy on a tractor. It was quite a pleasant hike, and the view from the crest of the hill was spectacular.

The pier was close to the oil terminal. Much further away than he remembered from the outward journey. At least it was all downhill from here. Danny could see the ferry making its way down the Flint Sound and broke into an unaccustomed jog. He didn't want to have to sleep on the MacLeods' couch, or in Mrs McAllister's so-called cottage.

Once onboard, the sun peaked out from behind the clouds for a while. Danny stood out on deck and enjoyed the view. It wasn't the most elegant of observation decks. The passengers who wanted to brave the outdoors had to share the space at the back of the boat with various pallets, crates, and barrels. It was worth it. The islands glistened as the sun disappeared below the hilltops and gave the lush green fields a golden orange hue. It was easy to see why people fell in love with these bleak northern islands.

Back in Kirkwall, it seemed a shame to rush back to his bijou B&B. He found a pub up the hill which advertised a beer garden. In reality, it was just a few benches in a paved backyard, but it had an excellent view of the harbour. Danny sat nursing a pint of Bigbreck Gold and watched the sun disappear in the line of grey clouds massing on the horizon.

Without the warmth of the sun on his face, the cold evening crept up on him. He finished his pint and trudged into town to find his B&B. His room was tiny. Fewer pillows and embroidered cushions might have helped. He tried to stuff most of them into the otherwise empty wardrobe, but all that did was create a soft-furnishing avalanche. Eventually, he managed to wedge a couple of pillows on top of the closet and make a wobbly giant Jenga tower in the corner with the cushions.

He opened Ross' laptop on the tiny desk-come-dressing-table and typed rossmac and then B0££0ck$ to access the account. It might not be the most secure password in the world, but it was memorable.

Most of Ross' emails were banal in the extreme. His posts on social media were not much better. He talked about games and TV shows and websites that were utterly alien to Danny. He was only fifteen years older than Ross, but fifteen years was a lifetime these days. Things he thought were cool when he was a teenager were museum exhibits now.

Marissa was mentioned by several of his male friends, generally associated with lewd suggestions and offensive images. There was a comment from a lass called Jaz, whose makeup looked like it had been applied by an over-zealous undertaker. She thought that Marissa was bad news and that Ross should dump her immediately. She was standing, ready to offer comfort and support should the need arise.

Of Marissa herself, there was no sign. No photos. No internet presence. Not even a mention of her surname on any of the posts. Danny searched for "Marissa" and "Orkney" and came up with a few women in New Zealand and Canada. There were none listed for the Orkney Islands.

She was a mystery. Usually, Danny liked that in a woman, but Marissa was bugging him. Did she exist, or was she a fiction created by Ross to impress his friends? Some of the posts implied his friends had met her, but it was hard to be sure.

Maybe Marissa was a virtual girlfriend. Someone Ross had met online and never in person. He only had Morag's word that she worked at the oil terminal. That could have been a lie that got out of hand. Ross bragging to his mates about how he'd met this gorgeous woman and then being too embarrassed to admit she lived several thousand miles away.

The more Danny thought about it, the more this made sense. Once he'd got access to the terminal, he would know for sure. His idea of asking Marissa for help was a non-starter. He needed another angle.

Danny put away Ross' laptop and got out his own. There was a message from Morag MacLeod amongst the myriad of marketing emails. Her spreadsheet was highlighted with a rainbow of eye-watering colours, but it was a damn sight easier to follow than the paper version. Hi-vis yellow appeared to be for family, glow-stick green was for close friends and Trump-tan orange was for Ross' work colleagues.

One name sounded familiar. Gordon Breck. Danny searched for his name on one of the business networking sites. Breck was a self-employed medic, currently on contract with Orcadia Oil Ltd. He also gave talks on occupational medicine in the oil industry. Danny recalled going to one of his lectures. He couldn't remember anything about it, apart from the fact that the guy behind him had an annoying and persistent cough. Danny pinged Breck a message and hoped he would pick it up soon.

Chapter Six

DOUG AND NANCY MET at the usual spot. A stand of windswept rowans on a headland at the northernmost end of the island. It had no name on the Ordnance Survey map, but islanders called it the Tongue of Scorn. It used to be an emergency evacuation route for the terminal, but erosion had made the clifftop unsafe. The way was still passable, so long as you hugged the fence line and kept away from the edge.

Nancy was late. She knew how much Doug hated that. She had a ready excuse, but it was unlikely to improve his mood.

'I came by the MacLeods' place, like you said. They had a visitor.'

'Who?'

'I don't know. No one local. Gudgie wee lad. Didn't get close enough to see his face.'

'Polis?'

'Maybe, but not fae Orkney. This laddie was in plain clothes. Maybe a detective from the Highlands.'

'Shit! That's all we need.' Doug picked up a rock and hurled it into the sea far below. A few startled gulls abandoned their perches, their cries of alarm echoing along the cliffs.

'The MacLeods know nothing about us.'

'Let's keep it that way. Did this detective speak to anyone else?'

'Ellen McAllister.'

'Why her?'

'She's a nosey auld sow. Maybe she saw something.'

'Maybe I should pay her a call.'

'I could send Lorna round for a wee chat. Ellen could never keep a secret. She'll want to share it with someone.'

'And you can trust Lorna?'

'She doesn't have to know the truth. She wanted to help with the search parties. Maybe Ellen can tell her where to start looking.'

Doug seemed amused by that idea. Nancy kept her concerns to herself. One nosey woman was easy enough to deal with. So was this lone detective, but if he found anything, more were sure to follow.

'Are you ready for the next collection?'

'Aye, sure. When will they come?'

'Not sure yet. Some problem with their distributor.'

'That's not good.'

'They'll get it sorted. They always do.'

'I don't like the way they operate. We need to keep to the schedule.'

Delays made Nancy nervous, but it was always risky to question Doug's plans.

'You just make sure you're ready, alright. I'll have words.'

That did nothing to reassure Nancy. They were dealing with dangerous people. She didn't trust them further than she could spit. Could she trust Doug to keep them in check? Their lives depended upon it. They were in too deep now.

Nancy watched Doug scurrying back towards the terminal. She turned away and scanned the horizon. She was alone, with only the screeching gulls for company. It was an ugly place. Nothing but barbed wire and gorse. No one would choose to come here out of choice. She picked her way back down the sheep track to the patchwork of fields below.

Chapter
Seven

DANNY'S LANDLADY RECOMMENDED THE Barrelmakers Bar as being ideal for the hungry visitor on a tight budget. He hated eating alone, but it was an inevitable part of the job. He picked up the book he'd brought with him. It was called *Manhunt!* and it was proving heavy going. The exclamation mark should have been a warning.

The pub looked clean and the menu surprisingly inventive. Some customers had cleared their plates and didn't look any the worse for it. There was a pie-and-a-pint special on tonight. Danny went for the mutton-and-Marmite pie and took his beer and book off to a table by the window.

In *Manhunt!,* ninja assassins with supernatural powers were hunting down a group of stereotypical mercenaries. By the end of Chapter Three, Danny was rooting for the ninjas. He was hoping they'd reserve an excruciating death for the macho leader of the mercenaries and his revenge related anger-management issues. The book had won an award for the exotic cover artwork rather than its literary merits.

Someone had left the local paper and a suitably dumbed-down science magazine on the next table. He grabbed them and flicked through the magazine. It left him confused but comforted by the thought that some people out there would understand this stuff. It was a good thing you didn't need to grasp the concept of quantum entanglement to find a missing person, or else Ross really would be in trouble.

It didn't look like any of tonight's punters was a closet genius. Such a pity. He could have used having a boffin around to bounce his ideas off. There was a smartly dressed older woman at the adjacent table. She looked his way briefly and he gave her his best winning smile. She immediately blanked him and went back to swiping through emails on her tablet.

Just as he was about to head back to the bar for a refill, the pie arrived. It wasn't bad once he'd cut his through the exploding puff pastry topping. He finished the last chip, brushed pastry detritus off his trousers, and reached for the newspaper.

Most of the articles were about Orkney politics and island events. A headline on page two caught his eye. "Local Man Missing" with a photo and an appeal from the parents. The young man's name was Aidan Fitzgerald. He was a few years older than Ross. A delivery driver. His parents said he'd been distressed lately. He'd left home three days ago, and he hadn't been seen since. Police were not looking for anyone else in connection with his disappearance.

Danny's heart sank. The article didn't mention Ross MacLeod, but two young Orkney men going missing in the same month? Of course, men in their early twenties were the most likely to have mental health problems and were most at risk of harming themselves. It really could be a coincidence. Serial killers were rare enough in mainland Britain. Despite what crime fiction would have you believe, on a remote Scottish island, they were almost non-existent.

He would have to talk to more worried parents, assuming they wanted to talk to him. Even the act of getting in contact would upset them. All the same, it had to be done. Surely the police would put two and two together and start treating these cases more seriously. Why should he be the one to tell Aidan's parents about another Orkney family waiting for their son to come home?

Later, he thought. First, he needed to contact his fellow medic, Gordon Breck. His profile said he lived near Kirkwall. Danny prayed he was off-shift at the moment and hadn't gone back to Mallach.

Danny ordered another pint and worked his way through the paper, looking for anything unusual. He should be able to access the back issues online when he got back to the B&B. However, some of the more obscure local features only appeared in print. They would have everything on record at the newspaper offices, but until he knew what he was looking for, he'd be wasting their time and his.

———

The following morning, Danny ordered another full Scottish breakfast. While waiting for it to arrive, he worked his way through the usual deluge of unwanted emails. He took a swig of lukewarm coffee and scrolled through the spam, looking for anything of interest. Near the bottom was a message from Gordon Breck.

> I'M AT HOME. HAPPY TO TALK ABOUT ROSS MACLEOD. DID YOU BRING PPE? I'LL COME INTO TOWN THIS EVENING. AULD GRAINSTORE 7 PM, OK? TEXT ME.

Breck had tacked his mobile number on the end of the message. Things were looking up. Though why Breck thought he would have dragged his PPE all the way to Orkney was a bit of a mystery. He hoped the Auld Grainstore wasn't a bar where you needed a hardhat and a visor.

The map on his phone directed him over the other side of the harbour to a pleasant cluster of buildings near the sailing club. It looked like Breck would rather not meet in town. Danny was just glad to have company. The Grainstore had some excellent reviews for its food. It would be nice to have someone to talk to over his meal tonight. He was too tired to face more quantum mechanics, and he wasn't yet desperate enough to return to Manhunt! for company.

In the meantime, there were a couple of the guys on Morag's list who lived or worked on the Mainland. Davie MacBride was an old teammate who played football with Ross for Mallach juniors. Davie was happy to answer Danny's call. In fact, Danny had trouble trying to get a word in edgeways. Davie was full of anecdotes involving Ross, most of them alcohol related. Unfortunately, he hadn't seen Ross in months.

'That boy's too busy by half these days. Working the weekends for double bubble. I blame that new bird of his. Expensive tastes, so I hear.'

And, no, Davie hadn't met Marissa or seen a photo of her. He didn't seem to think that was odd.

'All that talk about her being a stunner. Total shite. Probably too embarrassed to admit he's pulled another munter.'

'Has Ross ever gone off before? Without telling anyone?'

'Not that I know. It was only a matter of time, though. Have you met his folks, eh? All that religious crap. Drove him mad. Couldn't take a piss without asking Jesus for forgiveness. He was always talking about moving out. Getting a place of his own.'

'But what about his job? And his new girlfriend? Surely, he wouldn't just up-sticks and leave all that behind.'

'Aye, well, maybe that tipped him over the edge. His folks wouldn't like him seeing some foreign bird, I tell you. I reckon he had a bust-up with them and stormed out. Can't say I blame him.'

'Any ideas where he might hide?'

'No, pal. And I'm not sure I'd tell you if I did. Leave the lad alone. He'll be back soon enough. Once he's cleared his head.'

The other name on the list was Craig Scott. A schoolmate of Ross, according to Morag. He worked in a garage somewhere in Kirkwall. They had no website, and Danny had been trying to call them all morning. In the end, he scoured the mean streets of Kirkwall on foot.

Mainland Motors was hidden away in a tatty-looking industrial estate. They appeared to specialise in farm vehicles and milk wagons. A young guy with an oil-smeared face stood outside, lighting a cigarette.

'Craig?'

'Who's asking?'

Danny handed him his card.

'I'm looking for Ross MacLeod. He's gone missing. His parents are worried about him.'

'Aye, they would be. I've not seen him. He called me a few weeks back. We were going to meet up for a beer. Something was bothering him. Something he couldn't say over the phone.'

'Did it have to do with his work?'

'Aye. Or maybe he ran off with that lass Melissa, or whatever her name is. You should ask at the terminal about her.'

'Not yet. No one seems to know anything about her. Not even her full name.'

'Yes, aye. Something's not right there. Though her family's fae Malaysia, he said. She might have one of those Asian names that you can't even pronounce.'

'I don't suppose you have a photo of her.'

'Well, maybe. There was a picture in the paper when that fat eejit fae Edinburgh came to open the new power plant. Ross is there, gawping at this Asian bird. Could be her. Too much of a stoater for him, I reckon. I took a photo. It's not great, but I can send it to you.'

Craig couldn't remember anything about the accompanying article, but it was a start. Next, Danny needed to talk to the local paper. They should be able to dig out the photo in question if nothing else. Hopefully, they were well inclined towards private investigators. Of course, he could always offer to give them an exclusive interview when he eventually found Ross.

Chapter Eight

THE EVENING WAS PLEASANTLY mild. There was hardly a breath of wind as Danny strolled along the harbour road. Gordon Breck was propping up the bar when he arrived and insisted on buying him a beer. The room was filling up with diners ordering food and wine by the bottle.

Danny picked up a menu and, drinks in hand, they wandered off to a quiet corner. Breck spoke with a posh English accent. It sounded like there was a bit of Sandhurst in his accent. Danny wondered if he was also ex-army.

'RAF, actually. I served as a Medical Officer. I was born and bred in Orkney, but I trained at Cranwell and was based in Lincolnshire for most of my career. I came back north when my mother fell ill; God rest her soul. The kids had grown up, and the wife liked it here. So, we stayed. I worked offshore for a while, then I got the job at the oil terminal.'

'Do many locals work at the terminal?'

'Not many from Mallach itself. It's sparsely populated and most of the locals are farmers. Plenty of Orcadians from the nearby islands. The ferries are quite frequent and reliable, all things considered. A few guys lodge in Kirkwall during the week and go home for the weekend. The rest are guys who travel from further afield and they mostly stay in the dormitories onsite.'

'Sounds like a good setup.'

'It's a bit of a retirement home for ageing oil workers, to be honest. Me included. We get to stay away from our families just like we do offshore, but without taking a helicopter ride out to the middle of the North Sea in all weathers. Of course, it doesn't pay as well as offshore, but it suits me down to the ground.'

'So, you don't get to stay at home?'

'Fortunately, not. The medic has to man his post at all times. They tried to change the rules a few years back, but everyone complained. My wife included,' he chuckled.

Danny perused the menu and then pushed it across to Breck.

'Oh, I've eaten at home. Though I wouldn't say no to a bowl of chips. Mrs Breck is on a diet, so we both have to starve.'

While they were waiting, Danny steered the conversation towards Ross and his disappearance.

'Yes, well, I'm glad someone is taking it seriously. The police were very offhand. And as for the management, some of them seemed glad to see the back of him.'

'Was he not a good worker, then?'

'He was new to the job, but I thought he was very conscientious. More than can be said for his supervisor. Perhaps that was the problem. Ross was showing him up.'

'Would that be Kevan Knox?'

'That's the chap. Not the sharpest tool in the box and, just lately, he's been acting oddly. When Ross disappeared, he tried to get me to say he was depressed or some such nonsense. I refused, of course. He got quite aggressive until I pointed out that even Medical Officers get basic combat training. It's amazing how much damage you can do with a scalpel and a rectal thermometer.'

'Blimey. How did that go down?'

'Not well. He made a few threats, but I didn't take him seriously. Fortunately, I was going home the next day, and I left my back-to-back to deal with it. I told my boss — that's the terminal manager, Iain Grant. I warned him not to be too surprised if I came down with a mystery illness before my next rotation.'

'You're not quitting, are you?'

'Good Lord, no. I'll not let some jumped-up doorman drive me out. I just thought I'd let the dust settle before I went back. Hopefully, Iain will have a quiet word with Knox. Even better, he might show the doorman the door.'

'That's a real shame. I was hoping you might help me get into the terminal somehow. Or at least get sight of the personnel records.'

'I take it you didn't bring your PPE with you, then? Well, there's a workwear shop in Kirkwall. If it comes to it, you can borrow some of my kit, though you're a bit short and you might struggle with my boots; they're size twelve.'

Danny finally got the idea. He was slow on the uptake today.

'I see. Are you saying they'll give me the job? Stand-in medic.'

'Well, you're qualified. It's not easy to get hold of a medic at short notice and officially the plant can't run without one for long. If I give you a ringing endorsement, I can't see there being any problems. I assume you are up to the job? I heard about your exploits on Cuillin Alpha. That wasn't an unqualified success. From the medical perspective, I mean.'

'As long as they're not expecting any more DIY brain surgery, I'll be fine. I assume I won't be totally cut off from the emergency services on Mallach.'

'No. Though it can seem like you're a long way from civilisation sometimes. And by the way, I don't blame you for what happened to your colleague. I can't say I would fancy having to deal with a severe head injury offshore. I'm not surprised you decided on a change of career.'

'It was rather decided for me. No one wants a Jonah on their platform.'

'Well, you won't be the only misfit in Mallach terminal. I think you might find it a refreshing change. Get you back in the saddle, so to speak.'

'The last time I was on a saddle was on a donkey on Bridlington beach. I fell off. But thanks for the vote of confidence. I'll happily take the job for a couple of weeks if they'll have me.'

After the bombshell job offer, Danny felt he ought to buy another round. Breck declined; he seemed keen to get back home before Mrs Breck phoned to see what was keeping him. Danny wanted to explore one more line of enquiry first, though.

'I don't suppose you have any medical records with you here? Or a list of personnel?'

'No. I might bend the rules occasionally, but sharing medical records is a criminal offence. Why? Who are you looking for, apart from our missing security guard?'

'A woman called Marissa. Allegedly, she was Ross' girlfriend. Unfortunately, no one seems to know much about her. Apparently, she works at the terminal and she's a bit of a stunner.'

'Well, there aren't many women in the terminal, good-looking or otherwise. I'm sure I would remember someone like that. There are a few more working at the site on an ad hoc basis. Cooks, cleaners, chemical engineers. Could be one of them, I suppose.'

Gordon didn't sound convinced. It became more and more likely that the lovely Marissa was the product of a young man's fevered imagination.

Chapter Nine

GORDON BRECK GAVE HIS boss the bad news early the next morning and recommended Danny as his replacement. Orcadia Oil HR department called him later that morning and the confirmation email came through within a few hours.

Danny liked the idea that, effectively, Orcadia Oil paid him to investigate their own employees. At the same time, the Mallach fighting fund paid him to look for Ross MacLeod. He had thought of waiving his fee, but figured he would need some extra money to bribe Gemma.

Danny had a few days to kill before starting his double agent work at the oil terminal. There were a few unpleasant tasks to perform first. He sent a grovelling email to Gemma, promising a lucrative hourly rate and his undying gratitude. It included a link to the video clip on the local newspaper website showing the grief-stricken MacLeods. Their pleas for help would surely melt even Gemma's granite heart. Though even with the bribery and emotional blackmail, he wasn't confident of success.

Next, he called the Orkney police. He wasn't expecting a warm reception.

'Sergeant Robert Campbell speaking. How can I be of assistance?'

'Hello. My name's Danny Verity. I'm assisting the MacLeod family regarding their son's disappearance. I wonder if I could talk to someone about the case.'

'If you must. This is Sergeant Robert Campbell speaking. Are you some kind of solicitor?'

'Ah, no. I'm more of an investigator, so to speak. I specialise in oil industry cases. I'm ex-Royal Military Police, by the way.'

He was under no illusions about the esteem in which both private investigators and military policemen were held by the boys in blue, but he had to try something.

'Is that so, sir? Well, we humble civilian police are treating this as a missing person case. Ross MacLeod is not a child. He's not even a vulnerable adult, as far as we are aware. I'm not sure I can help you any further. Unless you have some evidence of foul play, of course.'

'I was wondering if you had considered a possible link with the disappearance of Aidan Fitzgerald? They are of a similar age and both had connections with Mallach. They went missing within a few weeks of each other.'

'Very true. And both purchased tickets for the ferry before they went. I think you find they left of their own accord, Mr Verity. Perhaps they were running away together. However, I wouldn't like to speculate on such matters, sir.'

'Were they heading for the same port?'

There was a pause as Sergeant Campbell checked his notes. Danny could hear him muttering under his breath.

'No, as it happens. MacLeod was heading for Lerwick from Kirkwall and Fitzgerald had a ticket from Stromness to Scrabster.'

'And did they get on their ferries?'

'You'd have to *investigate* that yourself. Try the ferry company. I'm sure they've got nothing better to do. I'm afraid you'll be wasting your time, though. My regards to Mr and Mrs MacLeod. I'm sure it's a difficult time for them, but looking for trouble where it doesn't exist will not help them. Young men wander off all the time. Sadly, some of them don't come back. There's very little we can do about that, I'm afraid. Goodbye, Mr Verity.'

With that, Sergeant Campbell hung up. Danny wasn't surprised by his reaction. He'd been ready to come to the same conclusion. Yet, some things about these disappearances didn't add up. Too many unanswered questions. And what about these links to the island of Mallach and its major employer?

His third and, hopefully, final task for the day was to talk to the Fitzgerald family. He didn't fancy asking Sergeant Campbell for their address. Instead, on the principle that everyone in Orkney knew everyone else, he asked the waitress in the cafe where he was having lunch.

'Oh, aye. Sheila Fitzgerald. She works in the Scapa Hotel, by the harbour. You can't miss it.'

She also informed him that Mr Fitzgerald had run off with a large American woman named MacDonald and was now living in Idaho.

'Blew in like a tornado. I doubt he had much say in the matter. Their boy was just a toddler at the time. Sends them money, so I hear, but he's never been back.'

Danny strolled down to the harbour. The hotel was an imposing Victorian building with a grand entrance lobby. Undoubtedly a step up from his humble B&B. He took a peek at the price of a one-night stay on his booking app and decided to stay put.

The receptionist smiled as he stepped into the foyer. Her name was Catriona according to her company badge. He handed over his PI licence, and she stared at it blankly. Danny pressed on regardless.

'I wonder if I could speak to Mrs Sheila Fitzgerald? I believe she works here.'

'I'm afraid she's on compassionate leave. Family reasons.'

'Of course. I understand. I'd like to talk to her about her son. I have some information that might be important. Is there a way I could get in touch with her?'

Important information, possibly. Welcome news, certainly not. The receptionist took another long look at his photo ID and picked up the phone. After a muted discussion, she hung up and wrote down an address on the back of a hotel business card.

'You can call by now if you like, but don't go upsetting her. She's enough on her plate without southerners and ferry-loupers knocking at her door.'

Sheila Fitzgerald lived in a flat over a gift shop in the town centre. Presumably, her absentee husband was not over-generous with his maintenance payments. Inside, the apartment was pleasant enough. From where Danny was sitting, you could just make out the masts of the fishing boats bobbing around in the harbour. Sheila asked him if he'd like a cuppa but then launched into questions before waiting for his answer.

'Catriona said you had some news about Aidan. Has he been seen? Do you know where he is?'

'Sorry. It's not that kind of news, I'm afraid.'

'What is it then? Bad news? Have they found a...'

'A body? No. Nothing like that. I'm a private investigator. Did Catriona tell you?'

'She did. I couldn't understand why you would be looking for Aidan. I mean, someone has to pay you to look for people, don't they?'

'I'm not being paid to look for Aidan. There's another young man missing. Ross MacLeod. Maybe you've heard of him?'

'No, I haven't. I mean, I daren't watch the news. Always expecting the worst. The police would call me first, I suppose, but still. I nearly had a heart attack when Catriona phoned. I thought it must be them or the hospital.'

She certainly looked on edge. If only he could help.

'I don't suppose Aidan knew Ross, did he?'

'If he did, he never mentioned it. MacLeod, did you say? There are plenty of MacLeods around here, but no Ross that I know of.'

'You know that Aidan bought a ferry ticket to Scrabster? Any idea why?'

'No. It doesn't make any sense. There's nought at Scrabster. I went there once. Thurso is close by, but even that's a tiny wee place. I could understand if he'd gone to Aberdeen. He has friends who stay there.'

'Well, we don't know for sure that he got on the ferry. I mean, it could have been a ploy to conceal his whereabouts.'

'What makes you think Aidan would do something like that?'

'Ross MacLeod also bought a ticket. He was supposed to be sailing from here to Lerwick. But he didn't pack a bag or anything. He just disappeared.'

'Aidan took some things with him. That's a good sign, isn't it? I don't mean his usual overnight bag. He always had that in the van, just in case. Other stuff. And his favourite jacket's missing. Not just that horrible hi-vis one he uses for work.'

'How long has Aidan been missing now?'

'Two weeks.'

'And what did the police say?'

'Not much. They say there's nothing they can do if a grown lad disappears. Not unless there are suspicious circumstances. I mean, he might have all sorts of reasons for not coming home. They asked if he was depressed.'

'And was he?'

'Not depressed,' Sheila said. 'More like worried.'

'About what?'

'The drugs.'

'He was taking drugs?'

'Not taking them. Transporting them. His new job. He's been driving for a living for years, but this seemed like a step up. More money and a bit of responsibility. I mean, you've got to get the right medicine to the right place at the right time. It's not like delivering all that junk that people buy online these days.'

'And who was he working for?'

'He did say the name, but it wasn't one I'd heard of. Medivax or something like that?'

'Does a company called Neptune Shipping mean anything to you?'

'I've heard of them. I don't think Aidan did any of their deliveries. Why do you ask?'

'The name came up during my investigation. Probably not related. I just have to cover every angle. Aidan was worried, you say? Worried enough to run away? Was he being threatened, perhaps?'

'No. At least he never said. He was determined to find out what was going on, though. He thought there was something funny about the drugs he was delivering. Not to mention those herbal medicines he collected from that supplier on Mallach. He wouldn't say, but it sounded like they weren't exactly what they claimed to be.'

Mallach again. He was having the same bad feeling about Aidan that he had about Ross.

'You mean the drugs were counterfeit? Even the herbal ones?'

'Something like that. Aidan didn't want to say anything until he was sure. I mean, he knew blowing the whistle might cost him his job. He needed the money.'

'I know the feeling.'

'Please, will you help me look for him, Mr Verity? I mean, I haven't much money just now. I could pay you later. When I get back to work.'

Danny looked around the room. His rates were cheap. But Sheila Fitzgerald clearly had no money to spare.

'Look, I'm investigating Ross' disappearance already. The family have a fund going to help search for him. Maybe you should talk to them about your lad. They might help.'

He didn't like to say that the family lived on Mallach. Mentioning the island would make her even more anxious.

She shook her head. 'I'm not prepared to take anyone's charity. I can't ask them to give money for a lad they don't even know. It wouldn't be right.'

Danny was about to get paid twice, or even three times, for this investigation. The least he could do was give her some ray of hope.

'Well then, let's look at it this way. Ross and Aidan disappeared within a week of each other. Two young lads from Orkney. What's the chance of it being a coincidence? It makes good sense for me to investigate both. When I find one of them, he'll be able to tell me where the other is. I'm sure of it.'

Sheila Fitzgerald thanked him. She looked like she was about to burst into tears. Although clearly grateful, she was still expecting the worst.

'That's if you find them. Orkney folk who go missing usually stay missing. The sea takes them. That's what they say. And what it takes, it seldom gives back.'

Chapter Ten

Danny woke early and headed down to the dining room, full of enthusiasm for the task ahead. One more day before he went back to full-time employment in the oil industry. Two more full Scottish breakfasts (with extra toast and no sliced haggis).

He wondered what the breakfasts were like in the oil terminal. The ones on the Cuillin Alpha platform had been excellent. Not to mention the mid-morning bacon butties, the three-course lunches and the afternoon cakes. He wasn't ordinarily nostalgic about his time offshore, but the food had undoubtedly been a highlight.

Danny tried to focus on the present. One more day to concentrate on the job he had come here to do. He was amazed that Highland Loss Adjusters hadn't been on his case already. They must have low expectations of recovering the money.

He hated cheats, but Neptune Shipping was sinking ever lower on his list of priorities. It would be nice to find some evidence of fraud, though. Something to prosecute the bastards. It might seem like a victimless crime, but someone paid for it via their insurance premiums. He had a nasty feeling that it was him and his fellow mugs.

He switched on his laptop and made himself a cup of coffee. It took ages to boot up these days. About the same length of time it took to drink a coffee and eat a complimentary shortbread biscuit.

He had no joy searching for Medivax, Aidan's employer, so he tried a few spelling variations. There was a company called Medifax with a head office in Stirling. He coughed up the fee to check their company records online and made sure he got a receipt. He read the file and then gave a small whoop and danced around the chair. Medifax were a wholly-owned subsidiary of Neptune Shipping and Distribution Ltd.

So, Aidan worked for Neptune, indirectly at least. And Neptune had links to Mallach. Their subsidiary made deliveries there and possibly collected some dodgy goods in return. According to Jockie Muirhead, they might also be hiding some stolen goods on the island.

Danny wondered if Neptune had any other subsidiaries. Unfortunately, the internet was unable to offer much information on the matter. Either there weren't any, or they preferred not to advertise the fact. Neptune's own company records didn't even mention the one he knew about already. That looks dodgy, he thought.

He tried looking for links to Medifax instead, but only one mentioned Orkney. It wasn't on Mallach, but right here in Kirkwall. A local company called Lock-n-Load Storage listed Medifax as one of their corporate customers. It might be worth checking out before he left.

Danny wondered if there really was any connection between Ross and Aidan's or their employers. Ross was a security guard. He was guarding an oil terminal, not a medical facility. Even if Aidan had delivered some fake tablets to the medic at the terminal, how would Ross have found out?

There had to be something he was missing. Well, it seemed like he was heading to the right place to find out.

Danny's phone rang. An unrecognised Aberdeen number. Someone calling not from Aberdeen, but maybe from a hundred miles to the east of Aberdeen. An oil platform in the middle of the North Sea, perhaps.

'Hi, Gemma.'

'And hi to you too, ya great Yorkshire puddin'.'

'You got my email then?'

'Aye. If you mean the one from the bawbag who wants me to spend ma downtime on a god-forsaken, pish-soaked island watching pishing dicky-birds, for fuck's sake. What do ya take me for? Chris Fucking Pack-ham?'

'Nobody would ever mistake you for Chris Packham, Gem.'

'And what's all this shite about a missing lad? I told you what it's like in those shitehole northern isles. Any same person would run away as soon as they learned to tie their shoelaces. That boy's got way more sense than you, Danny-boy. And you want me to come running up tae the frozen north? Well, you can fuck right off, laddie.'

'It's two missing boys now. Both disappearances are linked to Mallach and Neptune Shipping.'

'Aw shite! That's bad. See, I ken ya want to find these boys, but why drag me into it?'

Gemma was actually starting to sound concerned. He almost felt bad about asking for help. Almost.

'I need someone who can look after themselves and can ask questions without arousing suspicion. An undercover agent.'

'A bruiser and a bullshitter. I'm flattered.'

'I expect you've been called worse. So, will you do it?'

'Do I have to sit in one of those wee sheds? Watch bowfin birds all day?'

'The wee shed called a hide. And no, it's just a cover story. You do understand the concept, right? You might have to learn a few bird names and sound knowledgeable, but that's all.'

'Aye. That'll be the bullshitting then. I prefer the bruising, to be fair. And I get paid for this? Generous rates you said in the email.'

'Of course. Not like offshore, though. The same rates as the loss ad-justers are paying me.'

'I wouldn't pay you in washers, but I suppose these insurance wankers have money to burn, eh?'

'Looks like they do. So, are you in?'

'Aye. OK. I'm doing it for the lost boys, no for you. And I'm no getting straight off a chopper and flying up to Orkney. Give me a day to wash ma knickers and pack a bag. I'll be there soon enough. God help me.'

Danny was so relieved he promised to buy her a bottle of single malt to counteract the tedium of bird watching. As well as the binoculars, the bird book and a couple of other props. He drew the line at a top-of-the-range down-filled jacket. He offered her a woolly hat and a thermos flask instead. She hung up.

After some more fruitless internet searches, Danny headed down to the seafront for a spot of lunch. He found a café beside the harbour and sat by the window watching the waves roll up the Shapinsay ferry slipway and break against the lifeboat pier. Grey clouds were building from the west and rain began spotting and streaking the window, obscuring his view.

After a satisfying Scotch Rarebit (like the Welsh version, but with a dash of cooking whisky), he reluctantly abandoned the shelter of the cafe. It was time to seek out the ominous-sounding Lock-n-Load Storage. The rain was heavier now. He was thankful that he hadn't promised Gemma his waterproof jacket. He pulled up the hood and trudged along the seafront to a small industrial estate on the edge of town.

It looked like no one was at home at Lock-n-Load, but their side gate was unlocked. Danny ignored the irony and let himself in. Their state-of-the-art storage facilities turned out to be a row of shipping containers stacked two high in places. Most of them were padlocked, but he found a couple he could open.

He sighed. Was he wasting his time? Boxes and crates from someone's delayed house move, push bikes which may have been stolen, old furniture that was only fit for firewood and a dozen life-size cardboard cut-outs of Sean Connery. Nothing that looked like medical supplies or even purloined oil industry equipment.

Danny exited the last container. He was about to give up and head back to his B&B when he heard the crunch of footsteps on gravel behind him. Instinct made him duck as something solid struck him on the back of the neck. It was a glancing blow rather than the bone-cruncher it might have been, but he threw himself to the ground as if he'd been properly poleaxed.

He lay still as his assailant prodded him with his boot and rifled through his pockets. Danny felt himself being dragged over loose gravel. It looked like he was leaving the way he came in. If the guy decided to throw him in the back of a van, he was going to get a shock. Danny wasn't in the best shape, but he was damned if he'd let anyone abduct him without a fight.

The dragging stopped. He heard a vehicle start up and pull away. He waited for a good few minutes before opening one eye and surveying his surroundings. He appeared to be lying in an overgrown alley behind the industrial estate. Once he was sure there was no one else around, he pushed himself up onto his knees.

His wallet was lying next to him. His assailant had removed all the cash, but had thoughtfully left the credit cards behind. Not a professional thief then. His private investigator's card had been tossed in a shallow ditch and bore a distinct boot mark. Danny wasn't sure if this was a symbolic gesture. He scrabbled in the mud to retrieve it.

His phone was also in the ditch. He picked it up and took some crime-scene selfies, including a few of the lump on the back of his head. If he found out who was responsible, they might come in handy. He considered calling the police but decided against it. He didn't like to explain why he was trespassing. That would only reinforce the Orkney constabulary's already low opinion of him.

Danny staggered into town, calling into the nearest corner shop for paracetamol and a bag of frozen peas. He carried his vital medical supplies back to his B&B and lay on the bed, using the peas as a pillow.

He told his landlady he'd banged his head on some scaffolding. She offered to make him an omelette for his tea. She even poured him a bottle of stout, explaining that her late Uncle Bob always used this as a headache cure. It turned out that Uncle Bob had died from a brain haemorrhage, but Danny decided to risk it, anyway.

He tucked into his omelette. Gradually, the pounding in his head eased. Danny was sure this wasn't down to the drugs, or even the drink. An act of kindness at the end of a wicked day was the best cure of all.

Chapter Eleven

Danny checked out the next morning and made his way to the ferry. He was surprised by how anxious he felt. This was only a fortnight's assignment. Chances were, he'd have nothing to do other than hand out painkillers and sticking plasters. And yet, starting this job was fraying his nerves more than his first flight offshore.

His head was full of unwanted memories. Scott Viklund lying on the bed in the Cuillin Alpha sickbay. Gemma's vain attempts to resuscitate him. History never repeats, so they say, unless you're trying to sleep. Then it's on an endless loop.

It didn't help that he had ulterior motives for being there. That he would keep secrets from his new colleagues. Of course, undercover agents always kept secrets. But so did the people they were investigating. Killers were, by nature, professional liars. He, by comparison, was a mere amateur.

His cover story was almost true and Gemma's was a complete fabrication. She would still make a much better spy. He could imagine her pretending to be a medic, blagging and blustering her way through by sheer force of personality and her unwavering self-confidence.

The ferry journey to Mallach was short, but the sea was determined to make it as uncomfortable as possible. Short choppy waves rolled down the Sound, each one timed perfectly to pitch the boat straight into the next crest. It felt to Danny like they were dropping off a series of small cliffs.

It was still better than taking a helicopter ride out to an offshore platform. At least the ferry would not fall out of the sky. He might prefer to drown if this went on much longer, but his wish was unlikely to be granted.

It was a short walk to the oil terminal security gate. The only difficulty was staying upright in the gusting wind as he made his way along the pier. He had one hand on the guardrail and the other grasping hold of his kitbag as it span round with the swirling wind.

There was no reception building to speak of, just a cabin that was home to a couple of sour-faced security guards. They looked like an old and unhappily married couple. They weren't expecting him and made no attempt to make him feel welcome.

'I'd call the terminal manager, but he won't be there,' the male guard said. According to the photo ID clipped to his breast pocket, his name was Alain MacKay. 'Monday morning briefing. You'll have to wait here.'

There were only two chairs in the cabin, and they were both on the far side of the desk. Danny signed in and started checking emails on his phone.

'You'll have to turn that thing off.' The female guard's badge was harder to read. Janet, or Janie maybe? Different surname anyway. Not a MacAnything.

'Could I just put it in airplane mode? In case I need to check something.'

'No,' Mackay said.

'It's the rules,' NoMac said.

That was the end of that conversation. NoMac phoned the manager's office and left a message. They sat, or stood, in silence, for ten minutes, watching the wind blow leaves and litter down the road. Finally, a van driver pulled up, showed his pass and was waved through.

'I don't suppose you know my friend Marissa. She visits the terminal from time to time.'

'Couldn't say,' Mackay said.

'We get a lot of visitors,' NoMac added.

Another ten minutes of brooding silence. Eventually, Danny spotted a lone woman in bright orange overalls marching purposefully towards the security cabin. Praying that she had come to save him, he ignored the guards' protestations and headed towards her.

'Danny Verity? I'm Cara Douglas, the Operations Manager. Sorry, Iain couldn't be here to greet you. He's a bit tied up at the moment.'

'No problem. Just pleased someone came. Your security staff didn't seem too happy to see me.'

'Alain and Anna? Oh, don't worry about them. Probably just a bit fed up because they have to go out in the cold. Normally, they send the young guys out to do the rounds, but we are short-staffed. I expect Gordon told you about our missing security guard?'

'He mentioned something about it. I don't recall the guy's name.'

'Ross MacLeod. Nice lad. Local. We're praying they find him soon.'

'Anything I should be aware of? Mental health issues, that sort of thing.'

'I expect Kevan Knox will want to talk to you about it. He's the Terminal Security Manager. Ross was depressed, so he says. Perhaps I should have noticed, but I don't like to pry into people's affairs. If they prefer to hide their feelings, that's fine by me. Hopefully, there will be something in the medical records. Gordon has many fine qualities, but he isn't that thorough when it comes to paperwork.'

Danny thanked her and changed the subject. He didn't want Cara thinking he was too interested in Ross.

'It's a shame Gordon's a bit under the weather. His loss is my gain. I'm looking forward to spending some here. Makes a change from the offshore life.'

'It doesn't suit everyone, but I like it here. Let me show you the accommodation first. Drop off your bag and we'll get a coffee. Hang onto your PPE, though. There's a locker in the sick bay. The accommodation is supposed to be off-limits during working hours. There are a couple of night shift guys sleeping, so we'll have to be quiet.'

The canteen was small but clean and surprisingly modern. They sat in the manager's lounge, which had actual padding on the chairs. Cara took off her overalls, hung them on a peg and slipped covers over her work boots.

She wasn't a Mallach local, but she lived nearby on the island of Eday. She enjoyed the daily commute on the ferry, so she said. She showed him a selfie of her in front of a cottage, next to a stony beach. No sign of a family or a husband. Danny offered to buy her a coffee, but she declined.

'I get to use the magic card today. Free drinks for visitors. You can be my visitor until you start work, at least.'

Cara was quite an elegant woman, out of overalls. It wasn't so much the way she looked as the way she moved that he found appealing. He guessed she was in her early forties, but he was never a good judge of age. If asked, he usually knocked ten years off his estimates to be on the safe side.

As she sashayed back from the counter with two coffees, he tried his best to put such thoughts to one side. He had an important job to do. Two jobs, in fact, maybe three. He couldn't afford to add more complications to this already convoluted situation.

'How do you know Gordon?' she asked.

'The offshore oil industry is a small world. There aren't that many medics. If you stick around long enough, you get to meet everyone in the end.'

'But surely there's only one of you on a platform at one time? You just pass each other on the helideck and that's it.'

Danny wished he'd had time to think up a more comprehensive back-story.

'That's not the case for medics, I'm afraid. Continuous professional development. That means a lot of training courses. It's a downside of the job. I met Gordon at an emergency medicine seminar in Edinburgh. I told him I was going to be in Orkney this week. We were going to meet up for a beer. I didn't expect to be doing his job for him.'

'Well, it's lucky you were around. Rather a handy coincidence.'

'I suppose so. Though if I hadn't been there, I'm sure Gordon would have found someone else. He seems to know a lot of people in the business.'

'So, what brought you to Orkney?'

Danny paused. He hadn't planned to mention Gemma, but they would have to meet occasionally to swap notes. On this small island, someone was bound to spot them. Better to come up with a plausible reason in advance.

'I've got a friend who is mad keen on bird watching. She's coming to Orkney for a couple of weeks. I said I'd spend a few days with her. Probably in some draughty bird hide. Now I'm spending two weeks in an oil terminal instead.'

'Well, you can still meet up, I guess. I mean, we don't lock you in the compound.'

'I was going to ask about that. Gordon said they had to have a medic available all the time. I wasn't sure if I had to be on-site 24/7.'

'There's nothing to stop you wandering off for a while, so long as you tell security. We have other first-aiders on site. We'd rather you didn't leave the island, though, unless you really have to.'

'I've booked her into the holiday cottage on Mallach for a few days. She might not thank me for it. It looks a bit basic.'

'If she's a keen bird-watcher, she'll love it here. Those nature-loving types don't usually worry too much about home comforts. I'm sure she'll have a great time.'

Danny was not convinced. He hadn't got round to telling Gemma that there wasn't even a bar on the island. At least he now had official permission to visit her when he was off duty.

Chapter Twelve

CARA TOOK HIM OVER to the sickbay, at the far end of the single-storey office block. This facility was larger but shabbier than the one he had offshore. At least the equipment was up to scratch, even if the paintwork was not. She handed him a small mountain of health and safety paperwork and a handbook.

'That should keep you busy. I'm afraid I'll have to leave. I'm not feeling too good today either.'

'Anything I can help with?'

'Women's problems. Nothing you want to know about, believe me.'

Danny was happy to take her word for it. The offshore medic's course was pretty comprehensive, but there were limits.

'Iain will talk you through the incidents and priorities after lunch. He'll give you a tour of the plant as well. It's not as torturous as an offshore platform, but you can still get lost in the belly of the beast. There's a layout of the site in your safety handbook. It's not that easy to follow unless you have a degree in Process Engineering. In case of emergency, head for the comms tower. The muster point is in the car park, at the foot of the mast.'

Cara passed him her business card in case he needed someone to call. She really did have an MSc in Process Engineering. Plus a CEng and an IChemE, whatever those might be. It was comforting that someone knew what they were doing, even if it wasn't him.

He resisted the urge to rush off and explore. He'd be bound to get lost. That could be a handy excuse when he wanted to snoop around out of bounds, but he'd better save that one for later. He might need it.

Danny powered up the sickbay computer. Someone had kindly left the medic's username and password on a card wedged in the keyboard, along with the Wi-Fi password and Gordon Breck's phone number. Hardly the most secure arrangement. It was not surprising. Breck was a fixture here, but plenty of other medics must come and go when he was off shift.

There were desktop shortcuts to various folders on the company server. Danny spent a couple of hours doing some virtual snooping. The personnel files were protected, but there was a weekly list of who was on site. No mention of anyone called Marissa, but it wasn't clear if the list included visitors. Aidan wasn't on the list either, so clearly it didn't include delivery drivers.

Medifax were in the approved suppliers' register, but no mention of Neptune Shipping. Danny thought they might transport equipment to and from the terminal, but if they were, they were doing it on the sly, or through yet another subsidiary company.

Something had been done to the USB ports to block memory sticks and external hard drives. So instead, he had to print off the files he was interested in and grab them before anyone noticed. The printer was in the open-plan admin office next door and it wasn't easy to get to it unnoticed.

Danny struck up a conversation with Fiona, a woman in a kaftan dress whose grey hair was enlivened by turquoise highlights. He made the schoolboy error of telling her he was the replacement medic. Fiona had more ailments than the average A&E department. The printer started beeping and she hauled herself out of her chair and shuffled over to help.

'Doctor says I should keep mobile. Easy for him to say. Now, what's the problem here? This printer gives out nearly as often as my ankle. Did I tell you about my ankle? Doctor says it's gout, but I've been looking on the internet and I'm not so sure.'

Danny managed to extract the printout and stuff it in a manila folder while she pulled out various compartments and put them back together again. She jabbed the start button a few times and the printer spat out the remaining sheets concertina-style. They were just about readable. Danny thanked Fiona and hurried back to sickbay before she had a chance to expound on Dr Google's diagnosis.

The door was open. A tall, serious-looking man with a scruffy grey beard and suspiciously dark sideburns had parked his greasy orange overalls on the spare patient's chair. Danny was about to ask him to move until he caught sight of his security pass.

'Hi. I'm Iain Grant. The terminal manager. Glad you could come at such short notice. Ready for your grand tour?'

'Cara said you'd want to go through the health and safety forms first.'

'Cara would say that. She's my nagging conscience. Essential, but annoying. I'd rather get out on the plant. The sun's shining and there's an outside chance that we might make it round without getting soaked. That doesn't often happen on Mallach, so make the most of it.'

Danny stuffed the folder at the bottom of the paper mountain and fished his PPE back out of the cupboard.

Even the sun reflecting off the six giant crude oil tanks couldn't make the terminal an attractive sight. Everything he touched was covered with a thin layer of grit-laden grime. The smell wasn't as bad as he expected, but then the wind switched direction and he got a noseful of some noxious chemical that made him sneeze and cough.

'Dead crude,' Iain said, pointing at the tanks. 'All of our oil comes from the offshore platforms. That's the live stuff. It either has gas dissolved in it naturally, or the platform uses natural gas to make it easier to pump it out of the ground. Once it gets here, we extract the gas to produce the dead crude. Nasty, thick, black gunk, but it's easier to store and transport.'

Iain talked about storage capacity and how many barrels a day passed through the terminal. It meant little to Danny. He wasn't even sure how big an oil barrel was. He pictured an old-fashioned wooden beer barrel.

Hundreds of them, all stacked on top of each other. When did they stop using actual barrels? Iain was looking at him in a questioning manner.

'Sorry. Just trying to visualise all that oil. You were saying?'

'I was just asking if you knew anything about propane production.'

'Only what I remember from GCSE chemistry. Methane, ethane, propane, right?'

'Very good. I'm sure your chemistry teacher would be proud.'

His chemistry teacher would be amazed. He'd failed the GCSE spectacularly. That lesson must have been the only one where he stayed awake.

Beyond the crude tanks were large dome-shaped vessels for the natural gas and row upon row of smaller tanks holding refined products. Beyond was the propane plant and another security gate. Unmanned this time.

'We can take a quick look inside. You shouldn't need to access this area unless anyone raises a health and safety issue. Your pass will open the gate.'

His company pass card did indeed let him through the turnstile gate and into the process zone. He nearly swiped his PI licence instead. Both were credit-card sized and carried the same dodgy photo. That would have been hard to explain.

'If you need to get in here, please don't come alone. Get Cara or one of her team to accompany you. There are a lot of potential hazards. If you get to be a regular, we can bring you up to speed on the process side of things. Gordon seems to spend half his time on holiday or off sick these days. I'm worried he's about to announce his retirement. We need to get a replacement, or at least a stand-in, lined up.'

Iain wasn't exactly offering him the job, but he was undoubtedly dangling a carrot. Mallach oil terminal might not be everyone's idea of an ideal working environment, but it was the lap of luxury compared to life on an offshore oil platform. The regular income would please his bank manager and his soon-to-be-ex-wife. Of course, if he really wanted the job, Iain could never find out that he'd been spying on the terminal. Ross turning up without his help, dead or alive, would go a long way towards keeping his secret safe.

For now, he had the freedom to poke his nose wherever he wanted. Though his nose wasn't keen on spending too long around here. Most of the gas plant was out in the open air. A good thing, judging by the smell.

'That's the last part of the process,' Iain said, 'Natural gas is odourless when it comes out of the ground. We add mercaptan. Smells like rotten eggs. We do the same to the propane. You always want to know when there's a build-up of gas.'

Danny wondered why they couldn't use Chanel No 5 instead. Though rotten eggs would certainly do the trick if you wanted people to run away from the smell. Maybe you got used to it eventually. Otherwise, it wouldn't take long for this job to lose its appeal.

There were a couple of metal-clad buildings along the side of the plant furthest from the sea. Iain didn't offer to show him around.

'Testing, trials, small scale production. I leave that sort of thing to Cara and the chemistry boffins to deal with.'

Another gate led out onto a tarmac track with grass and weeds growing through the middle of it.

'That leads down to the substation and the emergency generators. I'd stay out of there if I were you. If you grab hold of one of those cables, there won't be much left of you.'

Danny had a nasty flashback to the electrified cat. The smell of charred fur was still imprinted on his brain. That was only a domestic substation. It was hard to imagine what the wires on one of those giant pylons would do to you.

There was another turnstile gate leading into the electrical compound. Danny wondered if his card opened that one as well. Pushing someone into a high voltage substation sounded like a good way of killing them and getting rid of the evidence.

Danny reminded himself that he wasn't yet looking for a body or even the atomised remains of one. Ross could still be alive. Propping up a bar in Shetland, maybe. It would be nice to think so, but his overstimulated investigator's nose told him otherwise.

Chapter Thirteen

THERE WERE A COUPLE of wooden benches next to the pier, weather-beaten and rotten in places. Danny selected the most intact one. He perched on the end with the fewest woodworm holes and waited for Gemma's ferry to arrive from Kirkwall.

He wished he'd brought something to read. Even Manhunt! was better than staring at his phone. There was no signal, anyway. He leaned back, closed his eyes and dreamt of home. Sadly, that wasn't the most uplifting train of thought.

After their separation, Danny had been obliged to move out of the house he'd shared with Kelly for the last three years. He'd tried to argue that they could be separated in the same house. They barely spoke anyway and avoided each other as much as possible. That cut no ice with Kelly or her solicitor.

One day, he'd come home to find all his stuff neatly packed into boxes and sitting out on the lawn under a tarpaulin. Kelly had even gone to the trouble of calling her cousin, Saul, who worked for a removals firm. Saul reluctantly took everything into storage but had refused to find somewhere to store Danny.

He ended up staying in the city centre lodgings-cum-dosshouse for two weeks while he searched for accommodation. Eventually, he found an upstairs flat for rent on St Michael's Road in Headingley, right behind the Leeds Rhinos' stadium.

'Gets a bit noisy on match days,' the rental agent had said. Like that was a bad thing. Noise meant the home team was winning. Music to Danny's ears.

You could see one end of the pitch from his bedroom window, plus the top of the other goalposts and the scoreboard. Occasionally, a stray conversion sent the ball bouncing off the rooftops and into his backyard. He kicked most of them back, but one he kept. He'd hoped to get it signed by the players, but was too embarrassed to hang around outside the changing rooms with the school kids.

In his youth, Danny played briefly as a winger for the Rhinos' under-15s. He had visions of sprinting down the touchline to score a try at Wembley one day. But he never grew tall enough to play with the big boys. He'd kept waiting for that promised growth spurt to kick in. It never did. In the meantime, he'd spent most of the game being trampled into the mud by bigger and stronger opponents.

His last match was a savage mauling by Hunslet. He'd lasted about ten minutes before the opposition hooker, who was about twice his size and missing several teeth, tackled him from the side and sent him crashing into the advertising hoardings. He'd spent the rest of the match sitting on the bench with ice packs on various parts of his body. After that, his parents had intervened.

'You're going to get yourself killed, Daniel,' his mum had said.

'Aye, and that's not the worst of it,' his dad had added. 'You're an embarrassment to the shirt. Give it up, lad. Do summat you're actually good at.'

That was the end of Danny's rugby dream. When he called the coach to tell him his doctor had told him to quit, he sounded relieved. The blue and gold shirt in question, once Danny's pride and joy, was smeared with mud and his blood. His mother had attempted to repair it; Danny still owned it, but never wore it since.

Danny spent the following winter playing football, and the summer crouched behind the stumps at his local cricket ground. He would never make the grade in either sport, but he was considerably less likely to end up in hospital. Ironic, he thought, given his subsequent career choices.

The arrival of the ferry snapped him out of his reverie. When Gemma came over to greet him, he realised why he'd been reminiscing about his short-lived rugby league career. Gemma would be right at home in a scrum. She was the only person he knew whose greetings required a risk assessment and protective equipment. He leaned in to give her a platonic peck on the cheek and instead received what he could only describe as an affectionate head-butt. She didn't draw blood, but it rattled his teeth and gave him momentarily blurred vision. She followed that up with a friendly volley of jabs to the chest, which felt like they might have fractured several ribs.

'Good to see you too,' he gasped, taking up a defensive stance, like a boxer about to be knocked down in the first round.

He was saved from more punishment by the arrival of Mrs McAllister on her death-trap motorcycle. She tooted her horn, and he helped Gemma load her bag into the sidecar.

'This is for you.' Danny handed her a rucksack containing some water-proofs, binoculars, and a book entitled Birds of Shetland and Orkney. Plus the bottle of scotch, of course. She slipped it over her shoulder and perched pillion behind Mrs McAllister.

'Hang on, dearie. It's not far into Bron. You can walk, can't you, laddie?'

It wasn't far, but it was starting to rain. He'd given his expensive cagoule to Gemma, and his work jacket was showerproof at best. He jogged behind the car, hoping to make it to the cottage before the heavens opened.

He wanted to be there when she saw the cottage. She might just punch him properly this time, but putting his personal safety to one side, someone had to stop her from turning around and heading straight back to the ferry.

He needn't have worried. By the time he arrived at the cottage, puffing and panting, Mrs McAllister had the kettle on. Gemma was laughing at a story where a birdwatcher mistook one of her garden ornaments for a glossy ibis.

'I hope you'll be comfortable here. I'm afraid it's a bit basic, hen.'

'Nae bother, Ellen. I'm used to roughing it. I mean them birds dinnae nest in five-star hotels, worse luck.'

Mrs McAllister had a first name. Who knew? Gemma, obviously. He congratulated himself on hiring a first-rate assistant investigator. He just hoped she didn't expect a pay rise.

'These fancy cakes are grand, Ellen. Just the job after a long voyage.'

Nobody offered him one, so he helped himself when Ellen's back was turned. A cuppa would have been nice, but there were only two mugs. And two chairs. He decided to leave them to it. The terminal lacked character compared to the cottage, but at least he could get a hot drink and sit down in comfort.

'Well, I guess I'll let you settle in. Let me know how you get on with the wildlife. Don't mind me. I'll dry off soon enough.'

They didn't mind him at all. The two women were back to chatting and laughing like old friends. He pulled up his hood and started back up the road. The rain was wicking up his sleeves, and his boots squelched as he walked.

On days like these, an investigator's lot was not a happy one. If he needed any extra incentive to complete his task quickly, the Orkney weather was providing it. He was going to find what happened to Ross and soon, even if he had to turn the terminal upside down and search every sodden blade of grass on this accursed island.

Chapter Fourteen

THROUGH THE COTTAGE WINDOW, Gemma watched Danny trudge up the lane in the driving drizzle. She almost felt sorry for him, but it was his own fault. Fancy asking her to spend her precious leave on this god-forsaken rock.

Constable Verity could do the plod work and the getting wet part. She would concentrate on interviewing suspects in the warm and dry. She was clearly the brains of this operation. Detective Inspector Gauld. It had a nice ring to it.

It was a shame that Danny had to be the one to go undercover. He'd be crap at it. Too honest by half. But the vacancy was for a medic, not a radio operator. He would probably blow his cover at which point, she would be forced to go rescue him: fists flying and steel toe-capped boots striking soft tissue. She hadn't had a good scrap in ages. She would be straight round there. So long as it wasn't raining.

Mother McAllister had started on another rambling tale of island life. Gemma was only half-listening, but she enjoyed hearing Ellen speak. Tea and cake. Stories by the fireside. It reminded her of the books she read as a child. Absolutely nothing like her own childhood, of course, but that was the wonder of fiction for you.

Her mother had preferred cigarettes and scotch by the flickering glow of the TV. She liked her soaps, and she liked her drink. That was about it. She had a temper, but had never struck her daughter. There was always food on the table. Packets and takeaways, mostly. She wasn't a bad mother. Just not a particularly good one.

That was more than Gemma could say for her father. He left home on her sixth birthday. She remembered it clearly. They'd spend some of it in A&E and the rest in a police station. Her ma and da were always fighting. Sometimes with words, sometimes with fists. To be fair, it was her ma who started the last fight. But her father was bigger and stronger and that time, he went too far. He'd knocked her down, removing her front teeth in the process. He was still apologising and begging for forgiveness when she hit him over the head with the scotch bottle.

It was Gemma who called for the ambulance. And it was the ambulance crew that called for the police. Social workers got involved. There was talk of Gemma going into care. Nothing much happened in the end. Her ma got new teeth. Her da packed his bags and never came back. Good riddance to bad rubbish.

She wondered idly what it would have been like to be brought up here. Milking goats and clubbing seals, or whatever they did for fun on Mallach. Crammed into the wee cottage with Ellen and her extended family. The idea was strangely appealing. It was probably too late to get herself adopted, though.

'Is there a Mr McAllister?'

'Long gone. Bored himself to death, I reckon. He was a good father to the bairns, but Jesus Christ, he was a dull man. Not a lot of choice on a small island. I should have left and married for love. Instead, I stayed and married for farm and family. It's not been a bad life, but I wish I'd had a chance to see more of the world.'

'What about the bairns?'

'They moved far away. I don't blame them. One's in Glasgow. He comes home often enough, but he never stays long. My daughter's in America, would you believe? Oklahoma. Like in the musical. I didn't even know it was a real place. I have a grandchild I've seen but once and another on the way. She says she'll pay for me to fly out there. Maybe I will, one day.'

'Aye, you should. You'd enjoy it. I don't suppose it's all cornfields and singing cowboys.'

'Maybe so. But what about you? No one special in your life? That Danny's not bad for an English lad. He ran all the way here to see you were alright. He must have taken a shine to you, eh?'

'Danny? Don't mind him. He's a bit soft in the head.'

'You could do worse, you know.'

'Aye, I have done. Plenty worse. I can certainly pick the wrong 'uns. I'm taking a wee break from men. I'd rather concentrate on the birds. It's a lot less grief.'

'Well, I'm no expert on our peedie feathered friends. They're all just whitemaas to me. Screeching gulls and cackling geese. I'll introduce you to Heather Anderson. She fae Edinburgh, but she not so bad for all that. I asked her to call round. She'll be happy to show you the best places.'

That's all I need, thought Gemma. An expert. Talk about Danny blowing his cover. It'll take her ten seconds to realise I know nothing about those feathered feckers.

'I would want to be any trouble.'

'No trouble. Heather is willing to talk to anyone about wildlife. The hard part is getting her to stop.'

Ellen wasn't exaggerating. Heather showed up after dinner. She was keen to show Gemma a colony of guillemot nesting on the cliffs at Bowcheek Ness.

'It's a bit late, eh?'

'Not to worry. It's not far from the village and it's a lovely clear evening.'

It might not have been far, but the walk up to the viewpoint had Gemma gasping. Heather must be fit as a lop. She hardly stopped talking long enough to breathe. She was undoubtedly a mine of information, but most of it went flying over Gemma's head. Much like the guillemots. The difference being that the birds were trying to crap on her head at the same time.

For once, Gemma was happy not to get a word in edgeways. She replied with the occasional rephrased ornithological gem while nodding knowledgeably. That seemed sufficient to reassure Heather that they were kindred birders.

'Aye, I see those pear-shaped eggs you were saying about. Fiercely territorial, are they? I would be too if I were clinging to the rock by my webbed toenails. Aye, it's a real bitch telling those juveniles apart.'

She ought to be bored senseless by all this bird chat, but she wasn't. It was weirdly fascinating. There were thousands of murmuring guillemots. More birds than she'd ever seen in her life. This vantage point overlooked the whole curve of the bay. Through the binoculars, she saw chicks poking their heads out from under their parents' webbed yellow feet. Entire families balanced on a ledge no bigger than her hand.

Adult birds dive-bombed the water, came up with tiny fish or crabs and carried them back to the nest. They were effortless flyers and expert divers. It was a wildlife spectacular. Impressive enough on old David Attenborough's programmes. Watching it live, the sheer scale of it, with all its attendant smells and sounds, was something else.

'Well, fuck me. That's a lot of fucking gulls.' So much for the intellectual birdie blather. 'Sorry, hen. I work offshore. The lads swear so much it rubs off on you.'

'Don't worry about it, Gemma. I said pretty much the same thing when I first came here. So many different birds. So much to see. And this is just one part of a small island. Wait till you get to Hoy and Westray and the rest of Orkney.'

Not much chance of that unless Danny pulled his finger out.

'I kept coming back to Orkney on holiday. For years. And then I decided to stay.'

'Please tell me you didn't shack up with some farmer, like auld Ellen.'

'No. A farmer's daughter as it happens.'

'Jesus! That must have gone down like a lead auk in these parts. Did the Wee Frees not come around with burning crosses and the like?'

'Most people just accepted it. Rona and I kept our heads down. I mean, we didn't exactly hide our relationship. But nor did we go skipping hand-in-hand to the Kirk on a Sunday, or organising the world's smallest pride parade. I got called a few names I don't care to repeat, but I'm used to that.'

'But surely you're not the only gay gals on the island.'

'I think we might be. There is one other, but she's so far in the closet, she can probably see Narnia. It's a shame. Most youngsters leave the islands for the bright city lights as soon as they can. Even the straight ones.'

'What about your Rona's family?'

'Grandpa Dow wasn't best pleased, but I don't think it was much of a surprise to Rona's parents. They might have kicked up more of a fuss if I'd tried to take her back to Edinburgh. Rona was all set to go, but I wanted to stay here. I've never regretted it. Not for a second.'

Gemma was starting to see why someone might choose a new life in Orkney. She still preferred the bright lights of Aberdeen, though. It would take more than new friends and a flock of seagulls to change that.

Chapter Fifteen

So, ELLEN HAD PERSUADED another mug to rent her tumbledown cottage. A twitcher. Did these people have nothing better to do? Nancy wasn't surprised to see Heather Anderson. The dyke from Auld Reekie. Orkney was getting overrun by outsiders. Queer tree-huggers and gender-fluid crystal gazers. Give them a proper day's work. It would kill them for sure.

It was hard making a living on Mallach. A hard life on any island, for that matter. The so-called Scottish government did nothing to help her and the other real workers. They wanted to encourage eco-tourism, did they? What about the rest of us? The ones that have proper jobs?

Ellen McAllister would never approve of her solution. Nor would the damn fool government. Her way might not be legal, but it was still far better than living off neo-pagans and bird-brain naturalists.

This new one looked as fat and stupid as the rest. She wasn't with the polis, even they had standards. No sign of the guy who'd snooped around. A detective? If so, he had found nothing worth hanging around for.

She was tired and bored of watching the watchers. The dyke and the tourist were up on the cliff now. With a firm helping hand, both of them would go flying with the birds. Until they landed on the rocks, of course. It was very tempting. No one would be any the wiser.

Those cliffs aren't safe, I told them. Something should be done about it. What a terrible accident, officer. There would still be broken bodies lying on the shore. If there was a body, the police would be involved. She liked the other solution better. No body. No loose ends. No problem.

Chapter Sixteen

DANNY SPENT A SURPRISINGLY comfortable night in the terminal. The accommodation block didn't look much, just a stack of prefabricated cabins behind the canteen. He had no complaints about the bed, though, and he had his own washroom and shower.

His main worry was having to share with a snoring oil worker. This was different to the offshore setup, where the medic had his own cabin next to the sick bay. Fortunately, there were enough spare beds for him to have a room to himself for now.

The canteen provided evening meals for the inmates. The food was basic, but okay. It wasn't like there were any other fine-dining options on Mallach. At six a.m., it opened for breakfast and Danny decided to go for a full Scottish breakfast again, just in case the snacking options were not as excellent or as frequent as offshore.

He strolled over to sickbay, grabbing a coffee from the machine on the way. He'd just settled into his chair and fired up the PC when there was a knock on the door. His first patient? Not that he wished anyone ill, but he wanted to make himself useful. Indispensable even.

It was Cara. He tried not to look disappointed. He was happy enough to see her, but not the pile of paperwork she was carrying.

'It's a shame about Gordon, but I'm glad you're here, to be honest. Gordon is a competent medic, but he can be rather casual with his other duties. I'm afraid it feels like Iain conspires with him. Neither of them seems very interested in risk assessments or even the health and safety aspects. I'm sure with all your offshore experience, it's second nature to you.'

Jack Clark, the OIM on Cuillin Alpha, had given him an in-depth introduction to health and safety paperwork. Danny preferred Iain Grant's approach. Still, if he wanted to make himself useful, this was one way of doing it. Hopefully, he could sift through the forms this morning and then get started on his investigation.

By the time he'd finished his third mug of coffee, it was clear that he was being hopelessly optimistic. He was only halfway through last week's safety report cards and the letterbox outside sickbay was already filling up with new ones. There were the medication records to update and the incident reports to review. The updates from the Health and Safety Executive could probably wait. At least he hoped so. The way Cara was talking, she might set a quiz for him at any time.

It was a good thing no sick people were banging on his door. He didn't have time to deal with them as well. His priority had to be finding out more about Ross and what happened to him. He would have to make time for that. His first target was the security supervisor, Kevan Knox. Gordon had reservations about him. Danny needed an excuse to talk to Knox without arousing suspicion.

His excuse arrived in the form of a safety report card highlighting a lack of safeguarding for staff with mental health issues. It didn't mention Ross by name but talked about absenteeism because of stress and depression. The company wasn't doing enough to help younger members of staff in particular.

Armed with the card and the company safeguarding procedure, he went in search of Kevan. Anna Jansen was manning the gatehouse by herself today.

'Alain is on an industrial espionage course.' She didn't seem to know if he was learning how to become a spy or how to stop one. 'Kevan's on patrol. He does a lot of his patrolling around the smoke shack. Try there first.'

Danny thanked her and consulted his site plan. The smoke shack was near the canteen. Their coffee was better than the machine-made kind, so he decided to accomplish two things at once.

A man was sitting at a picnic bench munching on a cheese sandwich. His sizable frame was squeezed into navy blue overalls with "SECURITY" emblazoned across the back in large white letters. Danny strolled over and placed his coffee on the bench.

'Kevan Knox?' The man nodded. 'I'm Danny Verity. I'm standing in for Gordon Breck. Sorry to interrupt your break. Could I have a word?'

Knox continued chewing his sandwich, but motioned for Danny to join him at the table. He was relieved not to have to buttonhole Knox while being asphyxiated in the smoke shack. This was a far more pleasant environment.

'I've been given a safeguarding issue to look into. It's a general concern, but Iain thinks it's related to a young chap who went missing recently. Ross? I didn't catch his surname. I believe he works for you.'

'Mmm. Aye. That's right. Ross MacLeod. Poor lad. He'd been down in the dumps the past few weeks. I dinna ken why.'

'Did you speak to him about it?'

'Aye. But it's not an easy subject. Mental health and all that. They're always on about opening up and not hiding your feelings. I was in the army for years. Start opening up about your feelings and next thing you know, you're cleaning the lavvy with your toothbrush.'

'How about Ross? Was he prepared to talk about his problems?'

'Not to me.'

'Anyone else? Did he have any friends here?'

'Not friends as such. He hadn't been in the job long. He was pally with one of the admin girls. Lorna Kerr. She's fae Mallach. I wouldn't say they were close, though.'

'What about visitors to the terminal? I mean, sometimes people open up to strangers easier.'

'I wouldn't know about that. He took a shine to the lass fae the revenue, but he's not the only one. I doubt she'd be a sympathetic shoulder to cry on. Too full of herself by half.'

'Maybe I should talk to her anyway? What's her name?'

'I don't rightly know. Something foreign. Are you sure this is all about safeguarding?'

Danny decided he'd pushed the questioning too far. It was time to back off.

'I'm just covering all the bases. In case Iain asks. He seems very concerned.'

Danny pulled out the company safeguarding process. Knox looked uneasy. Danny read out a few paragraphs at random, hoping to unsettle the man. He needed to distract him from wondering about his interest in Ross MacLeod.

Neither Gordon Breck nor the MacLeod family thought Ross was depressed. So how come his boss, a man with all the empathy of a stuffed carp, had come to that conclusion?

The woman "fae the revenue" with the foreign name was intriguing. Might this be the mysterious Marissa? Danny needed to find out when she was next visiting the terminal. In the meantime, he would talk to Lorna Kerr and hope that she was more forthcoming.

Chapter
Seventeen

IT WAS RAINING. A light drizzle. Little more than a sea fret. Even so, old fair-weather Gemma would have stayed firmly indoors, gaming or watching TV. New all-weather Gemma was a tougher prospect altogether. She pulled on her borrowed waterproofs and set out to survey the island.

There was no TV, no Wi-Fi and no phone signal in the cottage. Nothing else to do but walk around in the rain. The strange thing was that she was enjoying it. There is no such thing as bad weather, just unsuitable clothing. Some old Yorkshireman in a flat cap said that. She hated to admit it, but he might be right.

Danny was undoubtedly discovering that right now, with his cheap hi-vis jacket and his threadbare chinos. A shame that the fancy cagoule he loaned her was a bit long in the arm, and the waterproof trousers made her look like a pregnant penguin. She was warm and dry, and fortunately, there was no one on this poxy island she wanted to impress.

Heather could not join her today. Apparently, even hippy twitchers had to work. As much as Gemma had enjoyed her guided tour of the guillemot colony, having Heather tagging along would severely hamper her investigations. She needed to wander as lonely as a clown. A simple, ignorant tourist lost in the rain. That way, she was far more likely to stumble across something suspicious.

Not that she knew exactly what she was looking for. Her plan was to walk around the island trespassing on private property. If they were near nature reserves or nesting sites, so much the better. If not, she would just have to look stupid and feign ignorance. Then, she could hone in on the areas to investigate further by seeing how irate the owners became.

Come to think of it, that would have been an ideal job for Danny. Acting like a slack-jawed balloon was right up his street. Shame he had to stay at the terminal, doing some proper work for a change.

Gemma set out along the same road towards the bay that Heather had taken her along. There was a track on the left. It looked as good a place to start as anywhere. A few birds circled overhead. She stared at them through the binoculars. Crows, or maybe jackdaws.

She checked her new bird book. There had to be some logical order to it, but she was damned if she could see it. The birds were grouped in families with only a very tenuous link between them. All the gulls were together right enough. Crows, however, were hidden away amongst the jays and magpies. The corvids. Wasn't that the name of the beardy guy who used to run the Labour Party?

Crows anyway. Unless they were rooks. Or ravens. She didn't give a flying fig what they were. She just had to sound convincing in case anyone asked what she'd spotted.

At least this book only had Highlands and Islands birds in it. No chance of her saying she'd seen a flock of flamingos and then finding out they never came north of the Med. She decided to walk towards the coast and let the carrion get on with cleaning up the roadkill.

As she approached the cliffs, her opinion of birding went downhill fast. A mob of sleek white seabirds with black caps swooped past. Terns, according to the book. Probably arctic terns, given how bloody cold it was up here.

She must have strayed a bit too close to their nests because they started dive-bombing her. They were only small, but their beaks looked pretty sharp. She pulled up her hood, but one still managed to peck her on the head.

'Piss off, you ungrateful wee bastards!'

She started jogging along the coast path to get away from the terns. Gradually, the attacks became less frequent, and she felt confident enough to pull down her hood. A few scruffy-looking brown birds were swirling around the cliff tops as she rounded the headland. Through the binoculars, she tentatively identified them as great skuas.

The name alone should have been enough to warn her away, but she was determined not to be scared off by a bunch of birds. At first, they seemed to be happily flying around looking for whelks or whatever they ate. Then one spotted her and dived. It was considerably larger and faster than a tern and it was flying straight at her. Surely, it's going to pull up, she thought, but it just kept coming. At the last minute, she threw herself to the ground and landed in some fresh sheep shit.

'Low-flying loon. Could have killed me. And it wouldn't have done you much good either. I don't even like eggs, you bird-brain.'

She lurched to her feet just in time to see another skua plummeting towards her. She was reasonably confident that it wouldn't really fly headlong into her. Almost definitely. This time she had a much closer view of its powerful hooked beak as it screamed past her head.

'Alright, alright, I'm away.'

She ran, doubled over, towards a low stone wall, and sat there for a few minutes to catch her breath. The skuas seemed to have lost interest, now that their victory was assured. She made a rude gesture in their direction and headed inland on a stone-strewn track.

The first farmhouse she approached was surrounded by rusting machinery and old cars. There were piles of old bricks and rubble in the fields and what looked like a stack of broken asbestos sheeting. No crops to speak of, just a few mangy cows and bandy ponies. What her grandpa called a junkyard farm. The ideal place to reinforce her view of farmers. Guardians of the countryside, my arse.

She strolled, bold as brass, through the farmyard. Surely these guys would tell her to get tae fuck. She looked forward to turning this shitpile upside down. A young woman appeared from behind the remains of a barn. She had a faraway look, but at least she was smiling, displaying a set of uneven teeth in many shades of yellow.

'Hey there, hen. You lost?'

'I suppose I am. I was heading for Bowcheek Cliffs. Must have taken a wrong turn.'

'No, no. You're right enough. You see the peedie hill there with the gorse at the top?'

That described pretty much every hill on Mallach, but she nodded anyway.

'You stay to the right of the hill and follow the stream until you come to the woods there. You'll see a track that goes up to the cliffs. It's a bit wet underfoot, but you'll manage. Can I fetch you a scone? Homemade they are, hen.'

Well, appearances can be deceptive. Gemma continued her journey weighed down with a bag of scones and a jar of blackberry jam. She was grateful for the gift but, with a hill to climb, she would have preferred home delivery.

She had no intention of heading to Bowcheek. If Ross had jumped or been pushed into the sea, there was hardly going to be anything to find. From the hilltop, she could see two more isolated dwellings nearby. Checking to see that scone girl wasn't watching, she scuttled down the far side of the hill and made her way along the track to the nearest building, a tiny stone-built croft. It looked deserted. She knocked on the door. No sounds of movement inside. She turned the handle, and the door swung open.

Someone had been here recently. There was a half-drunk cup of tea and a half-opened tin of beans by the sink. The contents didn't smell too good, but they weren't furred with mould. The lights didn't work. Nor did the stove. Cold beans might be edible, but only Americans liked cold tea.

On the bare tiled floor, by the kitchen table, was a gas stove and a couple of pans. Behind them was a sleeping bag and a foam mat. Someone was camping in the croft. Could it be Ross?

She looked around but all she found was a dog-eared book on the floor next to the sleeping bag. A Georgette Heyer novel. Gemma didn't like to stereotype the readers of Regency romances, but it couldn't be a young lad, surely?

The croft was reasonably close to her holiday cottage. The best way to find out who was sleeping here was to track anyone she saw travelling this way. Easier said than done, but she didn't have any better ideas.

Gemma had already walked further today than she had since she was a bairn. There was one more house in sight. Assuming the access track wasn't a dead end, it looked like the shortest route back to Bron.

A dog barked as she approached. An inhabited property at least, but Gemma was not keen on dogs. This sounded like a big one. A Rottweiler or maybe a Doberman. She opened the gate and gingerly edged around the farmyard.

With a great woof and the whiff of damp dog, she was knocked to the ground. Giant paws pinned her shoulders to the floor. She stared into the dewy eyes of the biggest St Bernard she'd ever seen.

'Bernie! Get away! You want a battering, do ye?'

The dog's owner raised his stick and Bernie loped off and stood behind him, panting and drooling. Gemma clambered back to her feet. Fortunately, the only damage was to her self-esteem. Her rescuer was a pop-eyed elderly guy with a heavy drinker's red-veined nose and a mud-encrusted tweed jacket. Instead of an apology and maybe a tot of brandy, all she got was a torrent of abuse.

'What you doing coming through here? You're trespassing on private property. It's your own fault if the mutt has your leg off. No good you trying to sue me for it. For all I know, you're here to rob the place. I'm in my rights to set her on trespassers.'

'Hey, pal! Gi' me a break. All I want to do is get to Bron. Just show me the way and I'll be gone.'

'Go back the way you came. Go on. I'll set the bitch on you. See if I don't.'

Bernie was nearly the same height as her wizened owner. She looked around at her master quizzically and yawned. Gemma dusted herself down and stomped off across the dung-splattered farmyard and through the gate at the far side, making a rude gesture towards the farmer and his slobbery dog.

'You can haud yer wheest. Both of you. I'm going this way and you can lump it.'

Bernie barked, but there was no sign that she had a hidden vicious streak. Gemma hoped this track really did lead to Bron. It would be a bit embarrassing going through all that nonsense again.

The track was overgrown with brambles and deeply rutted in places. She wondered if it was leading to another muddy sheep field. There'd been no other way out as far as she'd seen. Not one suitable for the rusty Land Rover he had parked in the barn. Even that miserable bastard must go to the local shop now and again. No supermarket deliveries out here.

Eventually, the track widened out and met a tarmacked lane. Weeds were growing through the surface, but it looked like a proper road, one that might lead to civilisation. After half a mile, the track ended at a T-junction with a lane just wide enough for that old-fashioned Land-Rover. No signpost, of course. Working on instinct rather than information, Gemma turned left. After another half-mile, she arrived on the outskirts of Bron, from where it was a mere ten-minute plod to the cottage.

On the way, she passed the village's one and only shop. In the windows, there were a couple of faded Ordnance Survey maps. How come Danny hadn't thought of that? Piss poor planning, that's what it was. She noted the shop's opening times and added the maps to her shopping list.

Gemma staggered through the front door of the cottage and slumped into the nearest chair. All this exercise and fresh air could not be good for you. Every muscle in her legs was throbbing. Her hips ached and her feet felt like they'd been pounded with a meat tenderiser. She was looking forward to a hot shower, but before she even had time to take off her socks and check for missing toenails, there was a knock at the door.

'Let yourself in,' she said wearily. She wasn't getting up for anyone. Not even if it was the Jehovah's or the Grim Reaper himself.

A young girl poked her head around the door. She was wide-eyed and nervous looking.

'Sorry to disturb you. Ah'm Lorna Kerr. Ma auntie sent me. I was waiting with Mrs McAllister. She said you wouldn't mind me stopping by.'

'Aye, well, you better come in. I expect you've had a cuppa or three already at Ellen's, but you could make me one, if you will.'

Lorna was keen to help. She made Gemma a cup of tea with two sugars and even found a packet of biscuits secreted in the bedside chest of drawers, alongside a well-thumbed bible and a vintage chrome-cased hairdryer.

'Ma said to ask if you needed anything. I pass by on the way to work so I can drop by. It's no problem. Ma said you might need someone to show you around.'

'So, are you a birder then?'

'Aye, no, but I ken where they head. My cousin William goes with them on the weekends. There's a wildlife club. Heather Anderson is the treasurer. Mrs McAllister says you've met.'

'We have, but she didn't mention a club. Any braw lads in it?'

'Aye, no, not exactly. Will's no bad, but he's a bit of a geek. So are his pals, to be fair. Mostly it's butterfly botherers and bird nerds. There's Heather, of course. And her pal Rona goes sometimes. Will asked Rona out once, but ma says he's barking up the wrong tree there.'

Laura's ma had a lot to say, it seemed. It was kind of her to send her artless daughter around, but also somewhat suspicious. Maybe Mrs Kerr was naturally helpful. Or naturally nosy. Perhaps she had other reasons for wanting to spy on strangers. Lorna was such an innocent. She would be spying unknowingly, that was for sure. Her aunt would be pumping her for information. Much as she liked the idea of having Lorna fetching and carrying for her, she would have to nip this idea in the bud.

Chapter Eighteen

Danny poked his head around the admin office door.

'Hi, Laura. Could you pop round to sickbay when you have a moment?'

'Is there a problem?'

'No problem. I'm just hoping you can help me with some paperwork.'

Ten minutes later, Lorna Kerr was sitting at Danny's desk, acting like she was being prepped for surgery.

'Mrs McAlpine says she can only spare me for half an hour. Unless it's a medical emergency.'

'I just wanted to talk to you about Ross MacLeod.'

'Have you any news?'

'Sorry. I don't know any more than you.'

'Well, that *is* good, I suppose. Mrs McAlpine says I should prepare for the worst. Suicide and drowning are the most common causes of death for young men in Orkney, she says.'

'Mrs McAlpine sounds like a cheery soul. I'm sure he just needed to get away for a while. He'll turn up soon enough.'

Danny wasn't convincing anyone with his false optimism. Lorna's lower lip was twitching, and she looked ready to burst into tears. He tried again.

'Look, I know you're worried. That's why Iain Grant asked me to talk to you. I understand you were good friends with Ross?'

'Aye, well, we used to chat in the canteen sometimes.'

'You're both from Mallach, I see.'

'Aye, but he's fae Bron and I'm fae Quoy.'

Two tiny villages about three miles apart, but Lorna made it sound like they were on opposite sides of the iron curtain.

'I see him around when we go to the store, but that's all. His father's a farmer and mine's a fisherman. They don't exactly see eye to eye.'

'So, you're not, you know... involved with Ross then?'

Lorna had a pasty complexion, and her blush was obvious.

'No. Who told you that?'

'No one. But you're concerned about him. I thought there might be something more to it than just the odd chat.'

'Well, I wouldn't have minded him asking me out, but my pa would. Anyhow, Ross has a girlfriend. Not that he sees her much.'

'Not an Orkney girl, then.'

'No, she's foreign. At least her parents are, so Ross said.'

'Have you met her?'

'She comes here sometimes, but I've never spoken to her. She's always in with Mr Grant or out on the plant.'

'How come Ross got to know her?'

'That's what comes of working on the gate. He gets to meet everybody. He even met a real knight once. He did the ground-breaking ceremony for the new wind turbine.'

Lorna seemed to be without guile. Even so, if he continued questioning her for much longer, she might get suspicious. As might her boss.

'Well, thank you for coming to talk to me, Lorna. I'm sure Ross will be back home soon. If there's anything else, please come and see me anytime.'

Please don't tell your colleagues, he thought. Danny didn't want the entire terminal offloading their emotional baggage at his desk. His was supposed to be a caring profession but was far better at dealing with physical ailments than psychological ones.

So Marissa wasn't an imaginary girlfriend. Their relationship was still uncertain. She might just be someone he chatted to when he was guarding the gate. The only way to be sure would be to ask her. Of course, she might lie, but even lies could guide an enquiring mind towards the truth.

How was he going to contact her? He could hardly march up to Iain Grant and ask him for a visitor's phone number. Moreover, the records he could access were only for employees and contractors who worked directly for Orcadia Oil. There was no good reason why he should have details of occasional visit one.

Cara's office door had been closed for most of the morning. He took that as an unofficial "Do Not Disturb" sign. Rather than knock and face potential rejection, Danny tried lurking near the coffee machine. After half an hour, she finally emerged from her office.

'Hi, Cara? Do you have a moment?'

'So long as I can drink my coffee at the same time. It's the end of the month. I have to produce all the figures. It's always manic and I'm not exactly feeling at my best.'

Danny couldn't help but notice that her hand was far from steady. He offered his medical expertise again. She silently waved him into her office and closed the door behind them.

'If I leave it open, the "could you just..." brigade will be in here like a shot. Don't worry about me. I forgot to take my medication this morning. It will pass. Anyway, how can I help you?'

'I was wondering what happens if a visitor falls ill while they're here. It's not in any of the procedures, as far as I can see. We had a problem with that in my last posting. A visitor had a fit in reception. Apparently, I wasn't supposed to treat them, just call an ambulance. Their insurance company was all over it like a rash.'

'Hmm, well, you have a point. Are you volunteering to update our procedures? I'm sure there are several holes in there that an experienced eye might be able to fill.'

Danny wasn't volunteering for any such thing, but it might get him the information he needed.

'Sounds like a poisoned chalice, but I'll take a look if you like. Do you get many visitors, anyway? Maybe I'm wasting my time?'

'I'm not sure of numbers exactly. I expect Fiona could tell you. She issues all the visitor passes. She'll moan, of course. Tell her I sent you and she should be able to give you a quick estimate.'

'I think we've met. She wanted me to look at her ankle.'

'Yeah, that sounds about right.'

So Fiona was Lorna's demoralising line manager? That explained a lot. He found her in the admin office, checking her symptoms on the NHS website. She certainly lived up to her billing. She could have moaned for Scotland.

'I'm very busy just now,' she said, sliding a half-eaten jam doughnut out of sight behind her in-tray. 'I don't have time to go chasing any wild geese.'

'It's just that Cara wanted me to get a list of all the visitors to the terminal as soon as possible. Something to do with the month-end report. Security issues, she said.'

'Well, she could have given me a bit more notice. How far back does she want to go?'

'Oh, just to the beginning of the year.'

'Hmm. Well, at least that's all on the computer. We only stopped doing handwritten passes a couple of years back. Hard to believe we're supposed to be at the cutting edge of technology here. More like the blunt end of the stone age, if you ask me.'

Danny had to endure another ten minutes of anti-company rhetoric before she agreed to email the list to him. He wasn't worried about lying to her. She might go complaining to Cara, but he had the feeling that no one really listened to Fiona, especially when she was in full flow.'

The terminal had more visitors than he expected. Delivery drivers, sales reps, officials, fitters, and fixers of equipment and so on. Anyone who went on the plant had to get security clearance. Those just visiting the offices sat through a five-minute induction video, filled in a form, and were good to go.

It didn't look like anyone bothered to check the information. They were supposed to be escorted, but Danny had already seen at least one IT specialist wandering about on his own with a visitor's pass hung around his neck. Maybe there was a real security issue. Suppose he wasn't the only one working on-site under false pretences?

It took a while for Danny to find Marissa on the list. Fiona had written her name as Alesha Lynn. The scan of her signature was hard to read, but it looked more like "Missa Lim". Her job description was listed as "Energy Consultant".

Danny had no idea what an energy consultant was. Maybe she read the meter. Even in a big industrial complex, someone had to check how many kilowatt hours you were using, surely? Or perhaps she gave advice on changing your energy tariff.

The internet only listed two people named Marissa Lim. One of them was an eleven-year-old piano prodigy. The other was the retiring head-mistress of a girl's school in Kuala Lumpur. Neither of them could be Ross' potential girlfriend. She had to be using an assumed name. But why?

She had made three visits to the terminal in the last year at irregular intervals. There was no chance of being able to lie in wait for her. The only person who would definitely know how to contact her was Iain Grant. Could he trust Iain enough to ask him? Not until he knew more about what had happened to Ross.

Danny would have to fall back on traditional investigative methods. He would have to break into the terminal manager's office.

Chapter Nineteen

'LORNA? AYE, SHE'S A good lass. Green as grass, but she means well.' Ellen had at least waited until Gemma had time to clean herself up and put the kettle on.

'Her aunt sent her, she said. Nice of her, I suppose.'

'Maggie Kerr? She's a nosy sow, pardon my French. I shouldn't say that, but it's true. What did you say to Lorna?'

'Thanks, but no thanks. I'm alright at the minute, but I'd let her know if I need anything.'

'You did right. If that woman gets her hooks into you, there'll be no getting rid of her. A right piece of work. Her brother was worse. I used to think it was him that caused all the trouble, but there was precious little change after he died. As for her sons, the less said, the better. It's a wonder Lorna stays so sweet and innocent with that family around her.'

This sounded interesting, or was it just gossip? In any case, Ellen showed no sign of leaving, so Gemma offered her a homemade scone.

'Ooh, nice. Wherever did you get these from?'

Gemma tried to explain the route of yesterday's walk.

'My, you did get a bit lost, didn't you? Thanks for the offer, but I think I'll pass. That would be the MacDuff farm. They're nice enough, I suppose, but not quite the full shilling. And I don't think they are particularly hygienic if you know what I mean. I've got a weak constitution, see.'

Gemma considered herself to have a robust constitution. She slopped copious amounts of the insanitary jam on the unhygienic scone and tucked in.

'What doesn't kill you, eh...'

'Well, that's certainly one way of looking at it, Gemma.' Ellen did not look convinced. 'I'm sorry you ran into old man MacBrayne. He always was a misery. Even when we were wee bairns, he hardly ever smiled. The whole family were a cheerless lot, to be fair.'

'Does he live on his own?'

'Aye. He has a daughter, but she married and moved away to Hoy.'

Gemma asked her about the abandoned croft.

'Oh, there's no one lives there now. Not for twenty years or more. It's a hard life. Barely enough land at Harpy Croft to make a living, even in a good year.'

'I could have sworn there was someone in there. I'm sure it's been used recently.'

'Well, I can't imagine who by. You're the only visitor on Mallach just now. If there was another, someone would tell me soon enough. There are no secrets on this island, believe me.'

Gemma was prepared to accept most of the things Ellen told her, but not this. Someone was keeping secrets on Mallach. Maybe lots of people with many little secrets. Or maybe there was one big secret that the whole island was keeping from her.

'How about someone from the terminal? Trying to save a few pennies, maybe.'

'Oh no. That would never be allowed. The oil company doesn't like their people staying in the village. It's against policy. The islanders wouldn't have them, anyway. That might seem a bit harsh, but it's always been like that. The terminal is the terminal, and the island is the island. Ne'er the twain shall meet.'

'But what about the islanders who work for the oil company?'

'That's different. I'm sure everyone gets on fine at work, but they don't socialise with the terminal folk. No islander ever brings an oil worker home for tea. It just isn't done.'

Gemma decided she needed to write out her list of suspects. It was growing fast, despite yesterday being her first day as an investigator. She'd checked out three farms (if you included the wee croft), met two nutters and possibly a third mystery loon. Then there was Lorna's mad family. All suspects, as far as she was concerned. This might take a while.

'How many farms are there on the island?'

'Let me see. From memory, there were forty-seven farmhouses and crofters' cottages, of which only thirty-one are occupied nowadays. There are over a hundred other farm buildings in various states of repair. I don't remember how many other houses there are on the island, but there are around thirty in Bron, I can tell you that much.'

'That's a pretty good memory you have there.'

'Aye, well, I've been president of the Mallach History Society for so long I feel like an antique myself sometimes.'

Forty-seven farms? At this rate, it would take her more than two weeks just to check them out, let alone all the villagers and those isolated barns. Her plan was unravelling already, and she'd barely started. What she needed was an information-led approach. That was what the polis always said when they didn't have enough manpower to investigate properly.

'Well, thanks for the information. I was thinking of heading out again soon, but I seem to be a rocket magnet at the moment. I don't want to run into another fella like MacBrayne. Any other places I should avoid?'

'I'd stay clear of the north of the island if I were you. That's where the Kerrs stay. The Dows have land up there too, and they're not much better. They'll not give you much of a welcome if you stray off the path.'

North it is then. Lorna's offer of help was almost an invitation to pop around for tea, surely. What she needed first was the name of a rare but plausible bird to be chasing. Perhaps it made sense to have another word with her local ornithological expert.

'Heather? Aye, she'll be in, I expect. I doubt she'll be able to go out with you until the weekend. Works from home, whatever that means. I can't imagine she gets much work done. We're not exactly on your superfast broadband here. Lucky if you can get online half the time.'

So, there was at least some Wi-Fi on the island? She'd thought she might have to stand outside the terminal waving her phone in the air. Time to start collecting passwords.

'It's stonedelf. One word, no capitals. That's the name of the cottage.'

'Stoned elf?'

'Delf. It's an old word for a drainage ditch. It's thought that this house was the first one in Orkney to have proper drains.'

She still needed to find a suitable bird as a pretext for her wanderings. And to find out if any of her bird-spotting friends had seen anything unusual lately. They might save her some legwork.

Rather than search online for her alibi, she decided to call Heather, who was in and happy to talk, as always.

'I'm glad you called. There's a meeting of the wildlife group on Saturday. I thought you might be interested. Get to meet a few of our local experts. It's not all birds, you know. There's botany, butterflies, and lots more. We have some unusual species of beetle on Mallach. We've someone from Ronaldsay coming over to give a talk about them. It's in the memorial hall. Starts at six. I know that's really early, but he has to catch the ferry home. I hope you can make it.'

Gemma assured her she would try. A talk on beetles? They better have some strong coffee, or she'd be asleep in minutes. And it would no doubt be full of yet more weirdoes. Unlikely to be the criminal kind, though. Still, maybe some of them would know Ross.

'Any rarities I might see on the island at the moment? Birds, I mean. Not sure about beetles and the like.'

'Oh well, I did see some bearded tits the other day in the reed beds by Loch Kist. I think there are a few hawfinches around, too. And there's always the long-eared owl. One of the terminal workers saw a pair flying over from Twatt. It went right across Thieves Holm towards The Loon.'

Bearded tits? If it had been anyone else, Gemma would have assumed she was taking the piss. But Heather didn't seem the type. And surely there was no such place as Twatt or The Loon? Mind you, half the place names in Orkney sounded like a piss-take. She would have to check out this nonsense before turning up at the wildlife meeting. Couldn't have the entire Orkney wildlife-bothering community laughing at her.

Gemma left Heather to her "working from home". She was with Ellen on this one. Whatever kept Heather busy, it wasn't what she'd call work.

Chapter Twenty

'MORNING, DANNY. ARE YOU busy?'

Fortunately, his laptop was facing the door and Iain Grant couldn't see the screen. Danny had fully intended to read through the paperwork Cara gave him. Instead, he was checking Facebook to see what his mates in Leeds were up to. Eating and drinking to excess mainly, judging by the photos.

Kelly had unfriended him shortly after she'd booted him out of the house. However, her concept of online security was a bit hazy and most of her posts were publicly visible. She and her skimpily dressed posse looked far too happy. Danny hoped that was just a façade. He closed the laptop and put on his most cheerful, professional face.

'Just going through the safeguarding procedures. Nothing that can't wait.'

'Safeguarding. Good Lord. Who did I upset now?'

'No one, as far as I know. It's about Ross. The young lad who went missing. I wanted to be sure we'd done everything we could to help him. I mean, that's assuming he needed help. Kevan thought he was depressed, you see.'

'And I thought he was quite happy here. Enjoying the job. I only spoke to him in passing. I'm probably not the most sympathetic boss around, but you'd think I would have known if he was planning to... you know... do something stupid.'

So, the only person who thought Ross was depressed was his boss. Either Kevan was displaying the classic manager's twenty-twenty hindsight, or he was lying. Maybe he was just trying to cover himself in case there was an inquiry. Or perhaps he had something more sinister to hide.

'If anyone spotted a problem with Ross, they didn't record it formally anywhere. That's why I was looking through the procedures. Just checking they are robust enough. I mean, suppose someone had concerns and there was no formal process for reporting it?'

'Good point. Not something that's ever come up since I've been in charge. So, Cara's got you looking at the procedures. That's good. I've got a bunch of incident reports for you as well.'

Danny deliberately hadn't mentioned Cara's name. It was obviously the sort of thing she might have suggested. No one needed to know that he had an ulterior motive for looking into Ross' disappearance.

He followed Iain into the terminal manager's office, pleased to see no lock on the door. There were, however, locks on several filing cabinets and drawers. He ignored the stack of paperwork on the desk. A nasty feeling told him he'd see that soon enough.

'Do stop me if I'm telling you how to suck eggs. We have a standard form to report accidents, injuries, or near-misses. The safety coordinator is supposed to deal with them, but they nearly always end up on my desk when Gordon Breck is on shift. He's nearly as good as me for offloading paperwork on other people. Nearly.'

He scooped up the hand-high pile and passed it to Danny.

'You do realise I'm only here for two weeks? I thought all this stuff would be computerised by now?'

'It is, but the operators can't carry electronic devices with them on the plant. They're an explosion risk. So, we had to retain the hard-copy system for them and, to be honest, most of the reports come in that way. Gordon's supposed to scan them in, but computers aren't exactly his forte.'

'Sounds like a job for the admin team.'

'It certainly does. If you want to tell Fiona McAlpine that, you have my full backing. Just let me know when you plan to approach her. I'll be in my office wearing a hard hat and ear defenders.'

'How about if I found an unofficial assistant for a short while? Lorna Kerr was very helpful yesterday, and she doesn't seem overly busy.'

'Great idea. Just don't blame me if you get it in the neck from Fiona.'

Blaming Iain was precisely what Danny had in mind. He was relying on Fiona being too busy complaining to check with the big boss. He didn't want to get Lorna into trouble, but he wanted to be able to talk to her alone occasionally. She might know more than she was prepared to let on in front of her colleagues.

'I wouldn't mind putting in a couple of hours extra tonight if that's ok. It's not like there's much else to do on Mallach.'

'You're not wrong there. Be my guest. If you're staying beyond seven p.m., just let security know. That's the shift handover time. You might have to sign in again.'

Danny lugged the pile of reports back to sickbay. No wonder Gordon Breck was so keen to let him take over. He wondered how many other mugs had ended up doing his paperwork over the years.

He kept the door open and positioned himself so he could see the comings and goings. Finally, around quarter to five, Iain walked past wearing his company jacket and gave a friendly wave. There was a ferry to Westray every hour, on the hour, and several employees had already to left to catch it.

By five-thirty, the office block was almost deserted. There were two night-shift workers in the maintenance office, but that was about it. Danny assumed that security would make their rounds at some point. They were unlikely to spend long in the office building. Hopefully, they were more focused on areas of the terminal that were liable to explode or burst into flames.

Danny picked up a random folder and strolled back to Iain's office. As he let himself in, the light came on automatically. He swore under his breath, but it couldn't be helped. If anyone saw him sitting in a darkened office, they would be suspicious anyway.

The obvious place to start was the laptop. Danny assumed Iain would have locked it away in a drawer, but there it was, sitting on his desk, powered up and ready to go. Unfortunately, there was no handy sticky note with the password to be seen.

All but one of the drawers was unlocked, and he rifled through them for something to give him a clue. Iain was keen on golf and Ross County Football Club. There was a photo of him on a boat with a woman and a young boy, presumably his family. No names on the back. Apart from that, everything else was business-related. A stack of business cards from various companies, but no Marissa or energy consultants, or anyone "fae the revenue".

There were, however, a set of keys. None of them fitted the locked drawer, but they did open the two filing cabinets. Danny tut-tutted as he peered inside. Good thing he wasn't a spy or a terrorist. Come to think of it, if this was the usual level of security, industrial espionage must be a relatively cushy career. Easier than trying to catch the culprits, anyway.

The files were neatly labelled, but few of the labels made sense to Danny. It was too risky to spend long going through each file. Instead, he flicked through each drawer, looking for anything out of the ordinary. Only two leapt out at him. One was an IT file that contained some account information. The other was marked "Energy Theft" and included a letter from one M. Ling, Revenue Protection Investigator for Energy Security Ltd.

Danny shut up shop and took the files back to sickbay. Rather than risk using the photocopier, he scanned all the documents with his phone. Once he was sure he had copies of everything, he checked the coast was clear and put them back in Iain's office.

He exited the building and swiped out well before security handed over to the night shift. Back at the accommodation block, he set the phone to transfer his illicit scans to his laptop and headed over to the canteen for a well-earned meal.

Chapter Twenty-One

SMALL TIME, SAME PLACE, different weather. The sun was breaking through the clouds, but Doug was not here to admire the view. Nancy appeared over the brow, her face red with exertion. They hugged briefly. Nancy clearly had a lot on her mind.

'I spoke with Lorna.'

'What did she have to say?'

'Nothing much. A waste of time, but what do you expect from an airhead like her. All she got was the woman's name. Gemma Gauld. But if she's undercover, then that'll be false.'

'We can use Lorna as an extra pair of eyes, I suppose. Otherwise, it's all up to you, Nance. Where did this woman go yesterday?'

'She was with Dan Mackay.'

'What for?'

'He said she was lost. Told her he'd set the dog on her. She gave him some lip and off she went.'

'So, she didn't get into the house?'

'Not according to him.'

'Well, that's something. Have to hope the old fool's telling the truth. Anywhere else?'

'The MacDuff place. She called in at Harpy Croft on the way.'

'That's a shame. We'll have to clear out of there and find another spot. This lass is getting to be a nuisance. Maybe it's time to fire a shot across her bows.'

'My pleasure, Doug.'

'Nothing too obvious. An accident. Just serious enough to put her on the boat home. Don't get carried away like last time.'

Nancy grunted. 'Don't you worry. We know how far she can walk now. Let's see how fast she can run.'

Chapter Twenty-Two

In many ways, the village shop resembled an early black and white version of the Tardis. It was bigger on the inside than seemed possible given the tiny building it occupied. It had clearly travelled from another time, and was occupied by a madman with strange hair.

All Gemma wanted was a map. It appeared that she would need a map to find one. She could have just asked the shopkeeper, but he was busy talking to himself and she didn't like to interrupt. Eventually, she squeezed her ample posterior past stacks of carefully balanced tinned goods and came out by the grubby bay window.

With the help of a long-handled litter picker, she reached over and extracted an Ordnance Survey Map and a thin pamphlet called Favourite Mallach Walks from the display rack. Judging by the cobwebs, the author was probably long dead, but she bought it anyway. No expense spared. She was going to claim everything back from Verity Investigations for sure.

A brief glance of the map proved Heather wasn't taking the piss. There really was a place called The Loon. A spit of marshland about five kilometres from Bron. It covered most of the northern bandit country that Ellen had described. In addition, the map showed a viewpoint up at Green Hill. It might be worth scouting the area before she tackled Lorna's clan head-on.

A bus would have been nice. Even a taxi. She considered asking Ellen for a lift, but her only means of transport was that classic motorcycle with sidecar parked in her front yard. Calling it parked was being too kind. Abandoned would be more accurate.

In her head, Gemma conducted a risk assessment and decided to walk. She trudged up the lane towards the terminal and took the first north-going track she could find. There was no signpost, just a weather-worn milestone covered with lichen. It was three miles to somewhere, but the stone was so worn she did not know where.

Around the twentieth bend was another abandoned croft. A small rectangle on the map seemed to line up with its location. In theory, the rock-strewn track on the right would lead her to The Loon. The midday sun attempted to break through the bank of clouds behind her. It looked like she was heading in roughly the right direction, so she stowed the map and set off towards the nearby ridge.

A runner, wearing a baggy tracksuit bottom and a hoodie, appeared from nowhere and bounded down the track towards her. The youngster stumbled into her, gave a muffled apology, and carried on down to the croft.

'Watch where you're going, pal.' There were eejit joggers everywhere these days. Never looked where they were going. Nearly as bad as those fecking cyclists.

After half an hour, the track banked right and headed uphill past a ruined barn. As she approached, she heard barking. A pack of dogs was loose in the yard. Her enthusiasm for seeing the view from Green Hill vanished rapidly. One dog she could just about cope with. A small one. Maybe a Jack Russell. From the sound of it, these were much bigger. She turned around and headed back the way she'd come.

She'd only gone a few paces when she heard shouting and more barking ahead of her. An older, heavy-set figure was striding up the path with four or five hounds in tow.

To avoid the risk of being caught between the mutts and their barnyard home, she headed down the sheep track to her right. There was a funny smell. It had been growing stronger for a while. Not sheep shit. Something more pungent. It seemed to follow her.

After a while, the track reached a burn and disappeared. She carried on down, following the far bank as best she could. The barking was getting louder. Perhaps they were chasing foxes or deer, or whatever dumb creatures they enjoyed harassing in these parts.

Gemma looked around. No sign of any wildlife. Only her. The smell wasn't going away. She took off her rucksack and sniffed. It smelled like a bitch on heat.

'Bastards!'

With the rucksack slung over her shoulder, she started to jog. Gemma wasn't built for speed, but at least this was a downhill run. She hoped her weight and native strength would compensate for a general lack of athleticism.

She caught sight of the lead hound out of the corner of her eye and broke into a proper run for the first time since she left school. Bounding from rock to rock, heart thumping in her chest, she gasped at every leap. She was keeping ahead of the pack, but one slip would spell disaster.

As she leapt over a ledge, the burn vanished and was replaced by a dry bed of pebbles. Instinct made her glance back. There was a hole under the ridge. A cave of sorts. Barely big enough room to shelter a sheep. If she wasn't built for running, she definitely wasn't built for potholing.

Caught between a rock and a dog pack, Gemma unslung the rucksack and hurled it as far as she could. It was a good throw. The bag tumbled down the hill and rolled out of sight behind a thick clump of gorse. She ducked under the ledge and began wriggling into the fissure, her legs beating like a swimmer out of water.

Her midriff stuck on a knobble of rock. She reached down and yanked on the hem of her trousers. Praying to Saint Margaret, the patron of crash diets, she forced several kilos of unwanted flesh into an unnatural and painful position. Then, with one frantic wiggle, she broke free. She slid on her front down the far side of the rock, landing headfirst in a pool of brown peaty water. A shower of earth and grass followed her down the hole.

She came to a halt propped on her belly at an angle of forty-five degrees. Her forehead was resting on a slab just above the level of the water. It was hard to breathe, and she had no idea how to get out of here. She just hoped the dogs couldn't get in. Muffled sounds filtered down into her hidey-hole. Excited yapping and a gruff voice shouting.

'Come here! Away to me! She's not hiding in a gorse bush. I'd see her fat arse from here, you stupid mutts.'

Fat arse? The cheek of it. If it wasn't for the dog pack and the fact that she was stuck like a cork in a bottle, she'd have been straight up there and punched the dog-handler's lights out.

The barking got louder. One of the hounds began snuffling around the entrance to her hidey-hole. The rest of the pack started off down the hill after their owner and the straggler eventually followed them. Gradually, the barking and shouting faded away and Gemma could think about how to get out of here.

The cave in front of her was wider than the entrance, but not by much. Back in junior school days, Gemma had been a keen gymnast. Currently, she was doing an inclined headstand. She needed to shift her weight and turn that into a forward roll. All without getting stuck upside down inside a hidden cave.

Gemma braced her hands on the slab and tucked her head as far as it would go under the smooth rock she was lying on. She slowly lowered herself into the cave until her centre of gravity was over her shoulders.

The attempt to roll down gracefully was unsuccessful. At some point, everything sped up, and the roll turned into an ungainly flop. She struck her coccyx on the opposite side of the cave and swore. This was just like gym class. Not everything she'd learned at school had been a waste.

Now she was stuck on her back with her legs in the air like a stranded turtle. It was not a comfortable position, but it played more to her strengths. She braced against the rock and used her feet to force her shoulders further upwards. This brief chimney climb gave her enough space to spin around. She was the right way up and facing the entrance, at last.

Next, all she had to do was repeat her entrance manoeuvre. Easier sworn than done. The rock she was lying on was smooth, wet, and slimy. Her legs were only long enough to push her shoulders through the hole. Every time she tried to wriggle back through the gap, she slid back down to the soggy bottom of the cave and had to start all over again. Eventually, she was too tired to continue and perched on the damp slab of rock, the only part of the cave bottom not under several inches of water.

She had another flashback to junior school. That story about Winnie-the-Pooh, getting wedged in Rabbit's warren and starving himself thin to get out. No willpower required when you're stuck in a cave. All her snacks and sandwiches were in the rucksack in the gorse bush. Assuming the dogs hadn't got to them already.

Gemma didn't fancy the chances: the cave might not get any colder, but she would lay in an icy mountain stream. Hypothermia would likely be the death of her, long before she got to the stage of gnawing her own arm off.

Anything she could have used as a climbing tool was in the rucksack. All she had in her pockets was her mobile phone. It was wet but still working. The display showed a fifteen per cent charge and absolutely no bars of phone signal. Presumably, mobile phones were not designed for underground reception.

If she scrambled back up to the entrance, she might just be able to get one hand out far enough for the phone to be in free air. She wouldn't be able to keep that up for long, so who was she going to call?

The logical thing to do was to phone the emergency services. They must have some first responders on Mallach. Maybe even a cave rescue team. But what if the only responder was her pursuer or one of his friends? A real possibility on a small island like this.

No, the only thing for it was to call Danny. She would never live it down. Still, it beat dying down here. Just about.

Her muscles were stiffening, but she forced them to climb again. Finally, with her left arm at full stretch, she could see one bar on the display. She quickly checked her location, called Danny's number, and waited.

'Hi, Gem. How are you doing?'

'Shut up and listen. Stuck in a cave. Come alone. Bring rope. Broccoli. Albatross. Nuzzling. Shite...'

With that, she lost her footing and tumbled off the rock. She splashed down in the freezing water and sat there wondering how her day could get any worse.

Chapter Twenty-Three

BROCCOLI, ALBATROSS, NUZZLING, SHITE. What on earth was Gemma on about, Danny wondered. Some kind of code? Were there even caves on Mallach? A quick search online showed there were plenty. The island must have the geology of Swiss cheese.

Google couldn't make any sense of her random words. He tried deleting "shite" in case it was just an expletive. At the bottom of the third page of irrelevant nonsense was a link to the What Three Words website. That rang a bell.

Some guy had the idea of carving the world up into three-metre squares and using three words to identify each one. Crazy, but brilliant. All you had to do was use your phone app to find the relevant words. In theory, a rescuer could then pinpoint you within a few metres.

Danny fed "broccoli.albatross.nuzzling" into the website and it came out with a location a couple of miles east of the terminal. Nowhere near a road. Anyway, he didn't have a car and Gemma said to come alone.

He grabbed his first aid rucksack. One of the night-shift security guards was hiding behind his van, having a crafty smoke. Danny persuaded the bemused man to loan him a towrope and ran off, down the road with it. Having until the next morning to come up with a plausible explanation, he had to hope the guy's van didn't break down or get stuck in the mud.

He was halfway there before he thought of texting Gemma to say he was on his way. No reply, but that wasn't surprising. It was hard to imagine how she'd got a signal at all while stuck underground. The whole scenario made no sense. Knowing Gemma, she'd blame him.

Danny was guided by his phone down the stream to the designated location. No sign of a cave. He didn't want to shout for Gemma in case whoever had thrown her down the hole was still around. It wasn't until he'd walked down the hill and back up again that he spotted the dark space under the ledge. He leaned in, speaking quietly, and received a torrent of abuse.

'Took your time, didn't you? I'm soaked to the skin and bruised to hell and back. I had psychotic birds dive-bombing me all morning. This was your eejit idea getting me to come to this pox-rotted island. You can damn well get me out of here and on the next boat home.'

'I'm lowering the rope. Can you climb, or do I need to haul you up?'

'I can climb. I'm not that feeble. I might need a pull for the last bit. It's a tight squeeze.'

It wasn't until he saw her head poking out of the cave entrance that he realised quite what she meant.

'You know what this reminds me of...'

'If you dare mention Winnie-the-fucking-Pooh I'm gonna ram a honeypot where the sun don't shine, pal.'

That was one childhood image ruined forever. He maintained a steady pull on the rope and stared at the babbling brook. He tried to avoid watching Gemma's potholing contortions without success. With one hand on the rope, she used the other to rearrange parts of her anatomy until they fitted through the opening. He looked away and choked down the snorts of laughter.

'Oh, aye. Very amusing. It's not you trying to get your tits oot the mangle. You won't be finding it so funny in a minute, I'm telling you.'

Gemma made a couple of lurching belly flops and then, with a roar like a sea lion giving birth, popped out onto the rocky streambed. Danny rushed over to see if she was alright. He thought she was crying. Then he realised they were tears of laughter.

'Oh Jesus, my ribs! Don't look. You're gonna make me laugh again. I hurt too much to laugh. Oh, Christ, I've gotta lose some weight. Gods, I should have let those shitting dogs bite some lumps out of me.'

In between bouts of hysterical laughter and cries of anguish, Danny managed to get most of the story.

'This is serious, Gem. If someone is worried enough to set the dogs on you like that, they must have something to hide.'

'Aye, but what? They don't know I'm looking for the young laddie. How could they? I'm just some busybody from Aberdeen.'

'Maybe they think you're the police? Or the customs?'

'This is not Whisky Galore, pal. You've been reading too many books.'

'Well, maybe it is about Ross. He could be held prisoner in one of the barns around here.'

'More likely they buried his body on these moors.'

Danny had to agree. If they found the body, at least that would be some crumb of comfort for his parents. The peat would preserve a body. There might be enough forensic evidence for the police to find his killer.

Not the breakthrough he'd hoped for, but it was a start. Gemma had wanted to stir up trouble. To be the canary in the coalmine. She'd got more than she bargained for. How were they going to find the culprits and uncover their secrets without ending up buried in the peat themselves?

Chapter Twenty-Four

'You lost her. How the hell did you manage? She's not exactly hard to spot. What happened? Did she disappear down a fucking rabbit hole like Alice-in-fucking-Wonderland?'

Doug was losing it. Nancy feared where that might lead.

'Just think about it a minute, Doug. The dogs were tracking the fat bitch across open moorland. She somehow threw them off the scent and got away without a scratch. What does that say to you?'

'Well, she's no twitcher, that's for sure.'

'You can say that again. Nor is she fae the revenue. Orkney police might have sent a detective, but not in plain clothes. I'm thinking SOCA or whatever there calling themselves now.'

'She doesn't look the part. Those were your words.'

'Well, maybe that's the point. They're not supposed to look like police. They blend in. Undercover.'

'You better be sure.'

'Look at it this way. If she's not SOCA, she's a spook. Then we really are in trouble.'

'Don't shit me, Nance.'

'I am not. And I'll tell you something else for nothing. They never come alone. She has a partner somewhere on the island. Did you think about that, eh? She does the snooping and her pal does the shooting.'

'You're letting your imagination run away with you. They've got nothing on us. No body, no clues. Nothing.'

'Not until I set the dogs on her. Now they know something is going on.'

'Why would MI5 be troubled by our little business?'

'National security. It's the oil terminal, I'm telling you. Probably think we're terrorists. Sent in a team to flush us out.'

'That's crazy talk. What would you have us do? Shut up shop and move to Fair Isle? We've got serious customers. I'm not imagining them. If those lads are unhappy, they won't just leave a one-star review. We have to deliver on time or a visit from the spooks will be the least of our problems.'

Chapter
Twenty-Five

ALL GEMMA WANTED WAS a hot shower and a hot meal. The hot shower soon deteriorated into a tepid trickle. She'd left a trail of mud across the bathroom floor and she smelled like a caver's crutch. In the fridge, the steak pie she bought yesterday was looking at her. She recalled the rash promises to Saint Margaret. Fasting, followed by some mild starvation and then some more fasting.

She compromised, settling on a bowl of vegetable soup and a cheese sandwich. Dessert was one of the apples Lorna brought around on the way home from work. She grimaced. The number of bruises on the apple was almost equal to the number on her body. It still tasted good. She considered a second one when a knock on the door announced Heather's arrival.

'You haven't forgotten, have you? The meeting. We'll have to hurry, or we'll miss the start of the beetle talk.'

Gemma routed around for some outdoor clothes that weren't smeared with cave slime, and reluctantly followed her to the memorial hall. She was exhausted, but the shower had revived her and she was determined to continue her investigations.

The beetle talk wasn't as boring as she'd thought. There were four thousand different species in the UK alone. Who knew? Who cared? Not old city Gemma. New country Gemma was mildly interested. Plus, the speaker was enthusiastic and informative. Not quite the creepy-crawly geek she'd been expecting. Even better, there was a bar.

'It's only supposed to be open when there's an event on,' Heather said. 'That's what it says on the licence. They don't pay much attention to rules like that on Mallach. There are no police and most of the parish councillors are on the hall committee. That's one of them serving behind the bar. Stewart Jackson. He's fae Yorkshire, but he knows all the island gossip. Not much gets past Stew.'

Everyone on the island seemed to be an expert on gossip. You'd think it was impossible to keep a secret on Mallach. Someone was managing it. Of that, Gemma was quite sure.

Maybe she could ask Stew about her jogger and the bastard with the dogs. They had to be working together. There wasn't much else to go on. Hard to tell if the jogger was male or female with that hoodie and the baggy clothes. Nor had she seen much of the master or mistress of hounds. Something to be grateful for, she thought.

Anyway, those questions would have to wait. Heather stuck to her like a limpet and was three-quarters of the way through a bottle of Chardonnay. She kept slipping her hand onto Gemma's thigh. Gemma asked a few pointed questions about Rona's whereabouts, but the hand stayed.

She looked around the hall. Mostly men. Mostly elderly. A few younger geeky guys. Only one or two worth a second glance. To shake Heather off, she elbowed her way into the geek huddle and introduced herself. They appeared dumbstruck in the presence of a woman, but one of them plucked up enough courage to reply.

'Pleased to meet you, Gemma. I'm William. I hear you're visiting the island. Welcome to Mallach. We don't get many visitors. Especially not pretty young girls like you. Can I buy you a drink?'

Gemma was not one to reject a compliment or a drink, even if they came from a guy who appeared to have borrowed his clothes off a scarecrow. He wasn't that bad looking, otherwise. Shame about his dress sense and minimal grasp of social skills.

He returned from the bar with two pints of Dark Taing. His hand lingered on hers as he handed it over. She pulled the glass away quickly, and took a quick swig of rich chocolaty ale. Nice pint, but next time she would buy her own.

'So, what did you think of our beetle talk, Gemma?'

'I never knew there were so many of the wee bastards.'

'Exactly. I mean, you'd never be able to spot every single species. It would take forever. I prefer Lepidoptera. Did you know there are only thirty-two species of butterfly in Scotland? Plus a few occasional visitors. I've only got three left. There's the mountain ringlet and...'

'Aye, well. I think I'll stick to birds for now.'

'That's very wise. Of course, getting a complete list of native Scottish birds could take a long while. Even Orkney has about four hundred species.'

'My. Fancy that, eh? I'll be lucky to see forty. Especially if the landowners are all like the bastard I ran into today.'

'Really? Sorry to hear that. Usually, they're quite friendly. I can't imagine why anyone would take offence at you. Where was this?'

'Up by The Loon. Some wanker with a pack of hounds.'

'I think there are some farmers that still go deer stalking though they're not supposed to. The red deer do get a bit out of hand sometimes. There was this huge stag once that wanted to get sexy with my rucksack. Very embarrassing. Of course, that was in rutting season...'

'Any hunters in particular? I wouldn't want to run into them again.'

'Well, I wouldn't like to say, but if it's anything illegal, people usually blame the Kerrs or the Dows. Though I've never heard of them stalking at this time of year. Mrs MacDuff takes in strays, but I'd hardly call them a pack. Or hounds, for that matter. A mob of mongrels, maybe.'

William laughed about his own joke. He sounded like a hyena snorting cocaine. She might have found it endearing in a three-year-old.

The meeting wasn't a total waste, even if William wasn't the font of all knowledge. The same names kept coming up. They might be just the local scapegoats, but she had to start somewhere.

Chapter Twenty-Six

KEVAN KNOX CAME TO see Danny first thing in the morning. Presumably, his minion at the front gate had blabbed about him leaving early. He had meant to talk to the security boss again, but now he was on the back foot.

'I hear you left site without telling anyone where you were going.'

'Sorry. Domestic emergency.'

'Domestic?'

'I got an email from my wife's solicitor. Soon to be ex-wife. We're going through a divorce and things are getting messy. I needed to call her in private. Should've told someone, but I was in a bit of a state, to be honest. I can make up the time.'

Danny was happy to do some more snooping overtime. However, after the mention of divorce, Kevan became much less aggressive.

'Yes, well, I hope this will not be a regular occurrence.'

'I seriously hope not. I managed to calm her down, I think. Not entirely her fault, to be fair. Her solicitor's pouring petrol on the fire. She thinks it's all my doing.'

'Right. I know what you mean. My brother went through the same a couple of years back. His wife took him to the cleaners. Or at least her lawyer did.'

The security chief was quite chatty after that brief male-bonding moment. Danny just hoped he never checked the CCTV. It would be hard to explain why he needed a rope to make a phone call. Even Mallach's phone reception wasn't that bad. As casually as he could, he asked Kevan if there was any news about Ross.

'Nope.'

'That's good, isn't it? It means he might still turn up alive and well.'

'I suppose.'

'You don't sound convinced.'

'Like I said, he was pretty depressed. There's someone goes missing every year in Orkney, seems like. Young lads, mainly. They wash up on some beach a few days later. Lots of handy cliffs to jump off around here. Some never turn up, of course. But that doesn't mean there are any happy endings. None that I recall, anyway.'

'But you said Ross didn't want to talk about his feelings. Are you sure he was depressed?' Danny was interested to see how Kevan would react to the question.

'He didn't need to say anything. You can tell, can't you? He was never that cheerful, but I just assumed he hated the job. Most of them do, to be fair. It's cold and wet and boring most of the time. You need the right mindset. I didn't think he'd last long.'

'So, you think he was depressed about work?'

'Some folk like coming to work to get away from domestic troubles. Like your divorce, right? Some can't wait to get home because they hate it here. But if you've got problems at both ends, you've got nowhere to go. You either pack your bags and leave, or take a running jump.'

'And Ross never packed a bag, did he?'

'Exactly. I feel sorry for his folks, but it's time to move on. I need to recruit a replacement. Iain's pussyfooting around. Saying I canna take anyone on because Ross might come back any time. Wishful thinking doesn't make my job any easier. It may sound harsh, but the sooner they find the body, the better it will be for everyone.'

On that sympathetic note, he left and Danny could finally get around to checking the scans he acquired from Iain's office.

The letter from M. Ling was mostly generic spiel about revenue protection and energy theft. It explained how her company could save them millions if only they spent a few grand now. It sounded like a costly insurance policy for something that was unlikely to happen. However, the last paragraph spoke about having evidence of unauthorised energy usage. M. Ling was not forthcoming with the detail but wanted to talk to the man in charge as a matter of urgency. Under the signature was a phone number and an email address.

Danny checked the signature against the one from the security pass. It wasn't a perfect match, but it was close enough. It seemed like Marissa used a variety of names to protect her identity. He searched for her again, this time using the name "Marissa Ling". Bingo! The first link was to a profile of someone working for Energy Security Ltd.

Maybe it was time to give her a call. An exchange of ideas, investigator to investigator. First, he looked through the rest of the documents. Marissa's company wasn't the only revenue protection experts Iain had been in discussions with. There was a printout of an email from another company and a brochure from the Revenue Protection Authority.

Nothing in the folder told him what was going on. He needed to get access to the terminal manager's emails. He turned his attention to the IT folder. Iain seemed to have trouble remembering his password. On at least two occasions, someone had reset the account, with warnings about the need to create a new password.

Since the new password was a random selection of letters and characters, it seemed likely that Iain would have followed their advice. But surely a man who has forgotten his password twice would feel the urge to write it down somewhere?

He examined the scans at maximum magnification. Iain had handwritten some instructions to himself about how to connect to the Wi-Fi. There appeared to be some mirror writing at the bottom of the page. Something written on the back, perhaps. Danny flicked through the scans again. If there was anything on the back, he hadn't thought to take a copy.

Nothing for it but to sneak back into the manager's office and try again. He had six hours to wait until Iain left the building. It was hard to concentrate on anything in the meantime. He wanted to contact Marissa, but he didn't dare call her from the office. Her email address on the letter was a generic company one. In the end, he texted her with his name and a few details and asked her to call back.

A couple of hours later, she returned his text with the one-word message "OK". Better than nothing. Maybe she would call later. Assuming he could find anywhere that had a stable phone signal.

The afternoon crawled by and eventually, Iain scurried out of the door to catch his ferry home. By five-thirty, there was only him, the night shift and Cara left in the building.

'Overtime, Cara?'

'No rest for the wicked. I missed a few days recently and I need to catch up. What's your excuse?'

'New job. Just trying to look keen. I'd only be lounging around in my room, watching TV. I'd rather do something useful.'

'Well, good for you.'

'When's the last ferry?'

'Eight o'clock. After that, it's the water taxi and that costs a fortune at night. I never stay that late.'

He certainly hoped that was true.

'I'm going to grab an early dinner and come back. Can I get you anything?'

'No thanks. I'll have gone by the time you get back.'

Danny bought an extra cappuccino just in case, but when he got back to the office, it was empty and dark. He took both cups with him into Iain Grant's office and powered up his laptop. He unlocked the filing cabinet and, after a bit of rummaging, found the offending piece of paper. His heart sank. The password on the back was only the Wi-Fi code.

In desperation, he tried using the code on the laptop. To his surprise, the screen turned blue and the company logo flashed up. This was followed by an inspirational message about staying safe and respecting your fellow workers. Maybe this was Danny's lucky day, after all.

The same password fired up Iain's email account. There was no filing system as far as he could see. He had dozens of unread messages and all of his fifteen hundred saved emails were in his inbox. Danny searched for "Marissa" with no success, then "M. Ling", "Energy Security" and "Revenue Protection". The last two yielded a dozen results. He forwarded them to the medic's email and deleted them from the Sent folder just in case.

Danny logged out and took a sip of coffee from the chipped canteen mugs. The lights in the corridor blinked into life and Cara marched into view. Danny gagged on his coffee.

'You took your time. Is that my coffee?'

Cara gestured towards the untouched cappuccino on her boss' desk. Bemused by her lack of indignation, Danny picked up the mug and handed it to her. Cara pulled up a chair, sat down, crossed her legs, and leaned back. She seemed completely unfazed by his breaking and entering antics.

'So, did you find what you were looking for?'

Chapter Twenty- Seven

ONCE HE WAS SURE that Cara was safely on the ferry, Danny headed backed to the accommodation and called Gemma. He could just make out her voice through the static before they were cut off abruptly. Probably a short-eared owl nesting on the transmitter mast. After a few minutes, she called back.

'The only place with a signal around here is up by the vicarage. The minister must have done a deal with God. Or the devil more likely.'

'We need to talk.'

The reception was still appalling, despite any divine assistance, so she suggested he came to Bron.

'I'll meet you in the bar.'

'What bar? Iain told me this was a dry island.'

'Oh, aye. Apart from the unofficial off-licence at the back of the village store. And the open-all-hours bar in the memorial hall. Very hush-hush. Except that everyone knows about it, including the polis. They just don't let the likes of you in.'

Danny thought she was joking, but he came anyway, wandering the unlit lanes, trying to recall where he'd seen the hall. The entrance was marked only by a faded, empty noticeboard, but the door was open, so he let himself in. He followed the sound of laughter and the clink of glasses to a door marked The Wheelie Suite. As soon as he opened the door, the laughter stopped.

'It's alright. He's with me,' Gemma said.

There was a disgruntled muttering, but then the conversation resumed. He wandered over to the bar where Gemma perched on a stool, knocking back a large glass of red wine. She introduced him to Stew, the barman. Danny stared meaningfully at the rows of bottles, but she didn't offer to buy him a drink.

'So, how do you two know each other?' Stew asked.

'Common interests,' Danny said. 'Drinking and birdwatching.'

'So, I expect you'll be wanting a beer.'

'I could murder one.'

'I dare say, but Gemma tells me you work at the terminal. It's more than my job is worth.'

Stew didn't appear to have a job. Unless you counted being an unpaid parish councillor and volunteer barman. Like Heather, he claimed to work from home, but was always behind the bar. He didn't appear to own a laptop or a phone. In any case, the only way of getting a mobile signal in the hall was to stand on the rim of the ladies' toilet and wave your phone in the air.

'I'll sell you a can of Irn-Bru, but you'll have to take it outside. Best I can do.'

It was raining as usual. Not heavy, just a relentless drizzle that seeped through even the most technically advanced waterproof fabrics.

They perched on a lopsided picnic table, Gemma with her schooner of wine and Danny with his rust-coloured soft drink. They were partly sheltered by the eaves of the hall and an overhanging downy birch that dripped on Danny's head at irregular intervals.

'So what's your big news, Danny-boy?'

'I broke into the boss' office, and his oppo, Cara, caught me in the act. It looks like we've both been rumbled now. A fine pair of secret agents we are.'

'Hey! Don't blame me, Danny-boy. This is your operation. I've just rubbed up some local headcase the wrong way. That happens to me all the time. So, what did this Cara have to say?'

'She just sat there drinking her coffee. I didn't know what to say. I made up some excuse, but I could tell she didn't believe me. In the end, she said: "Your secret's safe with me". Then she finished her coffee and left.'

'Creepy. But you're still in the game? Can you trust her?'

'I don't know. I can't see any reason to suspect her. She's a chartered engineer and an MSc. But. she seems have some personal agenda. Perhaps she wants to stitch up her boss so she can take his job. I don't think she'll turn me over to security. Not yet anyway.'

'Well, you're going to have to tell her the truth. Some of it anyway. Bit of a looker? Got all her own teeth?'

'Yes, well, I mean she a fair bit older than me...'

'But still not likely to be desperate enough for you, pal. Try the sympathy angle. Tell her how you're helping Ross' family look for their poor lost wee son. Some women go for that sort of thing, I hear.'

What she said made sense. He would have to confide in Cara. She had obviously figured out he wasn't just there to tend to sick oil workers. Could she become an ally? He needed to find out how much she knew. It was hard to see how he could carry on his investigation unless she was on his side. Apart from that, he didn't want anything of a more personal nature from Cara. That would almost certainly mean trouble.

'So, how are you getting on, Gem? Cutting a swathe through the Orkney birdwatching community?'

'Oh, aye. Geeks, loons, and oddballs. You left me holding the shitty end of the stick, Danny-boy. You get the Malaysian Mata Hari and Cara the Cougar. I get William the Weirdo and Gay Heather. Not to mention the bastards with the dog pack.'

'At least you get to sit inside the bar and have a proper drink.' Another drip from the roof landed on Danny's nose. He tried to steer the conversation back to the dry details of the investigation.

'With any luck, I'll hear back from Marissa, and then we might make some progress. Even if she wasn't involved with Ross, she was in contact with him. So, she must suspect there's something illegal going on.'

'Three investigators are better than two, I always say. What's this revenue protection about? See yer oil companies? They never pay taxes anyhow.'

'Could mean lots of things. They might be under-recording the oil and gas they're storing. Or the amount they process. She really could be coming to read the meters. Or to check they haven't been tampered with.'

Gemma snorted.

'No one gets murdered for reading the meter here. This isn't Glasgow, you know.'

'We're talking millions of pounds here. And we don't even know that anyone's dead yet. Let's stick to the facts. If this is related to Ross' disappearance, then you're right: it's not likely to be corporate fraud. More likely, someone is stealing from the terminal.'

'Oh aye, the old wheelbarrow full of oil trick. If someone is thieving, then it's surely one of the local Mallach guys that work at the terminal. There's not so many of them.'

'True. I can get you a list. Could be a two-man job, though. One on the inside and one out. Someone working in the terminal with close ties to Mallach. A relative maybe.'

'I'll ask around.'

'Try to be subtle about it. We don't want them getting suspicious. Well, not any more suspicious than they already are.'

'Don't you worry. I'm the sole of discretion.' Gemma raised a muddy boot to illustrate the point.

Danny scrolled through his messages and showed her one he had received from Aidan's mother.

'I don't know what to tell her. I can hardly go looking for him when I'm stuck in the terminal.'

'You're embedded in the terminal. That's what you tell her. That's where all the answers are, right? Where's the lad supposed to have gone, according to your eejit polis pal?'

'Scrabster.'

'That sound like a disease. Where the hell is it?'

'Near Thurso.'

'Oh aye, the frozen north. No one goes there unless they're cycling fae John O'Groats to Land's End. Mad. I wouldn't even care to do that on ma motorbike. Stevie Dunn stays up that way, mind. Wick or thereabouts.'

'That's handy. I don't suppose he'd fancy a trip to Scrabster? The ferry company aren't very forthcoming at this end, but they might be prepared to talk to a local lad.'

'Aye, they might. I'll text him. Don't hold your breath, though. He spends most of his time wandering over the hills, disturbing the peace with those bagpipes of his.'

'In the meantime, I'll try to find out what Aidan was doing in the terminal. I've drawn a blank so far.'

'You must know something. Who did he meet when he visited, for instance?'

'I don't. Just the medic, I assume.'

'Well, you know what assume does?'

'Yes, Gem. It makes an ass out of *u* and *me*.'

'You can leave *me* out of it. It's just you, Danny-boy. Just you.'

Chapter Twenty-Eight

It took most of the morning, but finally, Danny managed to get Cara on her own. He saw her walking out towards the Research building and jogged after her, pulling on his hardhat and safety glasses as he went.

She slipped through the security gate, but his pass was rejected with a chorus of dismissive beeps. When he called out her name, Cara stopped and turned. After a quick glance around, she let herself back through to his side of the fence and motioned him towards a low building with a corrugated iron roof. It was full of cables and spare parts, but empty of people.

'Sorry I couldn't let you into the Research Zone. It's strictly no pass, no entry.'

'I was supposed to have permission to access all areas.'

'You'll have to take that up with Kevan. Or complain to Iain, if our security Nazi objects.' Cara perched on a reel of high voltage cable and gestured at the rows of shelves. 'This building is the electricians' store. No one comes here unless they blow a fuse. A good place for a little tête-à-tête.'

Cara sidled up to Danny and smiled at his discomfort.

'Come on. You're not the only one looking into Iain's affairs. Who are you with? Police or Customs? I don't believe Orcadia Oil would send an undercover agent.'

There didn't seem to be an alternative. He pulled out his private investor's licence and handed it over.

'I'm working for the MacLeod family. They want to know what happened to their son Ross. I think the answer is here in the terminal.'

'Ah, I see. That puts a different perspective on things. I assume you are a genuine, qualified medic?'

Danny nodded.

'Well, that's something at least. I wouldn't want some police reject giving me mouth-to-mouth resuscitation.'

She puckered up. For a moment, Danny thought she was about to kiss him. Instead, her pout turned back into that knowing smile.

He decided not to mention that he was an ex-military police reject. That was still a sore subject. He'd been seconded to Special Investigations to help with an internal matter. Then his former commanding officer found out what he was investigating. Six weeks later, he'd been drummed out of the regiment on a trumped-up charge. Whistle-blowers were never popular in the military. Or anywhere else, for that matter. He hoped to have better luck with this inquiry.

'So I can carry on looking for Ross?'

'Your secret's safe with me,' said Cara, patting him on the cheek. 'I won't stand in your way, so long as you do nothing to endanger me or the terminal. No clues to Ross' disappearance are here, sad to say. You're barking up the wrong tree. You might find a few things worth investigating, but it won't be what you expected.'

With that, she strutted off into the restricted zone, leaving Danny more confused than before. Cara knew something, but she wasn't prepared to tell him what. She reminded him of Kelly, who constantly expected him to have telepathic powers. They were both doomed to disappointment. He would just have to figure things out the hard way.

So, others were investigating the terminal, or its management. Presumably, that included Marissa Ling. And what about Iain Grant? Of course, he only had Cara's sly hint to suggest that he was up to anything. It was a reasonable working theory, though. Everyone has something to hide. Guilty until proven innocent.

And what about Cara? If he could get a look at the research building, he might feel a little less suspicious of her motives. Of course, that meant talking to Kevan again, something he had hoped to avoid.

First, he took a long walk around the plant, checking to see which other areas were inaccessible to him. Danny was careful not to go inside any of the "Authorised Personnel Only" buildings, but he made sure he could open each door in case he needed access. He encountered no more problems until he reached the electrical plant.

He poked his head around the door of the generator hall. The coast was clear, so he went inside. Two heavily cladded enclosures sat side-by-side on heavy steel plinths. They looked like the gas turbines used as generators offshore. Up a flight of stairs was the control room. Rows of push buttons and meters and display screens lined the wall. There was no one home and the machinery was silent, except for a ventilation fan humming away at the far end.

He scurried back down the stairs and out through the rear entrance. A narrow passageway brought him out by a chain-link fence and another security gate that rejected his pass. That wasn't surprising. This compound housed the main substation for the plant, including some gigantic transformers and heavy overhead cables that hissed and crackled in the damp Orkney air. The "Danger of Death" signs showed someone being struck by a bolt of man-made lightning.

Danny would have liked to investigate the long low building on the far side, but there appeared to be some construction work going on. Another reason they wouldn't want a newbie contractor wandering around.

Danny completed his tour and headed back to the office block. Kevan was at his desk. He made a big show of appearing busy, but at least he didn't ask Danny to go away and come back later.

'What can I do for you?'

'It's my pass. Unfortunately, I'm locked out of a couple of areas of the plant.'

'That'll be Process and Electrical. Access for authorised Orcadian personnel only.'

'That's a bit awkward. I'm supposed to carry out safety audits, check evacuation routes, that kind of thing.'

'Not in there, you don't. You can check the fire escapes from outside the fence. Or there are the plans on the server.'

'Sorry, but I'm a bit more hands-on than some guys. I guess Gordon is someone who would rather stay inside and check things on the computer.'

'You're not wrong there. But rules are rules. I can't upgrade your pass. You can only access those areas if you get permission from senior management. You'd have to be accompanied by an authorised member of staff at all times.'

This sounded like bullshit to Danny, but he had no way of checking it. He could talk to the terminal manager, of course. Iain was unlikely to say yes, especially if he had something to hide. If Danny had to be accompanied, it would severely limit his movements. It would also give people plenty of time to hide stuff.

'Could I at least get a list of authorised people? Maybe I can just ask one of them to check a few things out. It would save me the bother of going back out in the cold again.'

'Aye, that sounds like a better plan. You're getting the hang of this.'

Kevan was in no hurry to give him the list, but Danny was determined not to leave until he did. Eventually, after much muttering and cursing at the computer, he printed off the entire personnel list, complete with their clearances and responsibilities.

'I'm no good with these spreadsheets. You'll just have to pick the bones out of it yourself.'

Danny was quite happy to do that. The more information, the better. He flicked through the list, looking for someone with all area access who might not use it too often. One name stood out: Lorna Kerr. Why would an admin assistant need access to the process plant? As far as he could tell, she hardly ever left the office. She didn't even walk over to the canteen for lunch, said the food was fattening.

He waited until the rest of the admin team had gone for their lunch. Then, he marched into the office, acting distracted.

'Oh, hi Lorna. Sorry. I didn't realise it was that time already. I'll come back later.'

'It's no bother, Danny. What do you need?'

'Just a handful of those Q11 forms. I was supposed to get them all to Iain this morning, but I missed a couple off the list.'

'Aye, no trouble at all. They're in Mrs McAlpine's office. You wait there. I'll only be a sec.'

Danny knew full well where the forms were kept. He just needed a few minutes alone at her desk. Terminal personnel were supposed to carry their passes on them at all times. Lorna rarely wore hers. Sure enough, there it was, lying face down between a fruit bowl and jug of filtered water. He palmed it and replaced it with his own. Hopefully, if she noticed the switch, she would assume it was a genuine mix-up.

It only gave him a few hours to explore, but maybe that would be enough. If not, he would have to try a riskier strategy. When Lorna returned, he thanked her and headed out onto the plant with the useless forms and the stolen pass.

Danny was surprised to feel his heart beating fast. He felt eyes boring into the back of his neck. Glancing behind him like a frightened fox, he didn't see anyone. He was exposed now. If anyone caught him in the restricted areas, his cover was blown and he would be ordered off-site. His best chance of finding what happened to Ross would be gone.

Chapter
Twenty-Nine

THERE WAS NO ONE around. Presumably, the central control room and the main security gate were staffed, but everyone else seemed to have decamped to the canteen.

Danny retraced the route he took with Cara to have another look at the electricians' store. She hadn't lured him in there for anything sexual, so why had she shown him inside that particular building?

He let himself in through the side door and found himself in the unused storekeeper's office. An infra-red sensor clicked on and the overhead strip lights blinked into life. Danny stepped back in shock. Someone was standing by the desk. His first black ops mission and already he'd been rumbled.

He expected the man to rage at him, but instead, he crouched down with his back to Danny. In the flickering light, he caught sight of the intruder's hairy bare arse as he attempted to pull up his boxer shorts and struggle back into his overalls. The man turned around, looking shame-faced and confused. It was Kevan. The security chief stared at the pass hanging around Danny's neck. Lorna's wide-eyed photo seemed to have him spellbound.

'Ah shite. How did you find out? You canna go telling Iain. I'll lose my job and she'll kill me for sure.'

Danny guessed who "she" might be.

'Your wife?'

'Aye. I've been trying to tell her for a while, but I daren't. If I so much as mention another woman's name, she goes mental. I think she's getting proper paranoid. If I tell her I'm having an affair, she'll have my balls for breakfast.'

'I don't think it counts as paranoia if you really are being unfaithful.'

'Aye, no, I suppose not. She never suspected anything, though. Not until a couple of weeks back. You didn't tell her, did you?'

'Hey, I only just got here, remember.'

'But how did you find out?'

Danny enjoyed having a hold over Kevan for a change. He didn't want him to know that Cara had led him to this seedy love nest.

'It was that spreadsheet you gave me. I was trying to figure out why Lorna had an all-areas pass. So, I thought I'd borrow it for a while and check it out.'

'Shite. And I led you straight here, no doubt. That's what comes of thinking with your dick, right enough. Are you going to report me?'

'None of my business, mate. Unless you are endangering health and safety with whatever you get up to in here. But you upgrade my pass, right? And I get to go wherever I want without you, or one of your team, in tow.'

'Aye, aye, whatever you say. You'd better get that pass back to Lorna. She'll be going frantic.'

No, she wouldn't. If she had been planning to make this rendezvous, she would already know. Danny had no idea what Lorna saw in Kevan, but he guessed he was about to find out. That was going to be an awkward conversation.

'Ross asked me to go to the Christmas party with him. I mean, it wasn't a date or anything. It was just nice to have someone to chat to on the ferry. The company put on a minibus for the local staff. It's not like you can have much of a party on Mallach, see.'

Lorna seemed more puzzled than worried when he'd returned her pass. She'd followed him out to the smoker's shelter and seemed happy to tell him about the affair.

'Ross is nice enough, but really, he's just a boy. Three years younger than me.'

She made that sound like an entire generation gap.

'He was drunk before we even had our starter. He was spouting some awful nonsense. So, I ended up talking to Kevan instead. He's a proper man. Reminds me of my pa some ways.'

That sounded a bit creepy to Danny, but each to their own.

'He's married, though. Was his wife not at the party?'

'Aye, she was, but she was even drunker than Ross. She fell over and boaked on the dancefloor. Kevan offered to take her home, but she swore at him and took a taxi. We chatted for a while and then I took him back to my place. I felt bad in a way, but she deserves it, really. She takes Kevan for granted. Everyone says so.'

Especially her husband, Danny presumed.

'So, what's the plan? Is he going to leave his wife?'

'He says so, but I hope he never. I mean, we have a lot of fun and all that, but I won't move in with him. He's way older than me. If he leaves his wife, she'll probably take the house and all his money. I don't want to stay in a peedie flat at the arse-end of Kirkwall. Where's the fun in that?'

Danny wasn't aware that Kirkwall had an arse-end, but he took the point. Lorna was savvier than her vacant expression suggested. She had more common sense than Kevan, that was for sure.

That was one mystery solved, and at least he now understood why Cara had shown him the storeroom. Her first tip had turned up trumps, Danny was more willing to believe her other insinuations. However, he was no nearer to finding what Iain Grant was up to. Nor did he know what any of this had to do with Ross' disappearance.

Two hours later, Lorna came by with his new security pass.

'Kevan's gone off sick. I think we're gonna break up. It was our secret before. It's not the same now people know about us. The romance has gone right out of it.'

Danny didn't consider the electricians' store particularly romantic. There wasn't even a leather chair, just a manky-looking bench. Definitely nothing he'd want to sit his bare cheeks down on.

'Well, it's probably for the best. I'm sure you can do better.'

'Aye. You're right there. Will you be seeing your young lady this evening?'

Danny nearly choked on his lukewarm coffee, snorting some of it down his left nostril. He could imagine Gemma's reaction at hearing herself referred to as his "young lady".

'Aye, maybe. Though between you and me, things are not going so well there either. It's always been a bit of an on-off relationship. Definitely more off than on, at the moment.'

'Oh, I'm sorry to hear that. If you ever need to talk...' Lorna patted him on the arm, gave a sympathetic smile and left.

He wasn't sure what to make of that. Normally, he would assume he didn't stand a chance with an attractive young lass like Lorna, but she'd been having sex in a storeroom with a guy several years older than him. Was it worth all the complications and potential embarrassment? Probably not. One thing was sure, his "young lady" wouldn't care either way.

Chapter Thirty

TIME TO GO NORTH again, Gemma thought. Her last trip had been cut short by a pack of angry hounds. Someone wanted to keep her away, making Gemma keen to continue her search.

She considered another attempt to visit the Kerr family home. It was likely that one of the Kerrs or the Dows had been responsible for her impromptu potholing experience. To avoid misunderstandings, she'd rather go with Lorna Kerr to make the introductions. Unfortunately, that would mean waiting until she got home from work.

Looking at the map in more detail, she came up with an alternative plan. Below Blackfowl Geo was a tiny beach and a path snaking up towards the terminal boundary along the clifftop. Presumably, it had initially carried on to the jetty until someone had inconveniently built a row of giant oil tanks in the way.

She needed to consult Ellen for some local knowledge. She was relying on her landlady's lack of birding knowledge because she would have to blag this one.

'Hi Ellen,' she said, poking her head around the kitchen door. 'I fancied taking a trip to The Loon to see the fulmars. It'd be a sight easier if I could get a boat up to Blackfowl Bay.'

'Oh aye, you can land a boat there if you know what you're doing. I'd not fancy it myself these days. I used to own a motor launch, you know. That was a long old time ago, mind. We went fishing at Blackfowl or skinny-dipping from the old pontoon in Calf Sound. Those were the days.'

Most of the pontoon washed away in a storm, years back, but some of the fishermen still use it to store their nets.'

'I don't suppose you know anyone who could take me. I'd be happy to pay.'

'Aye, maybe. There's Jack Jansen. His ma works up at the terminal. The family has an old boat that they keep in the harbour. I'll give him a call.'

Jack turned out to be a strapping young lad in his twenties. Finally, things are looking up, thought Gemma. He had a bushy beard and a man-bun, but beggars can't be choosers. She was more focused on his enormous biceps. Probably took steroids and spent his life pushing weights. Still, she wasn't proposing to marry the big lump. He pointed to a vintage creel boat moored out in the bay.

'Tide's still on its way in. We have to fetch the tender out first.'

The tender looked nearly as big as the creel boat itself. Getting it down the slipway involved a lot of manual handling. Jack put Gemma in charge of the launch trolley, which was about as cooperative as the average supermarket trolley. Under her careful guidance, the tender snaked its way down into the water. At this point, Gemma realised she would have to get her feet wet.

'Ellen should have told you to bring your wellies. Tell you what, why don't you hop in now before it gets too deep. Shy me the painter once you're in.'

It took quite an effort to clamber on board, but it was better than wading out waist-high, which appeared to be the only alternative. Gemma had no idea what a painter was, assuming it had nothing to do with fine art or the Forth Road Bridge.

'Just hoy me the rope. Aye, the one at the front. And quick, before you float off tae Norway.'

Jack set the oars and steered them skilfully between the mud-banked shallows to where the creel boat was moored, out in the deep-water channel. He lashed the tender to the mooring buoy and helped his new crewmate on board. Gemma acted all weak and helpless to get the best view of those biceps in action.

'Are you married, Jack?' she asked once they were safely on board.

'Aye, no. I was engaged for six months to a lassie fae Westray, but she left. Took herself off to Stirling to study law of all things. Said she'd be back when she finished her degree, but she never.'

'I'm sorry to hear that. But, still, her loss...'

'Aye, so that's when I decided to dedicate my life to Christ. I'm training for the priesthood soon as they'll have me. Being married to the kirk is way cooler, eh?'

'Oh, aye. Cool. Frigid even.' Gemma toyed with the idea of trying to persuade him to one last fling before he donned his dog collar. She was probably wasting her time, but those muscles were really very impressive.

The boat rocked and rolled its way across the rough, exposed waters of Gutter Wick until they reached the rocky beach at Blackfowl Geo. Gemma could just about make out the footpath climbing its way through cracks and crevasses to the top of the cliffs. It was a lot steeper than she imagined from the map.

'I can take you around to Calf Sound. It's a better track up through the cliffs there.'

Gemma was tempted, but it was also much closer to the Kerr's farm. One of their clan might use the pontoon even. She preferred to sneak up on their turf from the other side of Kelda Hill.

It took Jack several attempts to manoeuvre the boat in close enough to allow Gemma to wade to shore. Even then, she landed crotch-deep in cold, murky water. She considered just climbing back in the boat and going back to her lodgings for a sulk. Sadly, Jack was already backing the boat out into deeper water and out of earshot.

'Aye, cheers. Thanks for nothing, pal.'

Jack smiled and waved, the roar of the engines drowning out her whining.

'Ah well. Best boot forward.'

She slung her rucksack on her back and picked her way across the slippery, seaweed-strewn beach to the cliff edge. The first part wasn't too bad despite the narrowness of the path. After that, there was a tricky section where an old rockfall cut across the route and then it really started to get steep.

It was more of a scramble than a proper climb, but then Gemma was not a proper climber. She had a rough idea of the principles involved, but had neither the footwear nor the physique to carry it off. Fortunately, the rock was stable, with plenty of handholds. There were dozens of birds wheeling around the cliffs. Nowhere near as many as at the guillemot colony, but enough to get her thinking. Maybe these really were fulmars. There was something important she ought to know about fulmars. Something that Heather had mentioned.

Gemma hauled herself over another ledge and found herself nose to beak with a very agitated seabird and its young chicks. Then she remembered. She had just enough time to close her mouth and screw her eyes shut before the fulmar regurgitated the entirety of its last meal all over her head.

If she hadn't known that the fulmar's diet was predominately fish, she did now. Half-digested skin and bones slid slowly and unctuously down her face. She couldn't keep her mouth closed forever. If only she'd learned to hold her breath longer.

When she finally took a gasp of air, the smell was gut-wrenching. She had to open her eyes and start climbing before the other fulmars decided to empty their stomach contents in her general direction. She slithered and crawled her way up the rest of the path in record time. Finally, she flopped on the cliff top, drenched and slimed, feeling like a modern-day Jonah emerging from the belly of the whale.

With the help of the antibacterial wipes in her first aid kit, she got most of the fishy residue off her head and shoulders. Unfortunately, her hair was still stuck together in clumps. The smell remained as revolting as ever, though now with subtle hints of lemon. Well, it wasn't like she was on her way to some posh restaurant for luncheon. If the damn birds could put up with the smell, so could she.

Gemma started walking along the cliff path, hoping that a bit of fresh air would help. It was very fresh indeed. She had difficulty staying on her feet. Fortunately, it was only an onshore breeze; there was little danger of being blown over the cliff edge.

She passed a couple of broken-down barns and poked her nose inside. The usual collection of rubble and rusting machinery, plus a rabbit and a few empty plastic drums of sheep dip. It looked worse than the backyards where she grew up in Aberdeen.

The next building looked more hopeful. There was a mud-splattered trail leading up to the main door. Some agricultural vehicle had been there lately. The building was more of a warehouse than the usual ramshackle barn. Not that it was in prime condition, but it was intact and it looked like some work had been done on the roof recently.

There was a substantial padlock on the door, making it even more interesting. No convenient windows at eye-level, of course, but a couple of skylights up on the roof. One was propped open. Gemma pulled out her binoculars and kicked her way through the bramble and gorse until she found the sweet spot.

From here, the line of sight just cleared the guttering and gave her a good view of the underside of the window. Some eejit had left the lights on inside, giving a clear reflection straight down to the warehouse floor.

With the help of the binoculars, Gemma could make out a row of heavy-duty pallets. She couldn't tell what kind of machinery was mounted on them, but they looked like pumps. The sort of shite you had to weave your way around on the main deck of the Cuillin Alpha. She never could figure why they always had to block her route to the tea shack.

It took some doing, but she managed to get the phone camera lined up with one eyepiece of the binoculars and took a few photos. They weren't bad, if she said so herself. She took a few more snaps and then scurried back to the cliff path before some bastard with a pack of dogs turned up.

She hadn't got far when she came to a barbed-wire fence blocking her path. Fortunately, she'd packed a selection of tools, in case she was required to do any breaking and entering. She pulled out a sturdy pair of wire cutters. They wouldn't have made much of an impression on the warehouse padlock, but they made short work of the fence.

Gemma squeezed sideways through the gap and set off again.

'Hey! What do you think you're doing?'

There was a big lass in dung-splattered dungarees striding towards her. She was carrying what looked like a pitchfork.

'Here come the hillbillies,' Gemma muttered.

'Did you not see the fence?'

'Aye, well, yes. It came loose in my hand.'

'This is private land.'

'Is that so?'

'My family's farmed this land for generations. You can't just come waltzing through here.'

'Well, I happen to know that this is a certified ancient path. Been here since MacAdam was a lad. Long before you or your neepheid family.'

She knew nothing of the sort, of course. According to Ellen, everything on Orkney was ancient. Put there by the picts or the celts or possibly the fairies, depending on her mood.

'Are you going to pay me compensation if one of my herd gets loose?'

'It's only a strip or two of barbed wire. You can knit it back together easy enough. I'd do it myself, but I have sensitive skin. I'm allergic to pricks.'

The woman was scowling at her now rather than glaring. It was a subtle distinction, but Gemma didn't think she had a wide range of facial expressions.

'You're that lass fae Aberdeen, are you not? The twitcher.'

'I prefer the term "birder".'

'My Lorna told me all about you.'

'I sincerely hope not. You must be Mrs Kerr, then. Mind if I call you Ruth?'

Gemma held out her hand. Ruth ignored it. Probably for the best. One of them had hands covered with cow shit and the other with bird puke. Ruth still seemed to consider whether to invite Gemma in or to push her off the cliff. In the end, she did neither and simply pointed inland.

'You can take yon path, away down there. It's not safe along the cliffs.'

Not safe because of landslides or not safe because of psychotic landowners? Ruth didn't elaborate. Gemma decided that discretion was the better part of valour. She had found something of interest today. It was time she went back to the cottage for a nice tepid shower.

'Aye, thanks, Ruth. It's been nice chatting with you. Say hi to Lorna for me. Maybe I'll pop round again sometime.'

Ruth grunted and stomped back over the field to tend to her herd. There was a quad bike parked by the far gate. Not big enough to have left the tracks she'd seen. The warehouse was on the wrong side of her precious fence. Maybe it didn't belong to the Kerrs. Just a coincidence that Ruth turned up right at that moment. There must be some way of finding out without arousing suspicion.

She strolled down the hill whistling a merry tune. She had Jack's number on her phone and a whole bar of signal here. He had offered to give her a lift back in the rib, but she decided against it. Despite the many obstacles standing in the way of their romance, she hadn't entirely given up the idea of jumping Jack. If she got onto his boat smelling like Aberdeen fish market, even she wouldn't be able to sustain that fantasy.

Chapter
Thirty-One

Doug perched on a rocky outcrop overlooking Harpy Croft. Nancy's quad bike was outside. There was no one else in sight. Since the twitcher had found this place, meeting here was a risk. But one worth taking. It had been too long.

They kissed only briefly. Nancy seemed distracted. Doug pulled away and stared into her eyes. Nancy's face was easy enough to read.

'Aren't you pleased to see me?'

'Aye. Of course. But we said we wouldn't do this. Not until this mess is all over and done with.'

'It won't ever be over, Nancy. Without a body, there will be no inquest. Just a missing person report filed on some dusty shelf in some police station. But it will still be there.'

'I meant not until the strangers leave.'

'Even after they've gone, people will still be looking. Suppose one of your sister's bairns was missing. You'd never give up looking, now would you?'

That touched a raw nerve, alright. Nancy looked on the verge of tears.

'Seen anything of the twitcher?'

'No. The dogs must have scared her off.'

Nancy was lying. Doug could always tell. She was forever scared of being the bearer of bad news. She had cause, right enough. But why now? Even if those spooks, or whatever they were, didn't find anything, they unnerved

Nancy. And that might lead to an urge to confess. Doug knew all about that.

Nancy loved Doug. It was strange, but true. Doug wanted Nancy. To have her and to control her. That was all. There might come a time when this relationship had to be terminated. That would be a pity, but not the end of the world. Not for Doug.

Chapter Thirty-Two

WHEELIE'S BAR WAS QUIET this evening. Through the lichen and spider's webs, Danny could make out Gemma, sat by the window reading. He tapped on the glass. She hid the book and waved him in. He crept inside and perched himself opposite her on a rickety chair.

'It's alright,' she said. 'I had words with Stew. He's fine about you coming in now.'

The barman nodded at him warily a . He didn't look fine, but slightly scared of Gemma.

'Any chance I could get a pint of IPA?'

'Absolutely none.'

Stew was prepared to sell him a ginger beer and a pasty from the pie warmer. He wasn't prepared to say what was in it.

'Mystery meat,' Gemma said. 'Best not to ask.'

There was a lot to be said for turning vegetarian. Though if he was relying on the oil terminal canteen, he'd be surviving on cheese omelettes and potato salad.

'You said you had some news.'

'Aye, I did. I reckon I found your missing shipment. If there's a reward, ken, I want my share. Fifty-fifty. We agreed.'

Danny didn't recall making any such agreement, but then he hadn't seriously expected Gemma to find anything.

'Hold your horses. We don't even know if you've found the right stuff yet. Did you get any photos?'

'Ay, but they're a bit blurry.' She handed her phone over to Danny and he scrolled through her reflected shots taken through the barn skylight.

'I see what you mean. Certainly looks like oil equipment. I could give Joey a call. I'm just worried this will compromise our other enquiries.'

'You think the poor lads are locked up in a barn somewhere on Mallach? You've been watching too much TV, Danny-boy. Chances are they're far away from here, or they're dead.'

'Yeah, I suppose you're right. I don't want something we do making it worse for them.'

'Get a grip, laddie. If the polis raid the Kerr's farm, that'll really shake them up. If it's some other clan that's taken them boys, they're going to be mighty nervy for a while. Fear makes folk do stupid things. I'm all for shaking the tree and seeing what falls out.'

'With my luck, it's probably a wasp's nest.'

It was a risk, but they couldn't just ignore Gemma's find. With any luck, the police might find something relating to the missing men during their raid. If not, perhaps the perpetrators would assume they'd been looking for the stolen goods all along. That might give them an advantage.

The half-dozen regulars at the bar seemed wrapped up in their own conversation, but Danny didn't want to take any chances. He wandered up and down outside until he got a stable signal and called Joey McAndrew. Joey sounded like he was in the middle of a family meal and wasn't overly pleased to hear from him.

'Wassup, Danny? Can it wait?'

'I don't think it can. I think I've found Neptune Shipping's missing cargo.'

'Fuck me!' The phone became muffled as Danny heard Joey apologise to his wife. He grinned, heard small children's voices chirp the F-word, snorting with laughter. Then footsteps. 'Aye, I'm in the garden now so the little buggers don't hear me. You serious, Danny? You had better be.'

'My colleague got a few photos. They're not great quality, but the guys who own the equipment should be able to recognise it.'

'Right. OK. Send me what you've got. I'll call the customer now. And the police, assume they confirm it. Shit. All hell's going to break loose. What's the location like?'

'It's a farm building. Pretty remote. Belongs to the Kerr family, I think. Local hard cases. I'll send you a grid reference.'

Danny rushed back inside and asked Gemma to email her photos to Highlander Loss Adjustors. Given the internet speed around here, that would take a while. She insisted it would go a lot quicker if he bought her another G&T. That created a few issues until he ordered a T minus G for himself.

By the time he'd sent the remaining details to Joey, it was getting towards closing time. Danny's phone rang just as they were leaving.

'OK. We're on. The customer confirms it's their kit in the photos. I've been onto Aberdeen Police. They went all Apocalypse Now. Ready to fire up the helicopters and fly straight up there. They must really hate Neptune. Sadly, calmer heads prevailed.'

'I'm sure the good folks of Mallach are pleased they're not about to be napalmed. So, what's the plan now?'

'Orkney Police will be moving in first thing tomorrow, along with an armed unit from Highlands and Islands and backup from a coastguard vessel. I'll keep you posted, but I'd keep my head down if I were you.'

Danny intended to keep well out of the way. Sickbay in the oil terminal seemed as good a place as any. But he had a nagging feeling that the raid would turn up more than a few palettes of stolen goods. Suppose they found a body or even two. Then, at least it would be up to the Orkney police to inform the parents, not him. That was scant comfort.

He ended the call and told Gemma the news. He was pretty sure she wouldn't be so easily convinced to stay away.

Chapter Thirty-Three

DANNY WAS RIGHT. GEMMA was desperate to witness the police raid. Her enthusiasm was dampened only by the earliness of the hour.

'So, when they talk about dawn raids, they really do mean dawn? I thought it was just a figure of speech. I mean, dawn tomorrow is five o'clock, for fuck's sake. Why not have an after-breakfast raid instead?'

'I think the idea is to catch the criminals napping.'

'Aye, but they'll be expecting it at dawn. Those crooks probably get up especially early. Wait till nine o'clock and they'd be off their guard.'

She was still determined to head up to The Loon, but there was no way she could ask Jack to take her in the rib without arousing suspicion. She couldn't face walking up there again, not that early in the morning.

Gemma wandered down the hill to see Heather. She was willing to bet that all her bowfin birds woke up at dawn, too. That would give her a good excuse, but why did everything have to start at the crack of sparrow's fart?

'Hey, Heather. I was fancying going away out somewhere to hear the dawn chorus. I wondered if you had a bike I might borrow off you.'

'Oh, what a wonderful idea. If I weren't working, I'd come out with you. Of course, you can borrow my bike. It's lovely to ride. Full suspension, disc brakes and it's got twenty-seven gears.'

It was also a bright raspberry colour with a glitter finish. Hardly the ideal vehicle for an undercover surveillance operation. Still, borrowers can't be choosers.

'Aye, well, I'm not going to lose it in the dark, am I now? Thanks, Heather. I'll be sure to bring it back in one piece.'

———

She set out at four a.m. to be sure of getting in position well before the birds and the flying squad. Ellen knocked together a pack-up breakfast that would have fed a family of four. Gemma had a bad feeling there would be haggis in it somewhere. She hated all traditional Scottish delicacies that weren't deep-fried.

Cycling along the coast road, she reached the turn-off for the Kerr's fiefdom. She didn't fancy taking that track in case she ran into the polis or one of the Kerr's making a run for it. Fortunately, there was a winding deer track a hundred metres further along the road. Despite the gradient, Heather's bike made short work of the hill with the help of the twenty-seven gears. Gemma found a convenient place to perch behind a chambered cairn and waited for the fun to start.

In the pre-dawn glow, a thrush began to sing at the top of its voice. It was joined by a duet of robins, then a cacophony of tits, finches, and God knows what else. Almost worth getting up for. It was positively deafening, though. So much for the peace and quiet of the countryside. Early morning at her city centre apartment was quieter than this, even on bin days.

Rumbling tyres on the rough track cut through the birdsong. A couple of Orkney polis Land Rovers were followed up the hill by a tactical unit in an armoured van. The Orkney boys stuttered to a halt just before the rise and let the van trundle on up to the bay doors. A bunch of gun-toting polis leapt out the back and lined up against the warehouse wall while some poor sod dressed in Kevlar tried to jemmy the door open. Finally, at the third attempt, there was a dull clunk, and he ran off to one side. Two officers, either side of the door, hauled it open and their pals piled in shouting 'armed police' and pointing their guns in all directions.

After a few shouts of 'clear', the lights came on and they lowered their weapons. The Orkney polis came jogging up the hill with an eager-looking German Shepherd. Gemma wasn't sure whether it was there to sniff for drugs or scare the villains. It tracked a few rodent trails and poked its nose in all the corners. Then, satisfied, it sat down and waited for someone to offer it a treat.

With the bay doors fully open, Gemma had an excellent view of the interior. Using Danny's expensive binoculars, she could even make out the manufacturer and part number of the pumps lined up on the warehouse floor. Exactly as per the loss adjustor's inventory. Someone would be happy. Danny could even get paid, and then might not whine so much about paying her.

There wasn't much else of interest. An overhead crane and a forklift truck. Some metal cabinets off to one side and a single table and chair by the fire exit at the rear. There were only three doors that she could see. The only windows were the skylights in the roof. If she ever had to break in, the fire door looked favourite. Unless the polis couldn't be arsed to fix the jemmied front door.

She swung the binoculars around and scanned back down the track. There was an ambulance parked up on the tarmac lane below. The driver seemed to have a well-earned snooze. Good news, so long as he stayed there.

She caught a flash on the horizon as the rising sun reflected off the headlamps of another stationary vehicle. It was a quad bike with a border collie perched on the back and a big lassie standing up on the footplate. Staring into the sun, it was impossible to make out the woman's face, even with binoculars. Gemma would have bet all of Danny's finder's fee that it was Ruth Kerr.

It was still only five-thirty. Danny would be fast asleep in his wee cot in the terminal. On the off chance that he'd forgotten to turn his phone off, she called him and was gratified when a grumpy voice mumbled, 'whozat?'

'Who d'ya think, you lazy wee bastard? I've been up for hours monitoring the situation up here on The Loon.'

'Oh, yeah. Ta. Well done you. Not that anyone asked you to go. In fact, I think the police specifically asked you to steer clear. So, what's the situation?'

'All done and dusted. The polis found your stolen goods just like I said they would. There's a low loader turned up just now and some eejit's playing dodgems with the forklift. He's moved one of the pump units out the door, but it's gonna slide off the forks if he's not careful.'

'They've not brought anything else out then?'

'Nope. There was no one in the warehouse. And no body bags if that's what you're asking. The ambulance is still away down the hill. All is calm.'

'Good. I couldn't see any link between Neptune Shipping and Ross. Maybe Aidan, but not Ross. We'll have to see what the police say. If they're prepared to talk to me. They've been pretty tight-lipped up to now.'

'Aberdeen police might spill the beans to your man Joey. He's handed them Neptune Shipping on a plate. Those boys have been after them for years.'

'Right. Well, I'll give the Macleods and Mrs Fitzgerald a call later. I mean, it's no news really, but it's better than bad news at least.'

On that cheery note, he hung up. Gemma opened up her breakfast carry-out and tucked into a cold Lorne sausage and a tattie scone. Eventually, the haulage company and the polis would be on their way. She might get the chance to take a shufty inside the warehouse. The polis might think they were finished, but she reckoned she had a better nose for trouble than any sniffer dog.

After two hours of sitting on a damp mossy bank in the cold morning air, she had finished everything in the breakfast pack apart from the sliced haggis, which she cut up and left for the carrion crows. There were still four Orkney officers hanging around outside the warehouse. The boys from the haulage company were still fannying about waiting to get the pallets onto their low-loader. Now the crime scene lass had arrived and was in the process of putting on her white onesie. It was time to leave.

Gemma climbed back on her raspberry-coloured fairy cycle and bumped her way down the deer track and back onto the tiny coastal road to Bron. Ellen was just coming back from the shop with a pint of milk and a loaf under her arm.

'Did you enjoy your dawn chorus, dearie? Fancy a cuppa and a slice of toast?'

Gemma was still pretty full of tattie cake, but she was never one to say no to a second breakfast.

'That's a pretty bike you've got there. Is it Heather's? I've seen her push it around the village, but I can't say I've ever seen her riding. I told her it was a lot of money to pay for a glorified shopping trolley. She could have borrowed one from the supermarket in Kirkwall if that was all she wanted.'

Gemma was too busy stuffing her face with hot, buttered toast to join in the conversation, but Ellen didn't seem to mind. Eventually, the last slice was consumed and the bread bin was empty.

'While I was up on Red Hill for the dawn chorus, I saw this big square warehouse up on The Loon. The polis started buzzing around it. Have the Kerrs been up to something they shouldn't have?'

'Oh no. I ken the place you mean, but it doesn't belong to the Kerrs or the Dows.'

'So, whose is it then?'

'I'm not so sure. Back in the day, there were plans for a wind farm on The Loon. The birdwatchers were up in arms about it. We had the chairman of the RSPB up here and all sorts. I signed their petition, and told the Islands Council chairman what I thought about it in the strongest possible terms.'

Gemma figured that would be enough to stop most developments. She liked wind turbines, but she wasn't about to tell Ellen that. They made an eerie noise, but at least they didn't stink of oil and exhaust fumes.

'They got as far as laying the foundations for one of the turbines. They even dug a big old trench to it from the terminal, right across the Kerr's land. I thought Ruthie would have kicked up a storm, but I hear she got a hefty handout from the Development Board. So anyways, we put a stop to it in the end.'

'How come the terminal was involved?'

'Their parent company wanted to show off their green credentials, but the local management was dead against it. It's probably the only issue that has united the entire island. Orkney wants to become a centre for renewable energy. The other islands have their tidal turbines and wave-energy machines and whatnot. Mallach would rather stick with good old-fashioned petrochemicals. There's no logic to it, though. Most of the islanders say they hate the terminal, but if anyone tried to demolish it, they'd have a mob waving their pitchforks at them.'

'What happened to the trench?'

'They covered it over. You wouldn't even know it was there now. Some Aberdeen company took over the wind turbine site and built that wacky warehouse. It was supposed to revitalise the economy of the island. No idea how. Anyways, it's been empty since it was built. They're always having plans for what to do with it, but they've come to nought.'

'I don't suppose you remember the name of the company. I might know them.'

'Aye, no, I don't recall. Heather, or rather her lady friend Rona, might.'

'How come?'

'She used to be Rona Dow before she and Heather got married. I never thought I'd live to see that. Two lassies getting married to each other. I've nothing against it, mind. So sweet to see them both in their wedding dresses. I imagined Rona would have a morning suit. She wears the trousers in that relationship, I'd say.'

'So, you went to the wedding?'

'Aye, I did. In the Grand Hotel. Very nice. I mean, there weren't many guests. Rona's ma came and her sister, but the rest of the family stayed away. Heather's friends and Ruth, of course, but that was it. I think they only invited me to make up the numbers, to be honest.'

'Why Ruth?'

'She's always been a bit more broad-minded than the rest of her clan. She was born in Thurso, see. She's only Rona's aunt by marriage. Her husband, Greig, is dead now, but he had two sisters and a brother, all with families. Not one of them came, though I know for a fact they were all invited. Her Auntie Morven called it an immoral union, but she's got five bairns and none of them by her husband, if you believe the rumours.'

Gemma wondered if Ellen might have started those rumours herself. She made her excuses and went back to the cottage to write up her notes. There was a lot to digest. Maybe super-sleuth Danny could make some sense of it. She would send him an email late, but right now, she needed a lie-down and a snooze.

Gemma shut the curtains and stuffed in her earplugs, but she could still hear those damn birds chirping away. She must be developing twitcher's tinnitus or something. She pulled the covers over her head and counted cars until, eventually, she nodded off.

Chapter Thirty-Four

D<small>ANNY WAS ABOUT TO</small> swipe into the office building when the door burst open and Iain Grant strode past him with barely a good morning nod. He was wearing a shirt and tie. It looked like he'd attempted to tidy his salt-and-pepper beard, but it was as dishevelled as ever.

Lorna was sitting alone in the admin office, so Danny sidled up to her desk to find out what was happening.

'Iain's looking very smart. Are we expecting VIPs?'

'No, no. Just the lassie fae the revenue.'

'Marissa Ling?'

'Aye, that's her name. She sounded pure posh on the phone. Maybe that's why Iain wanted to look his best.'

Danny could think of other reasons why a middle-aged manager might dress to impress a young, attractive visitor. He needed to find some excuse to talk to Marissa. He also wondered if he had time to sneak back to the accommodation and change his shirt.

She'd never returned his call. Her only reply had been a one-word text message. And yet, here she was in person, all the way from London. He decided to stay put and let her make the first move. He didn't have long to wait.

There was a knock at the door and Iain Grant shuffled in, escorting a short, dapper Asian woman with long, black hair, and a soul-searching stare. She was probably in her early thirties, but something about her eyes made her seem older.

'Danny. Hi. This is Marissa Ling. She's visiting the terminal today. I'm afraid she's not feeling very well. I'll leave her in your capable hands. If I'm not in my office, just put a call out on the PA.'

Based on Ross' photo and his friends' immature comments, he'd been expecting Marissa to be taller, slimmer, and more of a beauty. Not that he was complaining. He was hardly in a position to criticise anyone else's appearance. Danny closed the door and ushered her towards the cleaner of the two patient chairs.

'So, what seems to be the matter?'

'Oh, I swooned. Iain swept me up in his arms and brought me here. That's probably how he saw it.'

Her accent was even more disappointing. Made in Chelsea, with just a hint of Southeast Asia.

'Don't you worry about it, Mr Medic. I expect it is just nervous exhaustion. I should be used to it after all these years and yet I still find lying to people so very tiring. Don't you?'

'I try to stick to the truth as much as I can,' Danny said, keeping a straight face.

'Well, at least we can be honest with each other, Danny. What exactly is your interest in the terminal?'

Danny told her about his search for the stolen shipment and the two missing men. When he mentioned Ross MacLeod's name, there was a flicker of recognition in her eyes. Was she hiding something? If she had concerns about Ross' disappearance, she wasn't letting on.

'And what brings you here, Marissa? I assume you didn't just come here to talk to me about your imaginary ailments.'

'I must admit I was intrigued. A medic who is also a private investigator? Very unusual and a little concerning. But it seems your motives are rather better than mine after all. I am only here for the money. Quite a lot of money, actually.'

She pulled out a sheaf of printouts from her briefcase and showed them to Danny.

'Mallach Oil Terminal exports its nasty fossil fuel electricity to the grid whenever it has any surplus and imports nice green energy when it needs a top-up. That's good for Orkney and good business for the oil company. However, we've been monitoring this arrangement very carefully. There is a discrepancy between the exported power and the power delivered to the grid.'

'So, is Orcadia Oil fiddling the books?'

'That's what I thought originally, but I have changed my opinion. The export meter has not been tampered with, but the outgoing power is less than it should be. I think that power is being diverted illegally. Iain Grant does not agree and nor does his boss. They think my calculations are flawed.'

'How much power are we talking about?'

'In Orkney terms, enough to supply a small village.'

'Like Bron.'

'Exactly. But I checked. The good people of Bron are not getting their power for free. This is not Electricity Galore. I don't want to search the entire island for a secret whisky still or whatever it might be. That's definitely not in my job description.'

'Can't you just search the plant and trace any illicit wiring?'

'Unfortunately, no. I need a warrant. The Scottish authorities do not want to upset a huge taxpayer like Orcadia Oil, especially one that is also a major political donor. I have all the official electrical schematics, but there are many places where a power take-off might be. To find it, I would need someone on the inside. Someone with access to the entire electrical plant.'

Marissa lifted her gaze from the diagrams and spreadsheets and smiled at him. It was a lovely smile and Danny forgot his disparaging opinion of her charms. Unfortunately, the smile also spelt big trouble.

'Suppose there was someone who had such access? An undercover investigator, say. How much might he be paid for snooping around the electrical plant? I mean, he would risk losing his job. He might also risk failing in the task he came here to do.'

146

'I quite understand,' Marissa said, looking thoughtful. 'Worth considering, maybe. As I see it, Mallach is a quiet place, not normally a crime hot spot. Yet here, we have several incidents occurring in a short space of time. Don't you think they might be related?'

Danny had come to the same conclusion, but he didn't want to make it too easy for Marissa. Especially where she hadn't given him an answer as to any payment.

'I'll leave these documents with you. Please don't let your colleagues see them. I am afraid I can't pay you for your services directly, but there is always a reward for information leading to a conviction in such matters. Of course, they say honesty is its own reward, don't they?'

Danny snorted. People did say that, but, in his experience, it was seldom true. Maybe he should have asked her to buy him a drink instead. Ah well, better not.

'Look, I'm staying in Kirkwall tonight, at the Scapa Hotel. If you are prepared to help me, why don't you meet me there and perhaps we can get to know each other a little better. Here's my number.'

It was almost like she could read his mind. Was he that obvious? She stood up and Danny held the door open for her. As she left, she handed him a card and shook his hand.

'I am feeling so much better now, Danny. Thank you for your advice. Enjoy the rest of your day.'

With that, she swept out of sickbay, leaving him deep in thought. There was little doubt he was going to help her. The only question was which part of his body had made this decision.

Danny wandered over to the canteen for a coffee and a slice of millionaire's shortbread to restore his equilibrium. He was on his way back when Lorna's voice came over the PA saying he had a visitor in reception. He was puzzled. Surely it couldn't be Marissa again. He couldn't think of anyone else.

He marched down the weed-covered gravel path to the security cabin. Through the wire fence, he could see an Orkney Constabulary police car in the visitor's car park. Well, that was a turn-up for the books. They hadn't seemed very interested in talking to him before, let alone making a house call. The two burly policemen were taking up most of the available space in the security cabin. Danny introduced himself. Neither man seemed keen on shaking his hand.

'I'm Sergeant Campbell. We spoke on the phone. This is PC Flett. Is there somewhere we can speak privately?'

They picked up their visitor passes, and he led them over to the admin building. The appearance of two police officers drew a few concerned glances.

'It's OK, Fiona,' Danny said. 'They've not come to arrest you. Yet.'

Sergeant Campbell seemed surprised to be ushered into sickbay.

'Mr MacAndrew told us you were working undercover in the oil terminal. He didn't say what as. You do realise that impersonating a medical professional is a serious offence?'

Danny explained. The sergeant seemed unconvinced until he showed him his registration certificate.

'When I phoned, you told me to go off and do my own investigating. What's changed?'

'We're not here about any missing persons enquiries. We'd like to ask you some questions about the alleged stolen goods you found in the warehouse near here.'

'What do you want to know?' Danny was happy to let them think he had found the shipment. Gemma wouldn't thank him for giving her name to the police unless there was a reward, of course.

'First of all, how did you know to look in this particular building?'

'I didn't. I asked around. Someone suggested that the north of the island would be a good place to start. There's a couple of families up there who have rather dodgy reputations.'

'Yes indeed. We are aware of the individuals you are talking about. However, that doesn't give you the authority to go breaking into their building on the off chance that you might find something illegal.'

'I didn't break into any buildings. Give me some credit. Modern investigation hardware is a bit more sophisticated than your crowbar and sledgehammer approach.'

He was glad that Gemma had told him how the police got into the warehouse. He wasn't about to tell them how she got her photos. Let them think he had a fleet of drones with high-tech spy cameras.

'Is there anything else you can tell us about the warehouse? Was anyone else showing an interest in it?'

'I was told that it belonged to some company in Aberdeen. I don't know anything more about them. Originally, I assumed it belonged to the Kerrs. Ruth Kerr was watching you break in. She seemed very interested.'

'I'm not surprised. As for this supposed company in Aberdeen, I'm afraid it doesn't exist. The company was registered, but the address is fake, as are the names of the directors. Possibly it was a front for Neptune Shipping, but there is no way of proving that, I'm afraid.'

Danny told them about the wind turbine project and the trench from the oil terminal, but they didn't seem interested. When he mentioned the alleged energy theft, their ears pricked up.

'We are working on the assumption that the criminals had assistance from someone within the terminal,' the sergeant said. 'It would have been difficult to offload the goods without someone allowing them access through the site. One of the security guards, perhaps?'

This would have been an ideal opportunity to throw Kevan Knox to the lions, but Danny refrained. He didn't like the man, but had no evidence that he was involved. So instead, he tried to refocus their investigation on the missing men.

'Ross MacLeod was a security guard. Perhaps he was being pressured into turning a blind eye. And then there's Aidan Fitzgerald. He visited the site regularly and his company is linked to Neptune Shipping. They were both worried about something that was going on. If they could be found, they might tell you what that something was.'

PC Flett made some scribbled notes, but his superior just shook his head.

'Sadly, they both left Orkney of their own volition. Highlands and Islands are on the lookout for them, but I'm not holding my breath. If I were you, I would concentrate on finding out who is stealing power from the terminal and how they are doing it. And please let us know when you do. You wouldn't want to get into any trouble, now, would you?'

Chapter
Thirty-Five

DANNY STEPPED ONTO THE late afternoon ferry to Kirkwall. He'd let night-shift security know he was leaving site, but still felt guilty about abandoning his post. All the same, it was good to escape Mallach if only for a few hours. He wasn't sure what sort of evening Marissa had in mind. It would be simpler if she only wanted to chat about electrical schematics over dinner. Disappointing, perhaps, but a lot simpler.

The ferry chugged through the harbour entrance and tied up at the quay. Danny mooched along the waterfront for a while, not wanting to appear too keen. He even called Gordon Breck to see if he fancied a quick drink. The terminal's regular medic was in the Cairngorms with his family, sensibly keeping well away from any potential trouble. Eventually, he gave in and called Marissa.

'I'm sitting at the hotel bar. Terribly louche. Hurry along and save my reputation, Danny.'

She was wearing the same dark trouser suit she wore in the terminal. His hindbrain was disappointed she hadn't changed into evening wear. Her laptop was open on the bar, surrounded by several empty gin glasses. Danny wondered if she had headed straight here after work. She was certainly living up to the private eye stereotype.

'I'm sure there are some charming little restaurants in Kirkwall, but I'm too tired to go sightseeing. Can I buy you a drink?'

'It's ok, I'll get these.'

'No, I insist. This is one of the few jobs that allow you to claim booze and bribes on expenses. So let's make the most of it, shall we?'

Danny was planning to order a beer, but all they had were kegs of fancy craft ales, brewed with tongue-curling hops. He settled for a glass of Rioja in the vain hope that it might make him look sophisticated.

'So, Danny, what do you make of Iain Grant?'

This was going to be a business meeting after all, thought Danny. Oh well, if that was the case, he preferred a bar to a conference room.

'Seems like a nice guy. Very hands-on. Not the most dynamic manager I've ever met. His team like him. I like him.'

'But what is his secret? He's hiding something, I'm sure of it.'

'Who isn't? I heard his wife is ill. Cancer. He doesn't like to talk about it, but it's not exactly top secret.'

'How about Dougie Warnock? Have you met him yet? The Power Systems supervisor. Not that he has anyone to supervise, apart from some yokel who wanders around taking readings occasionally.'

Danny hadn't run into Warnock yet. He could see why the man would be on Marissa's radar, though. He'd be in the ideal position to divert power without anyone noticing. It was time to get out on the plant and do a few of those health and safety spot checks everyone hated.

He begged a pen off the barman and started making notes on a napkin before the wine befuddled his memory too much. Marissa was talking in quick-fire bullet points. He was struggling to keep up. Perhaps she could send him the PowerPoint later.

'Warnock is local. If the power is being diverted to somewhere on the island, there must be a local connection. But, of course, everyone knows everyone on incestuous little islands like these. They're all married to their cousins. Keeping it in the family.'

The gin was affecting Marissa's volume, and they were getting hostile glances from the regulars. It was alright for her. She was leaving in the morning. Danny tried to keep a low profile, but the mirror-backed bar gave him nowhere to hide.

Marissa ordered more drinks, and Danny made his choice from the menu. With a shrug, Marissa selected a sharing platter comprising mainly of adjectives and foreign words.

'I don't tend to eat much when I'm travelling. You never know what you might catch out in the boonies. Alcohol is much safer.'

She clinked her glass against Danny's and turned back to her laptop.

'I've made a list of all the employees and where they live. There aren't that many locals working in the terminal. The ones that are tend to have menial jobs like those Neanderthals in security.'

'Security staff have access all over the plant,' Danny pointed out. 'Like Ross MacLeod, for instance.'

No response again. Either she had a fabulous poker face or she had no idea of the rumours Ross has been spreading about her.

She continued, 'But what are they going to do with it? Smash up the substation with the jawbone of an ass? No, we are looking for someone with a bit more know-how.'

Danny tried to big up his own investigation. He told her about Kevan Knox and his doomed affair with Lorna Kerr.

'Oh, that's priceless. So, you caught him bare-cheeked? Do tell me you have photos? It's hard to take anyone seriously when you've seen them with their pants down.'

'No photos, sorry. I don't consider Lorna a suspect, but my source in Bron told me to be wary of the Kerr family. And their neighbours, the Dows.'

'You have a source? That was quick work.' She sounded impressed. Danny wasn't about to tell her about Gemma. He wanted to keep a few things up his sleeve.

'I suppose Knox could be involved, but he'd need help. How does Knox get on with his boss, Grant?'

'Not so well. In fact, no one seems to like Kevan. Apart from Lorna, that is, and she's having second thoughts.'

'Is Lorna the admin girl who brings the coffee? Pretty, I suppose, but rather vacant. It was Knox who showed me around the first time I came. Bit of a creep, I thought. I wonder what she sees in him. He must have a ginormous knob.'

Marissa snorted into her gin and returned to the laptop. Finally, the sharing platter arrived. She picked at a few morsels of calamari and spread hummus on her olive bread. The rest she left for Danny, who hoovered up everything apart from the hummus and the anchovy dip.

'I don't see any Dows in my database, Danny. So, who are they? The Orkney mafia?'

'Something like that.'

Marissa didn't have much more to offer, other than loud derogatory remarks about Scotland, Orkney, and everywhere north of Watford Gap. He decided to leave before the locals took exception. If she started a fight, it was bound to be him bearing the brunt when fists flew. Marissa shook him limply by the hand and promised to keep in touch. She slouched over her laptop and as he left, he heard her demanding another double gin. You had to admire her constitution.

As he arrived at the pier, the penultimate ferry of the night was preparing to leave. It had been a confusing but informative evening and he was ready to return to Mallach. He hopped on board and sat at the back of the boat. As they chugged slowly out of the harbour, he stared at their wash, mesmerised by swirling phosphorescence against the oil-black water.

Chapter Thirty-Six

WEARY OF TRAIPSING RANDOMLY over the island, Gemma decided to take a more scientific approach. First, she called Stevie Dunn and told him about Aidan Fitzgerald and his poor distraught mother. Stevie was a soft touch and didn't take much persuading to make the short trip up to Scrabster Harbour. She emailed him a photo of Aidan and a copy of his ferry ticket.

After a few fruitless attempts to get on the internet, she packed a rucksack and stomped up the lane to see about catching an inter-island ferry. The first boat that appeared was heading to Hoy and half a dozen other islands, all ending in "ray". Fortunately, she didn't have long to wait before the ferry to Kirkwall arrived.

It was a larger boat than the one she'd arrived on, with space for several vehicles on deck. Not that anyone in their right mind would bring their car to Mallach. There were more potholes than tarmac on the island's roads. Once onboard, she looked around for a bar or at least a wee cafe. Sadly, it was the same spartan facilities as the outgoing boat. An empty vending machine and a unisex toilet that smelled of diesel and disinfectant. She decided she would rather hang her arse over the side like sailors did in days of yore.

She hauled herself up the rusty iron steps to the deck above to admire the view. It was a grand sight, right enough. The sun was making miniature rainbows in the spray. It might even have been warm if not for a howling gale blowing down the Firth.

A lone gannet tailed the ferry. Gemma kept a beady eye on the bird in case it showed signs of regurgitating its breakfast or crapping on her head. She needn't have worried. It was far too busy scanning the water for a tasty snack to be concerned with the human interlopers passing through its feeding grounds.

With the wind came the waves, increasing all the time, until they passed Rewick Head and left the open sea. As they steamed down the Shapinsay Sound, Gemma expected the land to offer some shelter. Instead, all it did was funnel the wind, making the swell choppier and more confused.

Finally, they rounded Thieves Holm and headed into the calmer waters of Kirkwall Bay. The town was a welcome sight. Grey stone houses perched on the hill above a rocky coast. Gemma noticed a fine big hotel on the bay, built in the grand Victorian style. If her investigations turned up something interesting, maybe she should check in there for a few days. According to the tourist poster on the ferry, there were several historic pubs in the town centre and a whisky distillery nearby.

First things first. Gemma marched over to the ferry terminal ticket desk and demanded to see the manager.

'Aye, well, she's no here,' said a tiny woman with tied-back greying hair, perched on a high stool behind the counter. She was wearing a faded blue polo shirt, about three sizes too big for her, with Morag embroidered on the breast pocket.

'Well, you'll do then, Morag.' Gemma flashed her oil industry Vantage card at the woman. 'Aberdeen Social Services. I'm trying to trace a person under our care. Name of Ross MacLeod. I'm told he bought a ticket from here to Shetland. I need to know if he caught that ferry. We're all very concerned about him.'

With some difficulty, Gemma put on her most sympathetic expression. Morag took the ticket details and typed them into her computer without a murmur. After a few minutes, she shook her head and handed the piece of paper back to Gemma.

'I'm afraid there's no record of that ticket being used. I suppose he could have snuck on without showing a ticket. There's plenty who try to get away without paying, you know. It's a disgrace. We should have more powers to deal with them properly. If it were up to me, I'd drop them off at the nearest skerry and let them swim home.'

Gemma looked at Morag in a new light. A woman after her own heart.

'He had a valid ticket, though. It would be a bit odd to try and dodge a fare that you'd already paid.'

'True, true, but you said he was in care. Maybe he's a bit soft in the heid.' She tapped her temple. 'We get plenty of odd folks in the islands. It's the limited gene pool if you want my opinion. That's why I decided to marry a Shetlander. I've always had a thing about blonds.'

This wasn't exactly the sort of information Gemma was looking for, but once you got these timid types talking, it was hard to get them to stop.

'Speaking of Shetland, I don't suppose the guys at Lerwick could help?'

'Aye, well, I could try, but you know how it is, not exactly high-tech up there. They'd only know if he bought a return ticket, or he'd decided to travel on to somewhere else.'

Morag was on the phone to her colleagues in Shetland for quite some time. A queue was building up, but Gemma ignored the muttering behind her. Eventually, Morag put down the phone.

'Sorry, dearie. They've no record of that ticket. Fifteen MacLeods bought tickets in the last month, but not a Ross MacLeod. It's quite a common name, I'm afraid. There were plenty of MacLeods in my year at school and two lads called Ross, both ginger. Can you believe it?'

Gemma could believe it. She was less sure of being able to get away from Morag. Fortunately, an elderly man with sharp elbows pushed past her and demanded a ticket to Papa Westray. His surname was Ross, but it was hard to tell if his straggly grey locks ever had a tinge of ginger.

Gemma made a beeline for the tourist information, but no distillery tours ran that afternoon. She enquired after local pubs, igniting a debate amongst the staff and their only customer, who seemed to have visited them all during his stay. Once she explained she was after a nice spot of lunch, the list was whittled down to three and she got away while they were still serving food.

The Fisherman's Inn had a grand view of the harbour, slightly spoilt by a poster advertising incontinence underwear. After a satisfying pie and chips outside, Gemma made her way reluctantly back to the ferry terminal. Morag was nowhere to be seen and the wind had eased. Another rough crossing on a full stomach would have been unpleasant. As it was, she found a sheltered spot on the upper deck where she could call her new operative.

'Hiya Stevie, me auld pal. How's scabby Scrabster?'

'Quiet.'

'When is it not? Anything happen there? Ever?'

'You'd be surprised, Gem. There's a ton or two of monkfish and whiting coming through here most days.'

Her over-stuffed stomach flipped. Since that bastard fulmar had regurgitated its breakfast over her, the mention of seafood was enough to make her queasy.

'Sounds great, but I'm more interested in living people than dead fish just now.'

'Aye, well, the ferry just arrived. It got busy for a while at the Harbour Inn.'

'I might have known you'd be watching from the bar.'

'Where better? Anyway, most of the folk have gone now. A quick pie and a pint and then they all hop on the bus down to Thurso.'

'I don't blame them, though I don't suppose there's much there either. Except for the train to Aberdeen, that is.'

'A few people stick around. Tourists and the like.'

'Tourists? In Scrabster. Are they mad or just lost?'

'It's a nice wee village, Gem. I like it here. Very peaceful. You should come visit sometime.'

'I've enough excitement to deal with here on Mallach. There's still another colony of puking seabirds I haven't seen yet. On the other hand, the way Danny-boy's investigation is going, I might as well go wading in guano again. It's either that or take up potholing.'

She filled Stevie in on the latest developments. He was surprised to hear that Ross MacLeod might not have caught the ferry to Shetland.

'I've had a bit more success than you, Gem. I talked to a couple of lads who run a charter fishing boat out of the harbour here. They recognised Aidan Fitzgerald from the photo you sent. He was asking after a B&B or a cottage to rent. Somewhere off the beaten track, he said.'

'Sounds like our boy, right enough. And did they have some recommendation for him?'

'One or two. I'll check them out once I've finished up here.'

'Aye, no bother. You finish your pint first. I mean, it's not like the poor wee lad's life is in imminent danger or anything.'

There was no reply from Stevie, just some crackling followed by a loud pop. It was either a problem with the phone signal or someone scrunching up a crisp packet. Hard to be sure, but either way, that was the end of the conversation.

Chapter Thirty-Seven

THE FOLLOWING DAY, DANNY had his first proper patient. It was Kevan clutching his right hand, wrapped in a roll of blue paper towel.

'I came in early to check the perimeter. I tripped up and grabbed one of the high-pressure flanges to steady myself. Red hot it was. There ought to be a sign.'

Danny offered a few sympathetic words and examined the wound. There were two circular red welts on the edge of his palm. It didn't look too bad, but no way Kevan got that injury from a hot pipe. He might not be an expert on oil terminals, but Danny could recognise an electrical burn when he saw one. Presumably, Kevan had grabbed hold of some live terminals. So why the lie? He applied a sterile bandage to the injured area and handed the security chief an incident report.

'If you let me know exactly where it happened, I'll take a look later. There definitely ought to be a warning sign, or some insulation, especially if it's near an access way.'

Kevan was hardly likely to tell him where he'd really been injured, but it would be interesting to see what bogus location he came up with. He might give something away by accident. When first we practise to deceive...

Danny followed him out, ostensibly to get a decent coffee from the canteen. But, instead of going back to his office to fill out the report like a good little bureaucratic box-ticker, Kevan headed out through the security gate and onto the plant. Danny followed at a discrete distance.

He thought Kevan might be off to bolster his cover story by prising the warning signs off a genuine heat source. Instead, he headed straight toward the main generators. Now they were getting somewhere. Of course, there was no chance Kevan would lead him straight to the illicit power feed, was there?

It seemed not. The man had a bunch of keys and was opening a series of heavy-duty junction boxes in turn. He then glanced around and headed over to one of the turbine-generator enclosures. There was a larger key around his neck, which he used to lock shut a valve next to a row of gas bottles.

Kevan disappeared around the far side of the enclosure. Danny heard the metallic squeal of a door opening. He jogged over and saw that the main enclosure door was open. Rows of pipes and cables impeded his view. There was no sign of Kevan, but it sounded like someone was shouting for help. The voice seemed to come from inside, so he clambered into the dimly lit turbine compartment.

The door behind him clanged shut. He tried to open it, but failed to find the catch. Once his eyes had adjusted to the dark, the reason for his difficulties became obvious. The release bar was lying on the ground and there was no way of opening the door from the inside. He banged on the reinforced glass panel and yelled.

'Hey! Open up. Let me out of here, you bastard!'

The enclosure was lined with acoustic cladding designed to attenuate the noise coming from what was basically a static jet engine. No one would hear his puny efforts to attract attention.

After a few minutes, a motor behind him burst into life. Someone was starting the damn generator. The low whine emanating from the turbine gradually rose in pitch and volume. Danny counted the many ways you could die in here. It would get pretty hot shortly, and the noise was already intolerable even with earplugs. What about gas leaks or fire? And what were those bottles that Kevan isolated on the way in? Danny remembered a warning about CO_2 being used as a fire extinguishant. Not only would it put out the fire, but a high enough concentration would also suffocate anyone inside. Suppose Kevan had de-isolated the bottles after he'd locked the doors.

Danny could smell burning coming from the turbine casing. He dabbed his glove on the hot metal and sniffed. Kerosene had been sprayed over the exposed metal. It was highly flammable. As soon as it heated up, it was going to burst into flames. Was that enough to set off the fire detectors and release the CO_2? He didn't fancy hanging around to find out.

Kevan had come in here, but he hadn't gone out the way he came in. There had to be another exit. Under the turbine was a maze of oil and fuel pipes with no room to squeeze through. To the left was the spinning generator coupling, to the right an impenetrable forest of valves and instruments.

Up it was then. The hydraulic ram in front of him was attached to a complicated-looking set of levers arrayed around the turbine. The levers opened as the machinery increased in speed, presenting Danny with a rickety stepladder. He clambered swiftly up the hot metal structure. There was just enough room at the top to crouch with his shoulders pressing against the roof of the enclosure. A set of doors over the other side, identical to those he came in through, showed. They also had been sabotaged. There was no way out that way.

It was even hotter up here than it had been by the entrance. The ventilation fans did little to dissipate the heat from the roaring furnace beneath his feet. The howling gale they created made it hard to keep his footing.

He braced himself against the roof and it moved slightly. The panel was too heavy for one man to move unassisted, but the force of the air helped him ease one side upwards. It began to pulse and flap alarmingly. Danny wasn't sure if it would fly off or slam down on his head. He shuffled as close to the opening as he dared. It was all in the timing. As the panel lifted, Danny sprang forward and rolled out onto the roof. The panel banged shut behind him, narrowly missing his trailing foot.

Danny scrabbled for a handhold and his fingers closed around some thin metal tubing. It flexed and buckled as momentum sent him slithering across the oil-smeared roof. He rolled over the edge and dangled there, one hand still clutching the tubing. There was a creak and a twang as the tubing gave way, blasting him with high-pressure air and sending him swinging towards the ground.

He landed on his back on cold concrete, neatly sandwiched between two pipes. He lay there gasping like a patient with a punctured lung. For a moment, he thought he'd suffocate, but soon his breathing calmed and his vision cleared.

Danny heard running feet and the clank of a steel-toed boot striking metal. Someone was clambering over the pipes towards him. A tall figure, face shrouded by goggles and a bandanna, stood over him, an oversized wrench in one raised hand. Even if he had enough breath to move, Danny's body was still refusing to cooperate. He braced his head in his hands and waited for the blow.

Chapter Thirty-Eight

'WHAT IN HELL'S NAME is going on here?

The man put down the wrench and climbed over the pipe. Danny was in no condition to answer him. He could hardly breathe, let alone speak.

'What happened? Are you OK?'

'OK... just... winded... I think.'

'I'm Dougie Warnock, the power supervisor. Who the hell are you? Do you want me to call for the medic?' Dougie pulled down his mask. Now Danny could see his face. He looked more like someone's kindly uncle than a passing psycho.

'I... am... the medic.' His lungs seemed to work now, but words were still coming in gasps.

'Well, you should know better. What on earth were you doing in the turbine enclosure?'

'Thought I saw Kevan. Go inside. Followed. Door stuck. Couldn't get out. Then it started.'

'Aye, that's odd. This is the old standby unit. Not supposed to start unless the grid is paying for it. As for your pal Kevan, he's always putting his nose where it's not wanted. I saw him walking out of the building just now.'

Danny sat up. His back and shoulders were sore, but nothing seemed broken. His breathing had returned to normal. Not a punctured lung or anything serious like that.

'Well, it's a good thing I never finished fixing the catches on that access panel. Mind you, when the boss gets to hear about this, he'll have my balls in a sling.'

'Mine too,' Danny said. The two men looked at each other, weighing up their options.

'I suppose we could keep it between us. I mean, no one got hurt, right?'

'Suits me,' Danny nodded. 'I've only been here a few days. I don't want to report myself for safety violations. I'd like to know what happened, though. Just between you and me.'

Dougie agreed to find out why the turbine started and why the enclosure doors wouldn't open.

'I can fix the airline myself. I'll get those doors and panels sorted out, no problem. The turbine controls are another thing altogether. I can try to reproduce what happened, I suppose. If I can't figure it out, or there's a problem with the software, I'll have to report it.'

'Fair enough.' Danny was pretty sure there was no software fault. Someone had set a trap and started the turbine once he was locked inside. Could Dougie figure out how? Perhaps he already knew. Danny doubted Kevan Knox had the technical know-how. If the security chief was responsible, he must have had help. Despite their pact, Dougie seemed the most plausible suspect. If he wasn't the culprit, then who?

'Sure you're OK?' asked Dougie. 'I'm away to the stores to fetch some bits and bobs. I hope they have half-inch tubing. Otherwise, I'll have to send out for some. That'll take an age.'

Danny struggled to his feet and dusted himself off. His ribs hurt like hell. Unfortunately, there wasn't much he could do. Even if he went to A&E in Kirkwall, they'd just X-ray his chest, prod him in the ribs and make it worse. As long as he didn't laugh or sneeze, he'd be fine.

'If you don't mind, I'll just hang around here a while. Catch my breath. Maybe look and see if there are any more hazards.'

Dougie left with a list of parts and a worried expression. He left his adjustable wrench behind. Danny wondered what he'd been planning to fix. Based on his offshore experience, big wrenches were seldom used for their intended purpose. Mainly to hit things that refused to move.

Danny walked around the turbine enclosure. The vent fans were still running, but the turbine was silent. Both doors opened and closed from the outside, though the pressure generated by the fans made it hard work to close them fully. Inside, the bolts holding the door release bar in place were loose. Judging by the amount of corrosion, they had been like that for some time.

No wonder Dougie Warnock was worried. A safety issue like that should have been sorted out ages ago. Could it have been an accident? Danny didn't think so. Someone deliberately locked him inside and started the turbine.

So, Kevan has a peek inside the turbine enclosure. He leaves the door open. When someone goes in, he slams the trap closed. He jogs up the stairs to the control room, does some jiggery-pokery with the computer screens and starts the turbine. He leaves by another exit and goes on his merry way like nothing has happened.

It could have happened like that. The climbing part wouldn't have been easy for the big man. Surely, he wouldn't have had time to get back downstairs and out of the building. It sounded more like a two-man job.

Danny tried to retrace Kevan's earlier movements. He started with the junction box he'd left open. It was a solid, floor-standing unit labelled "Explosion Risk – No Unauthorised Access" and "Danger of Death". He gingerly prised the door open further. There were some huge cables inside. The colourful red, yellow and blue ones were coated with years of grime and grease. However, a set of brown, black and blue cables looked clean and new.

Three-phase power? That was the limit of Danny's electrical knowledge. He wasn't about to repeat Kevan's mistake and stick his hand inside. The new cables disappeared into an armoured casing and then up towards the roof. Tracing them would have to wait for another time.

Danny closed the door as best he could. There was no sign of the special key Kevan had used to open the boxes. He used some electrical tape to wrap around the housing. That would have to do for now.

Behind the junction boxes were open-grated steps leading up to the control room. Climbing them took quite some time. It felt like he was wearing a corset three sizes too small. Every time he got out of breath, sharp needles of pain spiked all around his ribcage.

Before going inside, Danny edged along a nearby access way. He rummaged through his rucksack and pulled out a small magnetic camera disguised as a security light. It looked incongruous stuck up here. He hoped no one would notice it amongst the obsolete crap lashed to the framework.

It felt good using proper monitoring kit for once. Spying on people remotely was better than being beaten up in person.

There was no one in the control room. All the selector switches were set to remote or automatic operation. A number of identical control panels were mounted along the far wall and, with the help of a tattered layout drawing, Danny eventually found the one which controlled his errant turbine. The alarm screen was full of flashing red messages. There was no way it would start again soon.

By randomly pressing buttons on the touchscreen display, he found another page labelled "Event Log". The last entry was "Emergency Shutdown Initiated at Enclosure", which Danny took to mean that it had been stopped using the big red button on the side. So far, so good. Finding how it had started was more challenging. "Manual Control" had been selected and then "Local Start", which made sense. A bunch of safety features had been overridden to get to that point. To do that, someone had signed in as "Maintenance Engineer".

Who would have that sort of clearance? Dougie, of course, but who else? Maybe someone had scribbled the username and password on the back of one of the panels. Even so, whoever started the turbine would need to know what overrides were required. The finger of guilt was still pointing firmly towards his new comrade, Dougie Warnock.

Chapter Thirty-Nine

THERE WAS AN EMAIL waiting for Danny on the medic's PC. Stevie the sparky had been busy. The email read like a poorly written travelogue. It seemed Stevie had been to every village in northeast Scotland and checked out every bothy, cottage and B&B. He'd also visited several hotel bars and pubs, seeking information and refreshment.

The email suggested that he had some important news to impart. Something that he wasn't prepared to share electronically. Stevie thought that undesirables were forever monitoring his online activity. He was probably right. Though the undesirables were usually more interested in scamming people out of their hard-earned cash. Danny doubted that Neptune Shipping and their associates were big into cybercrime.

After a few failed attempts and missed calls, Danny finally got through to Stevie on the phone. From the sound of wheeling gulls and the clink of glasses, he assumed Stevie was sitting outside a seaside pub somewhere.

'The Crab Inn. I'm in Sandiside. It's just a wee fishing village. There's a bonny view over the bay. You can just about make out the nuclear power station in the distance.'

'Nice. So, what's the big news?'

'I found him.'

'Aidan?'

'Aye. He's safe and well.'

Danny blew a kiss at the phone and drummed the desk with his free hand.

'That's brilliant news. Fantastic. I thought he was dead.' He let out a sigh of relief. It felt like he'd been holding his breath since he got here. Finally, he could come up for air.

'You Yorkshiremen are born pessimists. I always knew he'd turn up alive. He wasn't keen on being found, mind. I promised I wouldn't tell anyone.'

'Except me.'

'Well, I did mention you. I told him you specialised in finding lost bairns. How you were helping his mother out of the kindness of your heart.'

'And he believed you?'

'I may have implied that you'd taken a fancy to her.'

'Thanks. He definitely won't talk to me now. Has he told you anything yet?'

'This and that. The lad's scared shitless. He won't even call his mother in case it puts her in danger. Doesn't trust the police neither. Seems he's had a few run-ins with them in the past.'

'But he trusts you?'

'Gemma says I have a kind face.'

That was true enough. Stevie looked like Santa Claus without the red hoodie. He radiated a friendly calmness and good humour. Of course, Aidan would trust him. Whether he would trust Danny was another question altogether.

'Is there any chance you could get Aidan to talk to me? If he's worried about being traced, he could use your phone. We could have a quick video call.'

'A what?' Stevie sounded confused. 'I'm not sure my phone has one of those.'

'It's a smartphone, right? You can take photos with it?'

'Oh aye, the phone is smart. It's me that's not.'

'You know that's not true. This is probably a dumb question, but have you got any social media apps on your phone?'

'No, I don't think so. I prefer being social face-to-face.'

'Well, think of this as a modern way of doing that.'

The idea of signing Stevie up for a social media site was clearly a step too far. With some difficulty, Danny guided him through installing a video call app instead. He didn't fancy the idea of anyone being able to overhear this conversation. The office block had too many thin walls and prying ears. No one was allowed to take their phone out onto the plant with all those high-pressure gas pipes. Instant dismissal if you did.

Danny took himself and his phone off to the canteen for a coffee and then wandered around the scrubland behind the staff car park. It was a dull day, with only the occasional spot of rain. He found a place to perch on a broken-down wall. It was near enough to the building to pick up the Wi-Fi signal and far enough away to be out of earshot.

After half an hour, he was about ready to head back inside when the top of Stevie's head appeared on the screen.

'Hey, Danny! It works. I can see your ugly mug, clear as day. A technological miracle, eh?'

'Certainly is.' He didn't bother telling Stevie that only his left ear was visible. It was Aidan he really needed to see.

'I'll hand you over. Here's the lad himself.'

After some phone juggling, Aidan's face appeared on the screen. He looked terrified, like the proverbial rabbit-in-the-headlights.

'Hi, Aidan. You don't know how good it is to see you. Your mother has been in bits, you know. She had me convinced you were gone for good.'

'You can't tell her. If she thinks I'm dead, she'll be safer that way. I want the guys who are after me to see how upset she is. Then they'll leave her alone. You have to promise.'

Danny promised, on the condition that Aidan told him precisely what he knew and who he thought was after him. It took a while, but eventually, he agreed.

'One of my pals sent me a link about spotting fake medicines. He knew I was in the trade, so to speak, and he thought I might be interested. As it happened, the ferry to Westray was delayed. I got bored, so I thought I'd check through the stock I was carrying in the van. The big deliveries to pharmacies and hospitals are all boxed up and sealed, but I was doing the odd drop-off at care homes and the like. Sometimes the small batches are just loose in bags, especially if it's an urgent order.'

Aidan disappeared off-screen briefly and held up a box of benzodiazepine tablets.

'I found these. There's nay seal on the box. I was on sleeping tablets for a while myself and they always had a seal. They were a bastard to get open sometimes. Not these ones, though.'

'So, what did you do?'

'I spoke to my boss. First, he chewed my ear off for messing with the cargo. Then he said I wasn't to worry about it because the boxes didn't have to be sealed. The pills are all in blister packs, he said, so it wasn't necessary.'

'Is that true?'

'Aye, maybe. It's not the law, but most manufacturers do seal them up. Anyway, I figured the customers would have complained if there was a problem, right? So, I carried on as normal for a couple more weeks until I had to deliver a load of medicine bottles to a big house near Finstown. I thought it was a new care home, maybe, but there was no sign on the gate. I didn't have time to check in the bag, but I palmed a bottle when I was handing it over. I thought they wouldn't miss one.'

'And did they?'

'I reckon. My boss never said anything, but it felt like I was being followed. Even when I delivered to an out-of-the-way spots, I'd often notice a car behind me. Not always the same one. Maybe I was getting paranoid, but I don't think so.'

'Was the bottle fake?'

'I don't know for sure, but look here.' Aidan held the bottle up to the camera. 'See, there's no seal on the lid like there should be. It's Phentermine-Topiramate.' Aidan struggled with the pronunciation. The name meant nothing to Danny. 'I mean, they spelt the big words right, but it's supposed to be a slimming pill. Look here on the label. Says it's to help with sliming. How dumb is that?'

Danny asked him to send photos of the fake packaging. Aidan agreed reluctantly.

'I need something to show the police,' Danny said. 'In case anything happens.'

'Like when they bump me off?'

Danny didn't reply. Aidan already looked like a condemned man. So instead, he tried to convince him to share his information with the authorities.

'The more people who know about this, the safer you'll be. Are you sure you don't want me to call the police? They can protect you better than I can.'

Aidan shook his head.

'You haven't heard the whole story. You know I was collecting stuff for Medifax as well?'

'From Mallach?'

'Aye. I had to drive the van up a dirt track. Some warehouse in the middle of nowhere. I'd have never found it without satnav. It seemed very dodgy to me. There was no one around when I got there and then this woman came out through a side door.'

'Big woman? Angry looking?'

'No. Scrawny lass. Older than you, I'd say, but not real old, like.'

'Can you describe her?'

'Nothing to see. She was wearing one of those white romper suits, mask and all, like she'd just come out of a cleanroom.'

'Makes sense if they were manufacturing medicines there.'

'That's what I thought, but then why was she wearing it outdoors? She never even took off the mask. So, I started thinking: what if she just didn't want to show her face?'

'Did you go inside the building?'

'No. That's that weird too. She told me to wait outside and brought the boxes out to me. Heavy they were. I offered to help, but she said no. Health and safety or some crap like that.

'And what was in the boxes?'

'Loads of peedie glass spray bottles. I checked the contents and signed for them before I put them in the van.'

'What did the manifest say was in the bottles?'

'Some herbal potion to help with hay fever. You're supposed to spray it up your nose. I don't believe anybody makes that kind of stuff in a shed in Orkney. Good knows what was really in them. Damn things were clattering away down the track. Good thing none of them broke.'

'I don't suppose you kept one of these mysterious bottles?'

Aidan had been too scared to try and ferret away any more dodgy medicines. Danny asked Aidan to hand him back to Stevie, who wandered outside so they could talk in private.

'I hate to ask, but could you keep an eye on the young lad for me?'

'Aye, aye. Me and missus were thinking of taking the camper van up to the coast sometime soon. Sandiside seems as good a spot as any.'

'Is Mrs Dunn a big fan of nuclear power stations, then?'

'She used to work with radioactive waste. It'll be a bit of a busman's holiday for her. Don't worry, she'll be fine with it. I'd have to let her know what's going on, though. I'm useless at keeping secrets, especially from her.'

'OK with me, but you'll have to be discrete. I don't suppose Aidan will know you're there. He's hardly likely to go sunning himself on the beach.'

'What if we spot anything suspicious?'

'Then you can ignore what he says. Call the cops straight away. I don't want you and your missus putting yourselves in danger, understand?'

As soon as the screen went blank, Danny scrolled through his contacts to find Sheila Fitzgerald's number. Some promises demanded to be broken. The thought of Aidan's mother sitting at home heartbroken was more than he could bear. For the first time in a long while, he was able to give someone good news. He didn't plan to waste that opportunity.

'Is that Sheila? Hi, it's Danny Verity. The private investigator. Yes. Yes, I have. Good news. No, really. I've found Aidan. He's alive and well.'

Sheila broke down in tears, giving watery thanks to God and Danny in equal measure.

'I had a lot of help. No, I can't tell you where he is exactly. Overseas. Yes, I spoke to him on a video call. I saw his face. It was definitely him.'

'Why didn't he call me? I've been beside myself with worry.'

More tears.

'Aidan was worried about your safety. He thought you'd be safer if you thought he was dead. You *have* to act like you still do. For his sake and yours.'

'So, he's not out of danger then?'

'No one else knows where he is. If we want to keep him safe, I'm afraid we have to keep it that way for now.'

Sheila took some convincing, but eventually agreed. She was still distraught. Danny didn't think she'd have any difficulty keeping up the pretence.

'Aidan didn't want me to contact the police either. Is there any particular reason why he would be reluctant for them to get involved?'

'He's got a criminal record. Not his fault, poor lamb. My ex-husband, the bastard. He used Aidan to buy coke for him. Not the sort you get in a bottle, by the way. Normally, the polis don't bother stopping and searching the bairns.'

'But they stopped Aidan?'

'Aye. Someone tipped them off. Of course, the bastard denied everything and pinned it all on Aidan. He was only fifteen, so he never went inside for it, thank God.'

'Could his father be involved in this latest business?'

'If he is, he'll have more than the polis to worry about. I doubt it, though. I've not seen him since I kicked him out. I figured he was doing time for something. He wasn't the sort to stay out of trouble for long.'

Aidan's father sounded like your average addict. Thieving to pay for his habit. Not the sort of guy to be involved in a professional operation like this. Still, it would be worth trying to check out his whereabouts.

It took a while to get off the phone. Sheila kept thanking him and then bursting into tears again. You can't hang up on a woman while she's in mid-sob.

Eventually, her tide of tears ebbed away. Danny strolled back to sickbay, buoyed up by her reaction. A great weight had been lifted off his shoulder, but there was another, even greater one. If only he could give the MacLeod family the same good news.

He couldn't be that lucky, surely. The odds of finding Ross safe and well hadn't changed just because Aidan was alive. Still, it gave him hope. They'd found the stolen goods and one of the missing men. He just needed to solve the mystery of Aidan's medical supplies, Marissa's missing power and Ross' whereabouts. There was still an outside chance he could solve this case and go home happy. Just a chance.

Chapter Forty

THE SICKBAY PHONE WAS ringing as he opened the door. He prayed it wasn't a medical emergency. With all the distractions of the investigation and the health and safety paperwork, Danny had not enough time to do the routine part of a medic's job.

'There you are, Danny.' It was Marissa. 'I called your mobile, but I suppose that was expecting too much. Hard to get a signal on a godforsaken rock in the middle of the North Sea. How's it going? Still living the dream?'

He told her about his near-death experience in the turbine enclosure.

'Damn! I missed all the excitement. I should have stuck around longer. You are a bit of a lightning conductor, aren't you? That's a useful gift if you're an investigator. Until lightning strikes you, of course. I'm so glad to hear you're not dead.'

'I'll send you the photos of the junction box. You might be able to make more sense of it than me.'

'You're a darling. Do it now and we can talk about it over the phone. You show me yours and I'll show you mine! I've got some terribly interesting spreadsheets to send you.'

They might have been fascinating to Marissa. They meant nothing to Danny. Maths had never been his strong point. He always felt it was something the teachers had invented just to torture their students. Listening to the engineers in the terminal talk, he could almost see how to use maths in the real world. Shame that realisation had come about twenty years too late.

'I've created a few simple graphs for the hard of thinking. They're on the last tab. You do know where the tabs are, don't you, Danny?'

Yes, he knew that much. Her condescending tone was grating.

'If you look carefully, you can see there's a small, variable discrepancy between the incoming and outgoing power. That's the wiggly blue line at the bottom, Danny. It's been like that for yonks. It's barely noticeable compared to the huge load swings you get in an oil terminal.'

'But then it jumps up, right?'

'Bingo! Well spotted. About the middle of last year, someone turned up the wick on whatever candle they were lighting. Actually, not a candle, now I come to think about it. Let's see what happens if you superimpose a graph of the ambient temperature, like so. And now the inductance. Ta-da!'

She sent him the updated graph. Whenever the smooth red temperature line went down, the yellow line went down, and the wiggly blue line went up.

'It's an electric heater, I'd say. A jolly big one. Or lots of smaller ones. Like everyone in Orkney decided to boil a kettle simultaneously. I have a theory, but I'm keeping it to myself for now. I'd hate to prejudice your enquiries.'

Danny was quite happy to put up with that sort of prejudice if it saved him a load of legwork and brain ache. He told her about the failed wind turbine project and the alleged trench between the terminal and the warehouse.

'Interesting. Very interesting. Ooh, look! Your photos have come through. Lovely composition, I must say. Not much use, though. I mean, that new cable could be related, but you wouldn't use a skinny one like that. We're talking at least twenty kilovolts here. And it's likely to be underground.'

'So, where should I look for this cable? Do I need to borrow a shovel?'

'More like a pneumatic drill. Hopefully, it's buried under a layer of concrete. I'm afraid you will have to poke around in the substation. Not literally, by the way.'

'I assume twenty kilovolts can do you a lot of damage.' Danny thought about the poor electrocuted cat he'd failed to rescue.

'Absolutely. And there are a few four hundred kV cables running through. But don't worry. It doesn't make a lot of difference. Anything over ten kV is enough to vaporise you. It's a quick and painless death and it saves on those pesky funeral expenses. Worth considering if you were thinking of ending it all.'

'I'll bear that in mind. So, as long as I touch nothing, it should be safe enough, right?'

'Safe-ish. I'd wait for a dry day. Assuming they ever have those in bonny Scotland. There's always a chance of arcing, especially when it's wet.'

'How about I get hold of one of those rubber suits?'

'Very kinky, darling, but basically useless. Just carry a rabbit's foot and stay as far as possible away from anything that makes a crackly noise.'

She rang off before he had a chance to risk assess his way out of the assignment. The sun was making a rare appearance. He sighed; better head over to the substation and get the job over and done with.

Obscured from the offices and workshops by the windowless wall of the turbine building, he circled the substation perimeter. No one had a reason to come here unless there was a major fault. He took photos through the spike-topped steel fence of anything that looked like it was heading underground. Probably some of these were drainpipes, but he'd rather look stupid than do this all over again.

The part of the substation that faced north, towards the barn, was hard up against the chain-link fence surrounding the terminal. Without going outside the terminal and walking over the exposed moorland, he couldn't get through. Danny peered through the fence. If this was where the trench came in, there was no sign of it. The whole area was heavily overgrown with bracken and brambles.

There was nothing for it but to check inside the substation. He waved his all-area pass at the high barred gate with its array of warning notices and let himself in. The overhead lines were humming with power. The transformers occasionally clicked but he heard no crackling nor saw any sparks.

Fortunately, most of the equipment was out in the open air. There was one low brick building, but that was firmly locked. With had three different "danger of death" signs on the door, and a graphic of someone being struck by a bolt of lightning, he didn't feel like risking it.

He began taking a video of the layout and then stopped and scuffed at the ground with his boot. The base of the substation was concrete, with a thin layer of stones scattered on top. Here, the gravel was deeper. It was impossible to say how deep. The line of disturbed ground ran between the perimeter fence and the nearby transformer. Beyond the boundary, it was all gorse and scrub. Hard to be sure, but maybe this was the power line's route up to the proposed wind farm.

Danny took photos of the route and zoomed in on the tag numbers on the transformers and the incoming cables. Next, he attached another spy camera to the fence, pointing towards the brick building. Then, checking that there was still no one around, he let himself out of the substation compound and hurried away.

He had one camera left, which he had intended to hide somewhere in the office building. Now that he had free access to the offices, he wasn't sure that made a lot of sense. It seemed more logical to mount it somewhere out on the plant.

On the way back to the accommodation, he passed the single-storey research building. It looked somewhat incongruous amongst the giant oil tanks and high flare stacks. On a whim, he shinned up the chain-link fence and clamped a camera just underneath a security light. This involved letting go with one hand and holding the camera between his teeth. His foot slipped, leaving him hanging like Tarzan. Finally, after some frantic swinging, he got a toehold on a rusted and broken link. He hauled himself back upright and, with his free hand, offered the camera up against the flat metal underside of the light fitting. The magnet clanged it into place and he clambered swiftly back down to ground level, shaking his arms until the blood returned to his fingers.

Something made him look round. Out on the moor, he thought he saw a flicker of light. Was someone watching him from outside the terminal? He couldn't be sure. He took the long way back to the sick bay and sent the new photos off to Marissa. God knows what she would make of them.

He hesitated before picking up the phone and calling Gemma. He knew what kind of reception he was likely to face.

'You'll have to go back to the warehouse.'

'Says who? Has Mata Hari been working her wiles on you again?'

Either Gemma was psychic, or she was bugging his phone. Danny wasn't sure which option was more alarming. Maybe she just knew him too well. He swallowed his coffee dregs and told her what he'd found in the substation.

'I'm telling you, Danny-boy, there was nothing in that warehouse except for a few dodgy pumps and they were all wrapped in a plastic sheet. No way they were running or even plugged into the wall. It's all very well for you, sipping cappuccino in your comfy office. It's a long way up to The Loon. And anyway, yer warehouse is being watched.'

'The cops have gone. Even the lads from Kirkwall. They were kind enough to call in here on the way to the ferry. Gave me a right grilling.'

'It's not the polis I'm worried about. I need something to get Big Ruthie out of the way for a while. I need a diversion.'

'How am I supposed to do that?'

'I don't know. You're the private dick. They must have taught you a few sneaky moves in dick school.'

There was a way, but it was risky. Even if Ruth was fooled initially, she would find out she'd been tricked soon enough. It wouldn't take her long to figure out who was responsible. What would she do then?

He waited until lunchtime and snuck into the admin office. Since ending her affair with Kevan, Lorna had lunch in the canteen with the rest of her colleagues. Most girls of her age would have taken their phones with them, but Lorna wasn't like most girls. Danny rifled through her handbag and jacket before finally finding the phone plugged into a charger, over by the printer.

He wasn't proud of snooping on his colleagues, but he had been sneakily watching everyone unlocking their phones. In his unofficial line of work, you never knew when you might need information like that. Some used fingerprint recognition, which was rather inconvenient. The rest, including Lorna, used a four-digit PIN. He had a list of them in his notebook. The only one he hadn't figured out was Fiona, who kept hers clutched tightly to her chest. Staring intently at the admin manager's bosom was neither advisable nor desirable.

He unlocked Lorna's phone and found Ruth Kerr's mobile number. Now he just needed to compose a convincing text that would bring her running to her niece's aid. Ideally, something that would lead her away from the terminal and Danny. Lorna's moped helmet was hanging from the hatstand, which gave him an idea.

'Felt sick. Heading home. Run out of fuel on Tarf Hill. Help?'

It wasn't that far from Ruth's farm to Tarf Hill, as the crow flies, but there was an oil terminal in between. She would have to drive around the perimeter on what was little more than a dirt track. With any luck, Ruth would have to fetch fuel from somewhere first. And then she had to find a non-existent moped somewhere along a winding country lane. A light drizzle swept across the car park. That might work to his advantage. It was really going to piss off Gemma, though.

He removed the battery from the phone and discharged it with a paper clip. Then he prised the fuse out of the charger socket. He couldn't have Ruth calling back to find out the actual location of her beloved niece.

Chapter Forty-One

THE RASPBERRY BICYCLE HAD many fine features, but Gemma wished it had a more comfortable saddle. This one was more suited to those Tour de France lads with their shaved legs and aerodynamic bawbags. Surely even bony-arsed Heather must find it hard to ride for long. Gemma had a naturally padded backside. You would have thought that was an advantage. Apparently not. No amount of fancy suspension was going to save her from bruises in some sensitive areas. She would not be perching on those wooden bar stools for a while.

Just now, she had more pressing concerns. What would Big Ruth do when she found out that darling Lorna wasn't stranded by the roadside? Danny's cunning diversion was going to blow his cover for sure. She had one chance to find out what was going on at the warehouse, so she'd better make it count.

Underneath Heather's silver cycling gloves, she'd taped up her fingers and wound a couple of bandages around her knuckles. Gemma was a self-taught street fighter. You had to be where she grew up. After a couple of forced school changes in her teens, one of her teachers persuaded her to take taekwondo lessons and she even joined the local boxing gym. She'd harboured dreams of becoming a professional fighter, but sadly, her idea of mixed martial arts was considered unsportsmanlike, if not downright illegal.

She reached the top of the ridge in bottom gear, gasping to catch her breath. Under normal circumstances, it was challenging, but with a load of tools onboard, her overworked hamstrings couldn't cope. She abandoned the conspicuous bike under a gorse bush, out of sight of the warehouse and the nearby farm buildings.

The polis had gone, just as Danny said. All that remained was some of their useless black and yellow barrier tape. She scanned the horizon with her binoculars. No sign of any local farmers or any other jakey bastards.

Cautiously, she made her way up to the warehouse. The front bay door was locked with a big, hefty police padlock. Aidan said his mystery supplier came out of a side entrance. The only option was the emergency exit she had previously noticed.

It too was locked. Still, if this wasn't an emergency, then what was? She pulled out the Persuader, a metre-long crowbar that she'd lifted from the Cuillin Alpha in case any of the neighbourhood junkies paid her a night-time call.

There was just enough of a gap at the top of the door to squeeze in the claw end and wiggle it down closer to the release bar. She rocked on it a couple of times until she heard a creak, then threw all her weight against the door.

It flew open, and she tumbled inside. She made a lopsided parachute roll and staggered to her feet, still clutching the Persuader. Fortunately, no one was inside to witness her rather graceless entrance. She dusted herself off and looked around. Nothing. Just an empty building, bar a few shelving units and the overhead crane.

There was a fire extinguisher by the emergency exit. Nice to see that even criminals are up to speed with health and safety regulations these days. She used it to wedge the mangled door closed and started working her way around the inside of the building, tapping the walls with the Persuader as she went.

There appeared to be no hidden doors, no passageways within the wall, no secret compartments. Just a tiny office in one corner with a single desk. Nothing in the drawers. She moved the desk, but there was no hatch underneath. Next door was a toilet and handbasin. The only way out was the door she came in through. Unless you were supposed to flush your-self down, like in that Harry Potter film.

She had to be missing something. Something the polis would have overseen. There was an inspection pit in the middle of the floor, towards the main entrance. It was covered over with a sheet metal plate. She'd seen the polis lift it up and look inside. Well, there was nowhere else left, so she might as well give it a go.

The cover plate was heavy, but she managed to prise it open and slide it out of the way. It looked like a perfectly ordinary inspection pit, about the length of a large van and half an axle length wide. At the bottom were the usual shiny black puddles of engine oil and diesel. The only unusual feature was the metal liner. Inspection pits were usually bare concrete.

Gemma leaned over and struck the bottom with the Persuader. The liner tolled like a cracked bell as if she was hitting an empty tank instead of one resting on solid ground. She stood up and took another look around. The overhead crane was controlled by various buttons on a long pendant hanging by the far wall. Next to the pendant was a cargo sling with four hooks on long lengths of chain.

She powered up the crane controls and guided the hook over to the inspection pit like a big metal dog on a lead. She lowered the crane sufficiently to get the sling onto it and looked for somewhere to attach the hooks.

The inspection pit cover had two holes drilled into the metal on each side. Had she spotted them earlier, it might have saved her some effort. The metal lining had four bracing bars, one in each corner. She hooked the ends of the sling onto the bars and began to lift. She had to keep adjusting the chains to stop the liner from becoming wedged. Eventually, it came all the way out, making a hell of a racket.

Gemma swung the liner out of the way and peered down the holes. She expected it to be pitch black. Instead, it glowed brightly with UV light. A warm, damp updraft rose from the pit, turning to steam as it hit the chill Orkney air.

She waited for the cloud to clear. It took some time for her eyes to adjust to the glare. When they did, she couldn't believe what she was seeing. Underneath this sterile building, it was like the Lost World. Rows and rows of identical plants. An underground farm.

They looked very familiar. For a moment, she foolishly thought they might be tomatoes like her neighbour grew on his allotment. Then she remembered the other plants that her neighbour grew on his windowsill and everything clicked into place. The names changed with every generation. Grass, weed, bush, Mary Jane. Now she knew what this place was and why someone had gone to so much effort to hide it underground.

A vertical ladder led down into the illicit cannabis farm below. An overpowering odour of pollen and manure was carried upwards in the warm tropical air. She was about to climb down when she heard the fire extinguisher clatter to the floor.

She spun around. The door opened. In walked Ruth Kerr, carrying a wicked-looking hooked knife. She did not look pleased to see Gemma.

Chapter Forty-Two

Ruth marched across the warehouse towards Gemma. Mindful of the wicked-looking farm tool in her hand, Gemma backed around to the far side of the pit.

'You again? I should have known. You don't take a hint, do you?'

'I'm a bit pig-headed like that. Or so I've been told. How about you put down the wee scythe and maybe we can talk?'

'Haud yer wheest. I've nothing to talk to you about. I'll be hanging onto ma billhook, just for now.'

'Now then, violence never solved anything.' Particularly if the violence was directed toward her.

'I'm not a violent woman. Not unless I'm provoked.'

'Aye, is that right? Did Ross provoke you then?'

'Ross, who?'

'MacLeod. The lad who's missing, presumed murdered. Is this what happened to him? He came snooping around here and you sliced his throat with your nasty wee hook?'

'I never met the lad. If you don't shut it, I might just slice you, though.'

Ruth was holding the billhook in her left hand. It had a single-edged blade designed for the purpose of slashing weeds and the like. As the woman talked, Gemma edged left and then dived right. Ruth hit out with the blunt side of the hook and caught her a sharp blow on the shoulder. It hurt, but not enough to throw her off balance.

Gemma grabbed Ruth's arm and forced the hand back even further. The billhook clattered to the ground and skittered across the concrete floor before disappearing into the leafy pit below.

Gemma sprang back and took up her scariest crouching stance, one that she'd copied from an old Kung-Fu film. She didn't have the mad Kung-Fu skills to match, but Ruth wasn't to know that.

'Well, that evens things up, eh, Ruthie? Let's see how cocky you are without your cutter.'

Ruth said nothing. She took a boxing stance, jaw jutting out, her left hand at chest height, her right kept low to jab at her shorter opponent.

That complicated things. Gemma had fought a few southpaws. It was easy to lose track and walk into a swinging fist. Plus, this was a gross mismatch. Ruth was a heavyweight to her welterweight. Of course, since she'd given up competing, Gemma was closer to being a middleweight, but the extra pounds were around her hips instead of her upper body.

Still, she didn't need to land a knockout blow on the big lass. She just needed to keep out of the way of those big haymaker hands long enough to get to the door and make a run for it. Better hope Ruth isn't a sprinter as well as a boxer.

The plan was easier thought than done. For a heavyweight, Ruth was pretty light on her loafers. She had no trouble blocking Gemma's attempts to dodge around her.

Gemma tried mixing her martial arts and kicked out at her opponent's shins. She connected but was pretty sure she'd hurt herself more than Ruth. Another kick to the midriff was caught mid-air by Ruth, sending Gemma sprawling to the floor. She rolled up just in time to see Ruth's agricultural boot pass eye-wateringly close to her nose.

Deciding to change tactics, she darted in under Ruth's guard, got in a couple of jabs, and skipped back out. Ruth stepped forward to keep in range and she tried again. This time, Ruth blocked the jab with her right. Gemma leapt back again and Ruth followed. All she needed to do was to draw her a little further into the middle of the room.

The plan was working, but it required a lot of speed and stamina, and both were in short supply. Ruth aimed a straight punch at her head. She swayed back out of reach and Ruth followed up with a fearsome haymaker. It would be game over if that connected, so Gemma was forced to duck and go down onto one knee.

Before Ruth could press home her advantage, Gemma was back on her feet and another two paces towards the centre of the room. She was still no nearer to getting past her opponent, though. Ruth was starting to breathe heavily and her guard was dropping. That was a relief, but it didn't help Gemma, who would have needed a stepladder to punch her in the face.

Gemma tried another feint to the left and a jump to the right. Ruth, anticipating the move, lurched forward, launching a long sweeping uppercut toward her chin. It caught her with a glancing blow, but even that was enough to send Gemma staggering backwards.

She hadn't been paying attention to what was behind her, being more focused on drawing Ruth away from the door. The pungent aroma that suddenly surrounded her changed all that. She tried to regain her balance, but it was far too late. Arms wheeling like twin windmills, Gemma stepped back over the edge and plunged into oblivion.

Time slowed. This is going to hurt, she thought. Would she fall far enough to kill herself, or just far enough to break her back? Neither, apparently. The impact knocked all the breath out of her lungs and the pain shocked her back into real-time. Whatever she had landed on, it wasn't cold concrete, thank God. Instead, it felt plastic and pliable to her outstretched hands.

Her oxygen-deprived vision cleared. She could make out Ruth peering over the edge of the pit before marching round to the ladder and climbing down. Gemma had about five seconds to get her act together.

She was lying on a pile of hessian sacks piled high on the floor. She swung herself around and slid down to the side furthest from the ladder. Landing heavily on her feet, she stood there swaying like a Saturday night drunk.

Gemma could see the top of Ruth's head as she lumbered after her. She could barely breathe, let alone run away. Finally, in desperation, she pushed at the nearest sack. It slid away with surprisingly little friction, overbalanced and rolled, emptying several kilos of psychoactive herbs all over her assailant.

Disorientated, Ruth leaned against the stack, sneezing and coughing. Gemma waddled, stiff-legged, towards her and began pummelling her torso as hard as her fragile condition would allow.

Ruth backed away, her eyes streaming. Her heel struck a pipe, and she toppled backwards, plumping down on the concrete floor. Gemma aimed a swinging kick at her head. She connected with the woman's temple and drew blood, but Ruth remained sitting resolutely upright. They had hard heads in these parts.

As she was lining up another kick, Gemma heard a thud as something landed on the pile of sacks behind her. She turned around far too slowly. There was a whoosh of air and something solid struck the back of her head. The world span out of focus and she slumped to the floor.

Chapter Forty-Three

Doug stepped down into the artificial cloud forest and towered over Gemma, holding a wooden stake. A few blows to the head should finish off the nosey bitch, but Nancy was watching. That complicated things.

'What do we do now?' Nancy asked.

Doug shrugged and dropped the stake.

'She can help with the harvest. We haven't got much time.'

'And then?'

'You have to be ruthless, Nancy. Like the Amazons, remember.'

There was plenty to burn down here: palettes and crates mainly. And a pleasant draught of sea air flowing down the vents. With a few cans of petrol and a match, it would turn into one giant furnace. If Nancy was squeamish about feeding this one to the pigs, then an inferno would do the trick just as well.

'One final delivery, then we can close the whole operation down. We can go back to our normal lives. No one will be any the wiser.'

'We could let her go. It's only me she's seen.'

'Even if I was prepared to risk you going to prison, what about your family? What about me?'

'I'd never tell. You know that.'

'But the police would find out some other way. Fingerprints, DNA, whatever. We have to end this now. No loose ends.'

What if Nancy was a loose end? After all those hours of schooling, it would be a real shame to consign her to the flames.

Chapter Forty-Four

WHEN SHE CAME ROUND, Gemma was lying with her back against the curved concrete wall. Someone had made a lame attempt to put her in the recovery position with her hands tied together in front of her. She had no idea how long she'd been unconscious, but she didn't feel the least bit recovered.

Eventually, she clambered up onto her knees and look around. Two slack-jawed lads were shuffling their way along the rows of plants, zombie-fashion, cutting them down and filling more of the hessian sacks. An older man, with a passing resemblance to Mr Potato Head, was dragging the load towards the entrance, where he hooked them onto an overhead crane.

There was another figure in the warehouse above, operating the crane. Gemma could only make out a pair of boots with steel showing through the toes and the bottom of some dull orange overalls. Ruth was somewhere nearby. She could hear her barking commands to her minions.

One of the lads noticed Gemma watching and shouted out a warning. Ruth strode down an aisle of makeshift planters and pushed her way through the polythene screen.

'Nice to see you're up and about. We could use another pair of hands.'

'Seems like your boys have everything under control. Family business, is it?' It was a reasonable guess, confirmed by the scowl Ruth directed at her.

'Never you mind. If I untie you, do you promise to behave?'

'No. Why should I?'

'Your choice. You can work, or I can put you back to sleep.' She was carrying a wooden fence post, with blood smeared all over the blunt end. Mine, Gemma shuddered. No wonder her head hurt.

'If you put it like that...'

Gemma held out her hands, and Ruth loosed her bonds. She set her forced labourer to help Mr Potato Head, hauling bags from the growing area to the entrance hatch. It must have been thirty degrees with a hundred per cent humidity. Her head hurt like hell and the rest of her just felt like shit. If they were expecting her to keep this up for long, they had another think coming.

Ruth still had a beady eye on her, so Gemma made a token effort with the first bag. On her second trip to the entrance, she noticed some sacks had been hauled up to the floor above. The remains of the pile screened her from Ruth's gaze. She scouted around the scene of their scrap and spotted a flash of metal. Ruth's lost billhook was lying amongst the scattered cannabis chaff that covered the floor.

She picked it up and stuffed the handle down the back of her trousers. The blade was pressing against the small of her back, hampering her movements. Fortunately, moving like a robot was precisely what her captors wanted from her. It was hot, hard work. Whenever she stumbled, Ruth was there. Apart from the whip, she was a stereotypical slave driver in all other regards.

'Get back to work, you lazy fat sow.'

'Or what? You'll do to me whatever you did to Ross MacLeod?'

That hit a nerve.

'What do you know about Ross?'

'Only that you murdered him. How about telling me what you've done with his body?'

'I've murdered no one. Yet. Get on with your work. You're on borrowed time.'

Was Ruth telling the truth? Maybe Ross was still alive. After another hour of dragging heavy bags in tropical conditions, a quick blow to the head was sounding attractive. Ruth was still on her case. Surely, she must have noticed what state Gemma was in.

The next part of her plan wouldn't require much in the way of acting skills. She was on the verge of collapse, anyway. She feigned a stagger and got down on her hands and knees, crouching so the plant beds shielded her from sight. Carefully, she rolled over onto her back, trying not to stab herself in the kidneys. For a few uncomfortable minutes, she lay there spreadeagled until the slave driver arrived with two of her minions.

Ruth booted her in the side but with minimal force. Gemma played dead and prayed she wouldn't take a run-up next time.

'Oh, for Christ's sake! Drag her out of the damn way, will you? You'd best tie her up in case she comes round.'

The lads grabbed Gemma by her arms and hauled her unceremoniously towards the wall. The billhook was working its way down her trousers. If the dragging didn't end soon, she would end up with an extra crack in her arse.

They came to a stop and let go of her arms, smacking her head on the concrete. Her ears were ringing, and she was ready to puke. Ruth's nephews, or whoever they might be, were instantly promoted to the top of her shit list. The list was growing considerably.

They tied her arms painfully tight behind her back. For a panicked moment, Gemma was convinced they would find the billhook. Fortunately, these two seemed as unobservant as they were uncaring. When she was sure they had returned to their cutting duties, she opened one eye and looked around.

A few metres from where she was lying, a mouse casually sauntered out from under the nearest planter. Instead of scurrying away, it staggered towards her, then sat up and washed its whiskers. There was something wrong with it. Its eyes were wide and it seemed to have difficulty coordinating its paw movements. A stoned mouse? Whatever next.

'How're you doing, wee, steamin, cowrin, timorous beastie? More to the point, how did you get here? You didnae gnaw through concrete. Care to take me to your mouse hole?'

The mouse shambled past Gemma and trotted off, one shoulder leaning against the wall, like a drunk trying to make their way home. Gemma shuffled after it until a painful stab in the coccyx reminded her that she still had a sharp implement secreted in her nether regions.

With some difficulty, she pulled out the billhook and raised herself to a kneeling position. She wedged the handle between her feet. If she bent backwards, she could just about press the rope against the blade. However, sawing by swaying backwards and forwards was not easy. She dropped the billhook a few times and had to start the whole business over again.

The mouse was making unsteady progress around the curved wall, and then disappeared suddenly. She redoubled her efforts and eventually, the rope gave way. Not without having taken quite a chunk out of her wrist, though.

Gemma set off after the mouse. She was leaving quite a bloody trail herself. The Kerr family would have no difficulty following her. She crawled past three rows of decapitated plants and came to a halt by a plastic ventilation grill in the wall. A small section had already been gnawed away.

The grill was held in place by half a dozen screws. Gemma tried to loosen them with the end of the billhook, but all she did was to snap the tip off the blade and give herself another nasty cut.

She decided to take the agricultural approach instead and cut the grill open. The blade sliced through the plastic quickly enough, but it was a noisy business. Fortunately, the Kerr family firm were making plenty of noise. She kept glancing around. No one came to check on her whereabouts or her wellbeing.

Once she had cut through three sides of the grill, she could force her way into the ventilation duct. She found herself inside a concrete pipe, just wide enough to crawl through if she hunched her shoulders. Going forward was no problem, but it would be a nightmare if she had to retreat.

The bottom of the pipe was wet and scattered with moss and mouse droppings. A strong flow of air was blowing from behind. She worried it might blow her out the far end, like a pellet in a peashooter. More concerning was the prospect of running into the fans that were sucking fumes out of the underground farm.

All the while she was crawling, she could see light at the end of her tunnel. Not a precise circle, but rather a hazy green glow. As she got closer, she could make out the clumps of long grass and fronds of bracken covering the entrance. No sign of any fans, or even another screen, covering the exit. They must be using the ever-reliable island winds to draw the stale air out. Things were looking up.

Gemma pushed her head through the vegetation and peered out. The reason that this exit was unsecured soon became apparent. She was inside a small cave about halfway up the Cliffs of Loon. The cave floor was damp and slippery, sloping down towards the entrance and the turbulent sea below.

The route up looked possible for an experienced climber, which Gemma was not. There was a slight overhang. She doubted she was strong enough (or light enough) to haul herself over the edge. Downwards looked more promising. The cave was part of a fissure leading most of the way down and a few guano-covered ledges. If only she had some abseiling gear and something to attach a rope to, it would be a doddle.

She heard shouts from behind and the sound of someone forcing their way through the grill. Not Ruth, presumably. One of her family henchmen. With any luck, Gemma might get in a few good kicks to his head before he shoved her over the cliff.

Gemma had reached the end of the line. It was decision time. Up or down. Jump or be pushed. She peered out in the early morning gloom and spied something that made the decision a little easier. She eased herself out of the pipe, slithered to the edge of the cave, and gave a final two-fingered gesture of defiance to her pursuers.

Chapter
Forty-Five

NANCY WAS FRANTIC. DESPERATE to get Gemma back before news of her escape drifted upstairs to Doug. Why had she ever suggested letting their prisoner help with the harvest? Doug would think she had allowed her to escape. She grabbed one of her useless nephews and prised open the vandalised ventilation cover.

'Get yourself down there, Kenny. Don't let the bitch get away, d'ya hear me?'

Nancy clambered up the steps to the warehouse. Doug looked surprised to see her. She gave her partner a perfunctory wave as she stomped towards her quad bike.

'We're nearly done. I need a few more sacks from the farm. I'll be back soon enough.'

Doug shrugged and carried on craning the sacks onto the back of a lorry parked off to one side of the pit. Its driver, Liam, supposedly the brightest of her sister's lads, was meant to be helping. He was nowhere to be seen.

Nancy climbed onto the bike and started the engine. Instead of heading back to the farm, she took the narrow sheep track that led up to the cliff-top path. From there, she could look out towards the hidden vents, but the overhanging cliff made it hard to see what was happening inside the cave.

She heard a woman's voice shouting abuse, then a rockfall and a splash in the sea below. There was no one around apart from a small fishing boat further down the coast. It was motoring away from the scene and showed no signs of slowing down.

Kenny's head appeared briefly below her. He was trying to turn around and climb back up the ventilation tunnel. He slipped and then regained his balance. Nancy held her breath. He was a worthless piece of shit, but he was still family. Her sister would never forgive her if her youngest drowned.

She wondered if Kenny had pushed Gemma over the edge. From what she heard about his pathetic punchbag girlfriend, it wouldn't surprise her one bit.

Doug would be furious, but at least she had some good news now. Ruth leaned over the cliff edge and spat. Would she have had the guts to kill again? She was glad she hadn't had to find out. At least that nosey sow would not be troubling them anymore.

Chapter
Forty-Six

AN ANNOYING SOUND WOKE Danny out of a deep sleep. He slapped his alarm clock on the bedside table, and the display lit up. It was five a.m. He hit it several more times before he realised his phone was ringing.

'Danny Verity. Whadaya want?'

'Ellen McAllister here. I have Gemma Gauld staying with me.'

'Yeah. Sorry about that. She alright?'

'I'm not so sure. She wasn't back when I went to bed last night. I don't sleep too well these days. I'm always up at first light, so I checked on the cottage just now. No sign of her. She gave me this number to call if there were any problems.'

Danny shot up. 'Right. OK. Look, she might be in trouble. She said she was heading up to that warehouse the police raided.'

'Whatever for?'

'Curiosity, I suppose. I think you ought to call the police. I'll come over and then head up there myself.'

By the time he'd dressed and marched over to Bron, there was a small crowd outside Ellen's cottage. He assumed that the thin serious-looking woman was the birder with the mountain bike. He didn't know the two men. Ellen made the introductions.

'This is Heather, she's been showing Gemma around the island. William is from the wildlife club as well. Jack here is my neighbour's son. He's going to take you up to The Loon in his fishing boat.'

'Right. Thanks. I really appreciate that. This is not a birdwatching trip, though. Might be dangerous.'

Heather patted him on the arm.

'Don't worry, Danny, I know the Dows and the Kerrs pretty well. They're not as bad as they're painted, truly. Gemma can be a bit brusque with people. If she's got into some misunderstanding, I'm sure I can straighten things out.'

'Ok. I suppose that can't hurt. But what about your mate here?'

'William knows this coastline better than anyone. He did his thesis on the nesting colonies of the Skrowa Head cliffs. Plus, he's a bit sweet on Gemma. I couldn't leave him behind.'

William went bright red, but he had a determined look on his face.

'If she's been wandering around in the dark, you'll need all the help you can get. It's easy to get lost and those cliffs are treacherous.'

Danny gave up. It felt like he was about to lead a school outing. Or maybe he was just getting old.

'Did you call the police?' he asked Ellen.

'Aye, of course. They passed me onto the coastguard, and they said to wait a few more hours in case she showed up. That's when I decided to phone around the village.'

The tide was high, making it an easy row out to the main channel. The amateur search-and-rescue team climbed aboard Jack's creel boat and chugged through the tiny harbour, out to the open sea. Before they reached the end of the bay, Heather was already making plans.

'We'll have to split up to have any chance of finding Gemma. William knows a way up the cliffs. I ought to go with him in case we meet any of the locals. You can check further along the coast and then motor on down to the jetty in Calf Sound.'

Danny did like the idea one bit, but she was right. It was no good them all staying in the boat and a pincer movement sounded like the best plan. When they reached Blackfowl Geo, the shingle beach was entirely covered by the tide. Jack was able to ease the boat in until the port side was within stepping distance of a long shelf of rock. Heather and William hopped off and splashed their way through the shallow rockpools to the foot of the cliffs.

'Are you sure you'll be ok? I could come with you.'

'No, no, we'll be fine,' Heather said. 'I've my phone and a whistle. You concentrate on the coast and we'll head inland.'

'Call if you see anything. No heroics, you hear me?'

Jack backed the boat out and began tracking the vessel along the cliffs, as close as he dared. Danny perched on the prow to keep a lookout. Spray broke on a submerged rock a few metres in front, and he shouted in alarm. He needn't have worried. The little boat was surprisingly manoeuvrable. Jack backed them out of danger with a burst of reverse thrust and they moved onto the next inlet.

The sun was yet to rise, but it was light enough to make out the details of the narrow beaches and the rock face beyond. There was no sign of anyone on the cliff-top path and nothing on the rocks themselves, except the nesting seabirds.

At Skrowa Head, the beach disappeared. The water was deep enough for them to get right up to the base of the cliffs. Waves crashed on rocks close by. The creel boat held station in the clapotis, rising and falling with each passing crest.

From here, they had a good view all along the coast in both directions. Jack dropped anchor for a while. He seemed unconcerned by their proximity to the cliffs. However, the choppy waves reflecting off the rocks made their situation uncomfortable for a non-sailor like Danny.

'They call this inlet Twixt the Curples,' Jack said. 'Supposed to look like the devil's arse, but I've never seen it.'

The two rounded cliffs that made up the headland did look vaguely like giant's buttocks. Being moored between them did nothing to calm Danny's churning stomach. He tried scanning the cliffs with his binoculars. He could clearly see Blackfowl Bay, but the path up the fissure to his left was obscured from view. To the right was the broken-down old jetty that Ellen had described and the Calf of Mallach, an uninhabited rocky islet.

There was a small boat tied to what remained of the jetty. Unfortunately, there were no signs of its owner and it, too, looked somewhat dilapidated. Fixing his gaze on a distant point as the boat bobbed up and down made Danny feel sick. He lowered his binoculars and squinted up at the cliffs.

He was about to suggest that they moved somewhere more sheltered when he heard the clatter of rocks and saw a splash off in the distance. He shouted to Jack, who hauled up the anchor and motored at full power towards the source of the rockfall.

Beyond the jetty was a fissure in the rocks. Danny thought he saw movement. He squinted through the binoculars and, sure enough, there was a figure squatting in a small hollow in the cliffs where the fissure had partially collapsed. It was Gemma. He was sure of it.

Danny doubted she could see them, but he waved anyway. She waved back and called to them in her best foghorn voice.

'Hey! Down there. You in the boat. How deep is it?'

Jack threw the anchor overboard and watched the line pay out almost to its full extent.

'Four metres. Maybe five.'

She couldn't be thinking of jumping, could she? That was sheer madness. Her perch had to be two or three times the height of a swimming pool diving platform. He tried to call out. Too late.

'Good enough for me. Ready or not. Here I go. Geronimo!'

She launched herself from the cave, arms outstretched, like an overfed puffin taking flight. That illusion quickly dissolved as she plummeted towards them. She managed to hold a skydiver's stance briefly, then snapped her arms forward at the last instant and struck the sea with an almighty splash. A great jet of water shot up in the air and then splattered back onto the waves. Of the diver herself, there was no sign.

Chapter Forty-Seven

GEMMA'S ENTRY INTO THE water was more Apollo command module than Olympic diver. She was probably concussed, or she might have broken her neck on impact. Jack motored towards the site of her splashdown and cut the engine. Danny took off his boots. He didn't fancy his chances of finding her in these murky depths, but he couldn't just wait for her lifeless body to surface.

He leapt over the starboard bow, just in time to see Gemma's head surface away to port. He swam over. She was gasping and flapping like a fish on a hook. He put one hand under her chin and made an amateurish attempt at a rescue. Fortunately, they were only a few metres from the boat and Danny's life jacket was buoyant enough to support them both. Jack leant over and, with Danny pushing from below, hauled his catch onboard.

When Danny was out of the water, Jack headed, full steam, back towards Blackfowl Geo. Gemma lay sprawled across the creel traps, still struggling for breath. It didn't stop her from trying to talk between gasps.

'Did you see?'

'Are you OK? Any pain in the chest?' Danny tried to feel her ribs, but she slapped his hand away.

'Tom Daley? Eat your heart out!'

'Try to breathe deeply. You don't want to hyperventilate.'

'Nine-point-five at least.'

'Can you move your feet?' She tried to kick him on the shin and got her boot tangled in the netting.

'Might have over-rotated. Better next time.'

'Next time? Jesus Christ! You've really got a death wish, woman.'

He persuaded her to lie back and catch her breath. The next priority was to contact the land search party and get them back in the boat. If they came across whoever Gemma had been escaping from, they might be in serious trouble.

That was easier said than done. He called Heather's phone and then William's. Neither answered. They stood off from the old jetty, and Danny blew six times on his whistle. He hoped to see them hurrying down the path. There was no sign of anyone on the coastline or up on the cliffs.

Jack wanted to land and go looking for them. Danny told him to stay out to sea. If they had been seized, they would be safer if their captors thought they were acting alone. After half an hour of nervous waiting, a shabby open-topped boat came speeding round Skrowa Head and steered towards their position.

'Here comes trouble,' Jack said. 'That's the same one we saw tied up at the jetty, right?'

Danny trained his binoculars on the boat. It was approaching them with full force. It looked like there was only one person on board, but he couldn't see their face for all the spray kicked up as the boat crashed through the waves. Not until the boat swung round to come alongside did he recognise Heather. As it came to a stop a few metres from their vessel, William crawled up from the bottom of the hull, leaned over the side, and threw up.

'That was a lot of fun,' Heather smiled. 'We're playing pirates. We stole this ship.'

'Borrowed,' William corrected. He grabbed the side of the creel boat and Danny dragged him aboard.

'So, you're going to take it back then?' Danny suggested mockingly.

'No, I think we'll just leave it here. Or scupper it. They seemed a bit upset.'

Heather also clambered over the side, brushing aside Danny's proffered hand. She had an orange plastic kill cord tied around her leg with a key dangling from it. After a moment's consideration, she held it over the side and dropped it into the sea.

'Dreadful people,' she said. 'No manners whatsoever. And the sw earing...'

Once everyone was safely seated, Jack set off back to Bron at a steady pace. Danny was relieved that he didn't mimic Heather's driving style. He was keen to discover how they came by the "borrowed" vessel.

'We walked all the way over to the old jetty,' William said. 'Then a couple of men got out of this boat. They had a nasty, barky dog with them and asked us what we were doing. I said we were walking, and they told us to eff off back where we came from. Funny accents they had, and they looked rather grubby.'

'I didn't recognise them,' Heather said. 'Off-islanders.'

'Anyway, I pointed out that the path we were walking had been used as a right of way since the sixteenth century and this coastline is a site of special scientific interest.'

'That's when the big lad tried to punch him in the face.'

'So I hit him with my rucksack. I brought Sterry's Complete Guide to British Birds with me. Quite a hefty volume. Then the other lout set his dog on us.'

'I thought it was heading straight for us, but it was more interested in chasing an oyster catcher instead, thank goodness.'

'While they were trying to get the dog back, Heather jumped in the boat and started it up. So, I told them they could flipping well crawl back up the flipping bum-hole they came from. But, of course, they couldn't really go anywhere, not without a boat. It doesn't look much, but it's quite fast. Though I'm not sure it's entirely safe to drive in rough seas at those speeds.'

'We didn't find Gemma, I'm sorry to say. I hope those ruffians haven't got hold of her.'

'Aye, I'm fine, thanks for asking,' Gemma said, untangling herself from the fishing net. Heather climbed round from the wheelhouse and hugged her. William followed and hugged them both. They appeared to be having some difficulty getting him to stop until Danny stepped in.

'Best give Gemma some space. She's a bit sore. Been practising her cliff-diving. Very impressive it was, too.'

Heather squared up to Danny, arms crossed and frowning.

'First, the police raid the Kerr's farm. Next thing, Gemma's jumping off a cliff. There's a lot you aren't telling us here. I think we deserve an explanation.'

Danny glanced over at Gemma. They had led their new friends into considerable danger. It was probably time to tell them the truth. The expurgated version, at least.

Chapter Forty-Eight

IT WAS LATE AFTERNOON when Danny eventually made it back to the terminal. Iain Grant was waiting for him. It had felt good to unburden himself to his island allies. Danny had the same urge to confess to Iain. It might have softened the bollocking he was about to get.

'You can't just go wandering off round the island whenever it takes your fancy. And what's this crap about a medical emergency? No one's reported any incidents to me.'

'I got a call from the village.'

'Oh, for Christ's sake! Let me guess. Ellen McAllister?'

'How did you know?'

'Most of the islanders would have called 999. She calls the terminal. She and Gordon Breck go way back. I used to wonder if they were having an affair, but I don't think either of them could stop talking long enough. What was it this time? She tripped over the cat again?'

'One of her friends had a fall.'

'Serious?'

'Not really. I was more worried about hypothermia. She slipped and fell into the sea. I had to wait to make sure she was ok.'

Danny didn't enjoy lying to Iain, but this was as close to the truth as he was prepared to go. Could he trust Iain? Even if the man was on the side of the angels, at least one person in the terminal wasn't. Word would get around, which might put both him and Gemma in danger.

'Look, I understand you only want to help. There used to be a doctor on the island. Now they have to hop on the ferry to see a GP on one of the bigger islands. If it's an emergency, they send a paramedic over from Kirkwall. That's budget cuts and a declining population for you, sorry to say. Maybe we should set up a proper first responder arrangement. Gordon's been doing that role unofficially for years, but I hate to think what would happen if the insurers ever got involved.'

Danny promised to look into it. And to let Iain know if he got any more unsanctioned cries for help. When he got back to sickbay, he found a note from Lorna on his desk. Sergeant Campbell wanted to speak to him. He picked up the phone. It was one thing lying to your boss, quite another lying to the police.

'Thank you for calling back, Mr Verity.' The sergeant's voice was muffled. The wind was blowing across the microphone, and Danny could hear a marine engine chugging away in the background. 'Your associate, Ms Gauld, called. We are on our way to Mallach right now. She has agreed to meet us at the pier. I'd appreciate it if you would join us.'

It was unclear whether the sergeant was going to arrest them or ask questions first. Either way, Danny would be in deep trouble with his boss again. He checked the ferry timetable hanging outside the admin office. Iain's usual ferry home to Westray was due to leave about ten minutes before the Kirkwall ferry arrived. The timings were tight and weather dependent; with luck, Danny might just get away with it.

Danny waited until Iain left the terminal. He followed as far as a bend in the road, where the remains of an abandoned croft gave him a secluded view of the pier. The Westray ferry arrived a quarter of an hour late. The south-westerly breeze had picked up, slowing the little open-topped boat's progress across Flint Sound. He watched with relief as Iain walked down the steps and hopped onboard. There were no other boats in sight as he disappeared from view.

Fortunately for Danny, the wind had delayed the longer ferry journey from Kirkwall even more. He walked down the terminal road to the pier, arriving just in time to see Gemma strolling down the Bron road in the other direction.

'Aye, Ellen said it'd be running late. Local knowledge, Danny. I've got it. You don't.'

He didn't tell her how long he'd been sweating over ferry timetables this afternoon. Eventually, the Kirkwall ferry hove into view. The sea was getting quite lively now. The ferry pitched and rolled its way down the sound. It stood off the slipway until the waves sideswiped it onto the pier. The crew tied the boat off and set about getting the passengers ashore.

The police Land Rover was the only vehicle onboard. Its occupants were forced to stand to one side as it was hoisted off the boat. They looked rather green about the gills and watched with dismay as the crane operator dropped it from an unnecessary height onto the pier. Gemma thought it was all very amusing. Danny figured Sergeant Campbell would probably take his frustrations out on them.

'They only just got that Land Rover back to Kirkwall and now you've made them drag it all the way here again. Then that Neanderthal operator tries to break the suspension. They will not be happy.'

'Aye, but you've got to laugh, eh? They'd be on our case anyway, just because we know something they don't. Nobody likes a smart-arse.'

She was undoubtedly right about that. Sergeant Campbell had a face like thunder. His colleague, PC Flett, looked ready to arrest everyone that got in his way.

'These are serious charges, Ms Gauld. We'd like you to show us this mysterious cannabis farm and exactly where you were allegedly detained against your will. As for you, Mr Verity, we understand you were a witness to Ms Gauld's supposed escape from captivity.'

'Yes. I saw her jump off the cliff. You don't really suppose she did that just for fun?' Danny wasn't having it. 'Anyway, shouldn't we be having this discussion back at the station?'

'If we find any evidence to back up your allegations, we will be pleased to take your statements wherever you like. If not, you may well find yourselves charged with wasting police time. We can do that right here.'

Gemma and Danny climbed in the back of the Land Rover. It was a bumpy ride up to the Kerr's farm, even in a four-by-four. However, the track beyond was suspiciously well maintained, considering it only went to one unused building. The route followed the clifftop path for a while and then swung inland.

'Jesus, what's that reek?' wondered PC Flett.

'Smells like someone's lit the world's largest joint,' Gemma suggested.

'And you would know that how?'

'Passive smoking, officer. My neighbours are students.'

When they reached the warehouse, the source of the smell immediately became apparent. The warehouse was still intact, but dense black smoke billowed out from the four concealed ventilation intakes. Gemma pointed out more puffs of smoke rising from her diving platform out on the cliffs.

'Shit!' Campbell exclaimed. 'Best call in the fire brigade, Angus. Probably a waste of time, though. This place is going to be ash before they get here.'

He approached the warehouse with care and eased open the jammed fire door. There was surprising little smoke inside. Someone had thoughtfully replaced the fake inspection pit before torching the place, presumably to concentrate the fire down below.

Danny watched as Campbell stepped inside. It was a reckless move. The concrete floor could explode or collapse. He was about to warn him to get out of there, but Campbell was already running for the door in slow motion, the soles of his boots made tacky by the extreme heat below.

'Everyone get back! It's hot as hell inside. We'll have to wait until it cools down. Or blows up. Then it's up to forensics, though God knows what they'll make of it.'

'Well, there goes your evidence,' Danny said. 'Are you going to charge us with obstruction now?'

The policemen ignored him. Campbell was straight back on the phone to HQ while Flett mooched around, cordoning off the place with his blue and white tape.

There was nothing to do for Danny and Gemma. They would answer questions and give statements later. No doubt Sergeant Campbell was already thinking up reasons this was all their fault. There was no sign of him offering a lift anyway, so they set off back down the track to Bron. If this story didn't get him a drink in Wheelie's Bar, thought Danny, then nothing would.

Chapter Forty-Nine

WHEN DANNY POKED HIS head around the admin office door to say good morning, everyone was clustered around Lorna. Her eyes were bleary from crying.

'Her aunt's been arrested,' Fiona MacAlpine explained. 'Though I'm amazed her whole family wasn't locked up years ago, poor lass. Thieves and thugs, the lot of them.'

'What's she been arrested for?'

'Something to do with that police raid up on The Loon. Stolen goods, or some such. Did you not hear our peedie old fire engine racing up there? Someone set the building ablaze. Still smouldering. They had to send over to Mainland for a bigger truck. Arson, of course. Covering their tracks, the devious scoundrels.'

That prompted another flood of tears from Lorna.

'There, there, hen,' Fiona said. 'Arson and handling stolen goods? That's probably only a two-year stretch, so long as she pleads guilty. Could be far worse.'

Danny decided to leave before Lorna was completely overwhelmed by her boss' sympathy. He needed a coffee, but first, he headed to sickbay to find the medic's supply of paracetamol. Stew, the barman, had been sufficiently enthralled by Gemma's storytelling last night to let him sample both the local Orkney whiskies and the Highlands malts. They weren't miserly English measures, either.

Hopefully, pills and strong coffee would clear his head. He needed to know what Ruth had been charged with and what she had told the police. They were unlikely to tell him. He tried to call Gemma. There was no reply, but a few seconds later he received a text.

At polis stn - not arrested yet

Danny wondered if he should jump on a ferry to Kirkwall to stop her from saying something that would earn her a caution at least. He decided he had better stay and pursue his enquiries in the terminal. He was in enough trouble with his boss already.

As if he'd spoken of the devil, a rap on the door announced the arrival of Iain Grant. He was escorting the bedraggled Lorna. She stared ahead vacantly. Her eyes were swollen but dry, as if all tears had been wrung out of her.

'I told her to go home. Her mother's coming to collect her. Do you mind if Lorna stays here until she arrives? Fiona means well, but I don't think she's the best at dealing with a mental health crisis.'

That was a significant understatement. Danny was more than happy to look after Lorna. He just needed to think of an approach to questioning her that wouldn't cause another emotional meltdown. He needn't have worried. She seemed relieved to talk to an outsider. Someone who might not be prejudiced against her entire family.

'My ma warned Auntie Ruth not to get involved with those off-is-landers. They're up to no good, she said. I know money's been tight since Uncle Greig left, but she told us things were getting better. She'd started growing herbs for them quack medicines and the like. There was good money in it, so I don't know why she would help those whalps with their stolen goods. I mean, it's not even her barn. I blame that Doug for putting her up to it.'

'Doug?'

'Aye. I've not met him, but I've heard nothing good. Shy, she says, but my ma reckons he's got something to hide. He's around her place a lot, she says, but he's not local. I wondered if he worked at the terminal, but the only Doug we've got here is Dougie Warnock. He's alright. Doesn't keek down my top like most of the lads.'

Danny hoped she wasn't including him. He made a special effort to make eye contact in case his gaze had been slipping.

'My ma doesn't have a good word to say about this Doug. She said some awful things when she thought I wasn't listening.'

'What exactly did she say?'

'Nothing I'd care to repeat. She thinks he's some kind of perv. Like Uncle Greig maybe. When we were bairns, we weren't allowed to be in the house on our own with him. Not even the lads.'

The more he heard about Lorna's family, the worse they sounded.

'To be fair, it was what she said about Auntie Ruth that upset me. I don't know how she could say that sort of stuff about her own sister. I would never say anything like that about our Isla, even if she is a pure rocket most of the time.'

'What sort of stuff?'

'That she wasn't normal. That she would go to hell because of the sinful sex things she got up to. I don't believe it. Not Auntie Ruth.'

Danny did, but he preferred not to speculate about Ruth Kerr's sex life. It didn't look like Lorna was about to elaborate. He was saved from any further conjecture by Ruth's sister-in-law, Maggie Kerr, at the security gate.

He escorted Lorna out, partly because it seemed the gentlemanly thing to do, but mostly because he was curious to meet her mother. Maggie was an older, much rounder version of Lorna, with a couple of additional chins. If Lorna took after her, Kevan had dodged a bullet, for sure.

A young lad was waiting in the car. A few years older than Lorna. Her brother? He could easily be one of Ruth's thugs. Danny decided he would struggle to pick him out at an identity parade. Judging by the family photo

Lorna kept on her desk, there didn't seem to be much genetic variation in the Kerr clan.

Maggie ushered Lorna into the car. She thanked Danny for looking after her daughter, but her expression suggested she didn't trust his motives. Not surprising given the family history. He gave Maggie his number and told her to call if she needed anything. He felt sorry for Lorna. She obviously loved her aunt and she might not be seeing her for a long time. It was probably a long way from Mallach to the nearest prison.

As he wandered back to the office block, he noticed the main entrance doors were wide open. Alain was standing in the lobby, checking everyone's passes.

'What's going on?'

'Power cut, Mr Verity. The automatic doors always open like this when we're on emergency power. Safety first. Can I see your pass?'

'Sorry. I left it in sickbay. Anyway, you know my name. You just said it.'

'I suppose so. But we have to follow procedure, don't we?'

Power cuts made Danny nervous. They reminded him of being stuck on the Cuillin Alpha platform as the lights went out one by one. But it was still daylight. He was being stupid. He had no reason to suppose there was a saboteur in the terminal meddling with the power supply. Still, he would feel a lot happier if he had his first aid bag and a heavy torch to hand.

'I tell you what. How about you let me through to sickbay and I'll come back here with my pass?'

'And what if you don't?'

'Then you'll know I wasn't who you thought I was, and you can escort me off the premises.'

Alain frowned, then shook his head and waved him through. Danny considered borrowing Lorna's pass again just to see what he'd say. Alain didn't look like he had much of a sense of humour. He probably would throw him out, and Danny didn't want to miss his dinner. Tonight's special was venison curry and chips. It was too much of a risk. For once, it seemed better to follow procedure.

Chapter Fifty

Doug turned on his phone. It pinged repeatedly. A series of recent texts from Nancy:

> The police are here
> They have a warrant. I gotta let them in
> I swear I'll keep our secret

She'd better. They were bound to check her phone. Once they read those stupid texts, they'd soon figure out that someone else was involved. It was a good thing this phone was untraceable. It would be even harder to find if it fell in a crude oil tank.

The earlier texts were more interesting. Nancy had forwarded one from gormless Lorna. She'd gone home early and run out of fuel. Doug knew that wasn't true. Lorna had left the terminal at the usual time.

Someone must have taken her phone and sent a fake message. Now, why would anyone do that? Presumably, to send Nancy scurrying off to Tarf Hill to rescue her stranded niece. To keep her away from the warehouse while that fat, Scaberdonian sow snooped around inside. Nice plan. Shame it hadn't worked.

The real question was why Nancy hadn't mentioned this before. Fear? She had been stupid, and she was terrified of what Doug might do. Of course, that's the way he liked it, but that urge to keep Nancy on a tight leash had backfired this time.

No prizes for guessing who sent the text to Nancy. Doug had enjoyed their new medic's bumbling attempts to work out what was going on at the terminal. Now he was becoming rather less amusing.

Playing tricks like that on poor Nancy? Not funny. It was time to teach him a lesson. Who would the medic call for medical attention? It would be interesting to find out. Physician, heal thyself.

Chapter
Fifty-One

IT WAS A LONG time since Gemma had last been interviewed by the police, and she wasn't looking forward to repeating the experience. But, of course, she hadn't committed any crimes this time. Nothing serious anyway.

She was fifteen when she had her first encounter with them and she was innocent of all charges. They gave her an unnecessarily harsh grilling, anyway. It was a good thing they never found out about all the things she actually had done. Petty stuff, mostly. She wasn't happy about it, but she was quietly proud of never having been arrested. It gave her a bit of street cred.

It was a nice change to be a witness rather than a suspect. When you're a witness, they give you tea and biscuits. Weak tea and cheap biscuits, but still an improvement.

'Thank you for coming to speak to us, Ms Gauld.' They were polite to witnesses too. Though she wasn't sure how civil they would have been if she'd refused to come.

'No problem, officers. Always happy to assist the polis with their enquiries.'

Sergeant Campbell was accompanied by a plainclothes officer from Inverness, who introduced himself as Detective Inspector Gray. Despite outranking Campbell, DI Gray seemed happy for the local man to lead the questioning.

'Can you talk us through the events of yesterday? Right through to this morning when we were called in.'

Gemma ran through her story again. This time, they were recording her. After nearly an hour, Sergeant Campbell was getting restless. She wondered if she might have overdone her description of the fight. It was the best bit, though, and deserved some embellishment.

'You still haven't explained why you entered the warehouse. You knew we had searched the building already. There were police no entry signs all over it. Did that not make you think twice?'

'Aye, but you found nothing apart from the stolen pumps. We had information that there was more to find. Nobody seemed interested, so we decided to check it out for ourselves.'

'Who's "we"?'

'Well, you've met my colleague, Daniel Verity, right?'

'He was looking for two missing men, I understood. Not a drug ring.'

'Aye, well, you start looking for one thing and you find another. That's how it goes with this investigating business. You boys should try it sometime.'

Campbell glanced at DI Gray as if expecting him to react. Instead, he just snorted, wrote something on his notepad and underlined it. Whatever it said made Campbell even less pleased than before.

'So, explain your deductions. I'm all ears. And I'm not interested in stories about underground boxing matches or your cliff diving exploits. Just the facts, please.'

Gemma told them about the power line running from the terminal to the warehouse.

'Our associate, Marissa Ling, is a specialist energy revenue investigator. She spotted a potential energy theft from the terminal. We put two and two together and decided there must be more going on at the warehouse than meets the eye. So, I went up there to investigate. That's when I ran into the Kerr family and got into a punch-up with big Ruthie. You sure you don't want me to run through that again?'

It seemed they didn't.

'And what does any of this have to do with your missing lads?'

'Maybe nothing,' Gemma admitted. 'But Ross MacLeod was helping Marissa access various parts of the terminal. Maybe someone found out. And Aidan Fitzgerald made a couple of pickups from the warehouse; did you know that? I wonder what was in those boxes he was transporting. Nothing legal, I'll bet.'

'Is there any more information you've been concealing?'

'Steady on, pal. We've not been concealing. It's you who's not been listening.'

DI Gray cleared his throat.

'I'm sure Sergeant Campbell is not accusing you of deliberately withholding evidence. Nevertheless, if you have any information pertaining to this case, we'd appreciate you sharing it with us now.'

Gemma agreed to send them the spreadsheets and graphs. Of course, Marissa wouldn't be happy about it, but that was Danny's problem, not hers. She also promised to get Danny to send over his findings on Ross and Aidan. After that, it was his decision how much he shared with the boys in blue.

'There were a few other members of the Kerr clan in the warehouse along with Big Ruthie. One of the jakey bastards hit me over the head with a stake.'

'Yes, you mentioned that several times,' DI Gray said. 'I don't suppose you saw your attacker afterwards.'

'I did, but I only caught the odd glimpse. The bastard was upstairs loading the wagon. Slim, a bit taller than Ruthie, that's about it.'

'Man or woman?'

'I couldn't even be sure of that. Skinny lad or a flat-chested lass. Those overalls weren't exactly figure-hugging. Masked and hooded, too. Whichever it was, they took a good swing, just look at this lump on my head...'

She leaned over to show Gray. He didn't seem impressed.

'What about her other accomplices?'

'A couple of the Kerr boys at least, probably more. I'd say one was in his early twenties and the other one a teenager.'

'And would you be able to identify them?'

'Well, I've met a few Kerrs now and I'm telling you these boys were schucked out the same mould, no question. She's got dozens of nephews and cousins and I'll bet they all look exactly the fecking same. Why don't you just round up the fecking lot of them? They must all have done something.'

'That's very tempting, but there are a few human rights issues involved in arresting an entire family. Especially when it's based only on your testimony and some weak circumstantial evidence.'

'What about the warehouse? There must be some evidence left in there. I mean, you could smell the weed burning a mile off. Once the fire's out, surely your forensics crew will pick something out of the ashes.'

'Scene of Crime officers are on their way to site now. I don't think they will find much evidence, Ms Gauld. The inside of that concrete cellar was like a blast furnace. I'm not sure there's even much ash left.'

'The prosecutor fiscal will take your account into consideration,' said Sergeant Campbell. 'I've no doubt you're an acknowledged expert on sniffing out marijuana. However, as good as your nose might be, I doubt very much it would hold up in court.'

Figuring this was an insult, Gemma got up to leave. She was rather sensitive about her nose. One bridesmaid at her cousin's wedding broke it during a scrap. She'd never managed to get it straightened out to her satisfaction.

The polis had run out of bourbon biscuits anyway. Just those nasty pink wafers. Campbell terminated the interview and escorted her to the door. Gemma gave him her smarmiest smile and left with as much composure as she could muster.

Chapter Fifty-Two

ALL ROADS LED TO the terminal. Judging by the map spread out on Danny's desk, Mallach had been effectively cut in two when the terminal was built. The main gate led out onto the old road from Bron to the ferry and from there you could get anywhere on the island. The bulk of the island lay to the south. The Loon, to the north, could only be accessed via the narrow coastal road that passed along the eastern boundary of the terminal.

As far as this investigation went, all roads led to the terminal as well. Ruth Kerr was in custody, but she had to have accomplices. At least one who worked at the terminal. How else had the power been diverted to the warehouse in the first place? And then there was the mystery assailant who knocked Gemma unconscious.

Ruth wasn't saying much by all accounts. By locking up Gemma, she'd given the police a link between her and the stolen goods. Depending on how much of Gemma's testimony was admissible, they could also finger her for assault, kidnapping, and arson. Ross was dead, of that Danny was sure, but Ruth was still adamantly denying any involvement in his death. However, much Danny disliked the woman, he just didn't see her as a cold-blooded murderer. Had she killed him by accident?

His phone rang. It was Sergeant Campbell.

'This is just a courtesy call.' The police being courteous to a private investigator? That was new. It didn't bode well. 'We have finished searching Ruth Kerr's farm. We found something.'

'A body?'

'Not exactly. Remains of one. In the pig field. It's a common mis-conception that pigs eat absolutely anything. That's not true. They can certainly grind their way through flesh and bone, but they are not partial to teeth for some reason.'

'Human teeth? Whose?'

'We don't know yet. It's not easy to extract dental DNA, but it is sometimes possible. We will have to obtain a sample of Ross MacLeod's DNA. Or failing that, a sample from a close relative. Hence the call.'

'You want me to call the MacLeods and let them know you're coming?'

'You know them. It might soften the blow. But, of course, if you'd rather not, I quite understand.'

Danny did not want to make that call, but Campbell was right. It would be better coming from him. He wandered out of the building to find a private place and dialled the MacLeod's home number with a heavy heart.

'Mrs MacLeod. I have some news. Not good, I'm afraid.'

'Have they found a body?'

'Not exactly. The police have found some evidence. They'd like to get a sample of Ross' DNA to confirm if it relates to his whereabouts. A hairbrush maybe, or something like that?'

'He liked his hair cut short. I don't think he even owned a hairbrush.'

'Or they could take samples from you and Mr MacLeod.'

'Nae the both of us. Just me. Can you tell them that? They could make up some excuse about how it's better coming from the mother.'

This call was getting worse and worse. He was praying she didn't press him on why they needed the DNA sample. He would leave that to the police.

'Are you saying that Mr MacLeod is not Ross' father?'

'I'm not rightly sure. It was a difficult time. One of the lads from the dairy was very understanding, ya ken? That all stopped when I fell pregnant. We've been happy since Ross came along. I mean, we were happy. I don't want to make things worse.'

'Don't worry, Mrs MacLeod. Even if the police take samples from you both, I'll ask them just to use your DNA. I'm sure they can handle it sensitively.'

These days, the police got sensitivity training, didn't they? Hopefully, Sergeant Campbell wouldn't accidentally put his oversized police boot in it. He hadn't shown much sensitivity up to now, but he agreed readily enough when Danny explained the situation.

There was little else he could do for the MacLeods. The police would confirm a DNA match. Then, they would be told that all that was left of their son to bury was his teeth. It didn't bear thinking about.

At least he could try to find out who else was involved in his death. Was it murder or a gruesome accident? Even if Ruth Kerr was not prepared to come clean, there must be other ways to get to the truth.

Danny went back to sickbay and donned his overalls. It was time to check his snares and see who or what he'd caught on camera. He was about to leave when the lights went out, pitching the windowless room into darkness. He felt a tightness in his throat and his pulse quickened.

After a couple of seconds, the dim emergency lighting flickered into life. He opened the door through to the medic's office. The water-colour sun flooded the room with calm and normality.

Two power cuts in two days? That was par for the course for some of the old oil platforms, but not for an oil terminal, even one on a remote island. Surely not another saboteur? No one could be that unlucky.

With renewed urgency, he headed out onto the plant. The first stop was the substation. Danny downloaded all the camera footage to his tablet. It took an inordinate length of time. Someone was sure to spot him. Fortunately, the substation was not a popular destination and frequent showers were dissuading anyone from heading this far from their workplaces.

The camera in the turbine hall was more of a problem. A bored technician had been tasked with monitoring various parameters in the control room. He came and went at random intervals. Danny had just enough time to take down the camera, plug it into the tablet, and hide it in a cupboard.

He hung around badgering the technician with tedious health and safety questions in the hope of driving him away. Eventually, the tactic had the desired effect, and the man left long enough for Danny to retrieve his tablet, remount the magnetic camera, and make his escape.

He decided to remove the camera from the research compound and take it with him on the way back. He wasn't even sure why he'd gone to the trouble of installing it there. Fortunately, climbing up to extract the camera proved considerably easier than putting it up.

Back in his office, Danny sat watching the footage and was nearly as bored as the technician. These spy cameras were only supposed to record movement in the vicinity. However, that movement included two male gulls in the substation who spent most of the day displaying their eligibility to potential mates by hopping from one high voltage line to another.

He was fast-forwarding through the videos at such a rate that he almost missed the gulls flying off. They were replaced briefly by Kevan Knox. Fortunately, he stayed away from live wires this time. It was hard to tell why he was there. He seemed to look for something. After a while, he gave up and left.

Several hours later, Dougie Warnock arrived and did pretty much the same thing. He at least had some excuse for being there. He went up to the brick building, removed the Danger of Death sign and checked something near the entrance with some heavily insulated test equipment. He then fetched his toolbox and began fiddling around inside.

Danny was expecting to see a big flash and Dougie's remains splattered all over the camera lens. Instead, in the absence of any seagulls or sparks, the camera stopped recording. It started again as Dougie exited the building. Danny checked the recording time. It was very recent. He had only just missed catching the power supervisor in the act.

He couldn't understand why anyone would go to the substation to cause a power cut. There had to be easier and safer ways of sabotaging the electrical network or the generators. Danny might not know much about electrical systems, but he had first-hand experience of how simple it was to cause a blackout.

He locked the tablet in a drawer and marched back out to the workshop building, where the power systems supervisor had his desk. Dougie seemed surprised but unfazed when Danny marched into his office unannounced.

'What can I do for you, pal?'

'I was wondering what you can tell me about these power cuts we've been having lately.'

'Aye. A bit embarrassing that. Should have figured it out straight away.'

'How do you mean?'

'I took a meter down to the substation to check the impedance. We have a major earth fault. Kept tripping the protection relays. I've been searching all around the terminal for the damn problem. But, of course, it wasn't inside the terminal, was it?'

'Where was it then?'

'Up in that warehouse. The one they built on the old wind turbine site. I mean, the feed should have been isolated, but it weren't. There was a fire up there, I hear. Must have melted the insulation.'

'I bet it did. But you've fixed it now? No more power cuts.'

'I damn well hope not. I disconnected the cables altogether. I've been getting it in the neck from Iain and Cara all day for messing up their precious propane production. I just want to get home to my bed if it's all the same to you.'

So, no saboteur. Danny breathed a sigh of relief. Even on dry land, the thought of someone messing with high voltage power lines filled him with dread. Then, of course, there was still the question of what Kevan was doing in the substation. That would have to wait for the morning.

One more set of tedious recordings to sit through. At least the sex-mad seagulls couldn't get into the turbine hall. If it was full of mating mice, he was calling it a night.

Chapter
Fifty-Three

DANNY'S HEAD WAS STARTING to nod as he fast-forwarded through endless footage from the turbine hall. No rodents, thank God, even so, the video kept running. The building appeared to be a handy thoroughfare for every Tom, Dick, and Harry. So many people accessing a hazardous area like this? He could feel a risk assessment coming on and probably a few more of those fluorescent "Danger of Death" signs.

No suspicious behaviour, though, unless you counted the lass from the maintenance department trying to light a cigarette as she strolled past the turbine fuel tanks. Danny switched his attention to the last camera, the one he'd extracted from the research compound. A couple of swooping seagull shots and then Cara hove into view. She moved like she was on a catwalk, even with no one watching. Well, that wasn't exactly true, of course, but surely she didn't know that. He still felt guilty for gawking.

When she reached the door of the research building, Cara gave a knowing look over her shoulder towards the gate. He fast-forwarded to where she came back out, some two hours later.

Cara walked towards the camera without looking up and quickly disappeared. Danny was about to speed through another seagull courtship ritual when the gate opened again. The considerably less attractive figure of Kevan Knox appeared on the screen, lumbering towards the building.

He pulled out his impressive set of keys and opened each door. When he reached the door that Cara used, he glanced around and went in. According to the timestamp on the video, Kevan spent nearly an hour inside. What the security chief was up to in there? It certainly wasn't research.

Kevan wasn't around to ask. The two night-duty security guards were still on site, but he would get more sense from talking to the seagulls. Danny decided it was time he inspected whatever was going on in the research building. Cara wouldn't be happy, but the last ferry was already disappearing up the Sound and even she must have left for the night.

There was plenty of time. Danny had the place to himself. He called by the canteen first. It was just closing. He had to make do with a smorgasbord of congealed meatballs, flaccid veg, and lumpy mashed potato. At least the coffee was hot.

Next stop was the security cabin. From the footage, it looked like breaking into the research building would be tricky. He needed a better option. The night-shift lads were nowhere to be seen, and the cabin door was unlocked. Danny wasn't surprised. No one expects a break-in from the inside.

He hoped to find Kevan's keyring hanging on a hook, but there was no sign of it. After rifling through the drawers, he eventually spotted a tarnished metal key safe hanging on the wall. It was flimsy enough to prise open, but that would raise some awkward questions. Instead, he turned his attention to the combination lock. The four-digit number was likely a date. The Battle of Hastings or George Orwell's best-known novel were the usual favourites. No such luck. He got onto his phone and searched for significant dates in Scottish history. When he reached 1314 and the Battle of Bannockburn, the lock clicked open.

There were two bunches of keys. One had a tag labelled "Patrol" and the other just the initials "KK". Taking both was risky, so he lifted the KK keys and locked the box. Torchlight flashed up at the window. The night watch was back. There was no time to sneak away and nowhere to hide.

The two uniformed guards lumbered into the cabin and stared at him in puzzlement through their thick glasses. They looked to Danny like an overweight Proclaimers tribute act.

'Oh hi,' he said as casually as he could. 'I don't suppose anyone has found a phone? It's an old Motorola. Nothing special.'

'And you are?' the first Proclaimer said. His twin just slumped in the doorway, slack-jawed and bleary-eyed.

'Danny. The stand-in medic. I didn't notice it was missing till I tried to call the wife just now.'

'Nothing's been handed in. I'll leave a note for the day shift. Best I can do.'

Danny wasn't sure they believed his story, but they moved aside to let him go. He glanced back and saw them searching the desks for something. Probably checking he hadn't run off with the chocolate biscuits.

His stomach was still complaining about the leftover food and the recent unexpected surge of adrenaline. It continued grumbling anxiously all the way to the research compound. He avoided the route through the turbine building and followed the official path around the stores and along the terminal boundary, shivering in the chilly evening air. The only thing between him and the bracing sea breeze was a chain-link fence. Not surprising that most people preferred taking the shortcut. The whine of the turbines was ear piercing, even from this distance, but at least they were warm.

He was relieved that his pass still opened the gate into the research compound. The tips of his fingers were going numb, and he was desperate to reach some kind of shelter.

The door that both Cara and Kevan used was in the building's lee. At least he would be out of the wind while he fumbled through the half a dozen keys that might conceivably fit the door. By the fifth, he was wondering if he would have to go back and try for the Patrol keyring. It might be easier to just kick down the door and deal with the consequences.

Key number six was a close fit and almost jammed in the lock before turning with a satisfying clunk. The door swung open, creaking like the entrance to a haunted house, and Danny stepped inside. The room reminded him of school chemistry lessons. Bunsen burners, glass beakers, and jars of noxious ingredients. He also recognised several stills, although distilling had not been on the school curriculum. Unlike school, the floor was a mess, and the walls were tacky with oil residue. Only the metal work-benches had been cleaned recently.

Some of the cupboards against the far wall were locked. None of KK's keys fitted. The rest were empty or filled with discarded packaging. He rifled through the desks. Just the expected chemistry paraphernalia: tubes and funnels and spatulas. No keys, apart from a bunch of hexagonal Allen keys, which he found in a drawer along with a ring spanner and an adjustable wrench.

Danny turned his attention to a large metal box standing on a pallet near the roller door. It was big enough to fit a body inside, maybe two. According to the embossed label, it was certified to be flameproof. There were dire warnings of the dangers of opening it in a hazardous environment.

The door was held shut by a dozen or more bolts. He went back to the drawer for the tools and began the laborious task of unbolting the box. His arms were aching by the time he finished. He prised open the door, expecting his efforts to be in vain.

To his relief, no bodies were inside, only four wooden crates. The first three were nailed shut, but the fourth was only held down with gaffer tape. He peeled off the tape and peered inside.

The box was filled with tiny glass spray bottles neatly packed with bubble wrap. He picked one up. No label, but he was willing to bet these were more of Aidan's supposed hay fever remedies. He wondered what was really inside.

There were many illegal substances that people sprayed up their nose. Drug dealers weren't usually so particular about presentation and pack-aging, though. These looked like the bottles you got from the pharmacist.

He slipped a couple of bottles into his pocket and knelt to collect up the bolts. There was a distinctive aroma of gas, stronger the closer he got to the floor. He could also hear a loud hissing noise. Danny didn't like it one bit. He sprang to his feet and made for the door. It was stuck.

The handle turned freely enough, but the door itself would not move. He ran over to the roller door and jabbed at the raise button. No response. There were no windows other than the unreachable skylights in the roof.

The smell of gas was permeating the entire room. Trying not to panic, he followed the hissing. It seemed to emanate from a metal cabinet behind the row of desks. The cabinet was locked. Of course.

There was no time for any delicate lock-picking. Danny braced himself against the desk nearest to the cabinet and kicked out with both feet. The door buckled, but the lock remained intact. He tried again, hammering his heels against the metalwork with all the force he could muster.

This time, it bent inwards enough for him to prise the lock open. It took several more kicks from a steel toe-capped boot before he could pull the mangled door open and see where the leak was coming from.

Inside was a propane cylinder, nearly as tall as him. Fitted to the outlet was a solenoid valve and a cable which disappeared out through the wall. There was a knob on top of the cylinder. Danny frantically screwed it down until the hissing stopped. At least the maniac who had rigged this up hadn't thought to disconnect the hand valve.

That left the minor problem of being locked in a room full of asphyxiating gas. He was already finding it difficult to breathe. How long before the gas escaped through the cracks would cause him to stop breathing?

Another gem from chemistry lessons popped into this head. Propane was heavier than air. Or was that methane? No. Propane was the heavy one. He was almost certain. That meant it was never going to leak out through the roof. It also meant the air higher up would be clearer. Danny clambered onto the desk and stood with his head on one side pressed against the ceiling. His brain cleared a little. Unless he passed out and collapsed onto the floor, he should be able to breathe.

Another more pressing problem became apparent. From his elevated position, he could see into the bottom of the cabinet. Inside the plinth was another cable. This one was attached to a metal cylinder with a ceramic tip.

It looked very much like a spark plug. If that was energised, it would ignite the propane, and air quality would be the least of his problems.

Danny took a deep breath, leapt from the desk and dived inside the flameproof box. He climbed on top of the wooden crates and pulled the door closed behind him as tightly as he could. He realised was standing on top of a box full of glass bottles. There was another bottle in each of his overall pockets. It was not a good place to be, but the alternatives were far worse.

He felt the explosion rather than heard it. The pressure wave thumped him in the chest and his ears were filled with white noise. The box lurched, then toppled forward. His head struck the metalwork. His mouth filled with the metallic taste of blood. Flashes of light span around him like fireflies and dragged him down into unconsciousness.

Chapter
Fifty-Four

IT WAS PITCH BLACK inside the narrow box. Danny was lying face down. The smell of propane had almost dissipated. Maybe he was dead and some thoughtless undertaker had buried him upside down. Or maybe the explosion had burned most of the gas away.

His head hurt and he felt sick. His ears were buzzing like he'd just stepped out of a heavy metal gig. If he was dead, surely he wouldn't feel so sick.

He wondered if this box was airtight as well as flameproof. If so, was this just a painful interlude before asphyxiation finished him off? Was that a bad way to go? He couldn't recall. His training hadn't covered the Ten Worst Ways to Die. He felt surprisingly calm. There was absolutely nothing he could do to save himself. Much better to just lie there in the dark and drift slowly back into oblivion.

A loud crash and the sound of splintering wood. Followed by a lot of shouting and the roar of an approaching engine. Could they not leave him to die in peace? He kicked the metalwork and shouted at them to keep the noise down. It seemed to have worked. Everything went quiet.

'Are you sure? I canna hear anything.'

'Aye. A voice. Coming from over there. By the far door. The one that's all bulged out of shape.'

Danny drummed his heels on the box. He tried to shout 'go away' but it came out as an incoherent bawl.

'Hold on, laddie, we've got you.'

'Jesus, this box weighs a ton.'

'Fetch a rope. Maybe we can haul it up with the van.'

After several false starts, Danny's world began slowly to right itself. As the box lifted, his legs refused to support him and he slid to the bottom. When the door opened, his rescuers found him crouched on a bed of bubble wrap and broken glass.

'Are you alright, laddie? You just stay there. We'll fetch the medic.'

Danny lifted his head. The two faces peering at him were blurred, but he recognised the uniforms and the bottle-bottom glasses of the night-shift security team.

'Get tae fuck. It is the medic. What do we do now?'

'Well, he's awake, and he's breathing. I went on a first aid course once, but I don't remember what you do next.'

'Let's get him to sickbay. Maybe he'll come round.'

'Can you walk, pal?'

Danny swung his legs round and the two security men helped him to his feet. He could walk, just about, but would rather have gone back to sleep. The men assured him he could lie down once they got him to sickbay. He allowed them to manoeuvre him into the van's passenger seat and drive back towards the main entrance.

There was a great deal of debate about whom to contact. Neither seemed keen on calling the police or the Health and Safety Executive. Without bothering to ask their casualty, they decided he didn't need an ambulance. In the end, one of them tried calling Kevan Knox on his mobile. There was no reply. He left a long and confusing message.

'No point in waking anyone up, eh?' his twin said. 'Only a couple of hours and we can hand this over to the day shift.'

By the time they reached the admin building, Danny had come out of his mental fug. He wanted to be left alone to process what had happened, but his rescuers insisted on laying him out on the sickbed and making him a cuppa.

'We gotta keep an eye on you, pal. Concussion protocols and the like.'

He noticed they'd made themselves drinks too and helped themselves to his chocolate digestives. They didn't offer him one. It was a safe bet these masterminds hadn't rigged up the booby trap. So, who did? He asked them if they'd seen anyone else around.

'In the research place? At this time of night? Never seen anyone go in when we're on duty. We was amazed to find you in there, I can tell you. Usually, there's nobody on site except a couple of the process boys and us. We only came out here to see where the noise came from.'

'So Cara or Iain never come here? Or maybe Dougie the sparky?'

'Not likely. Dougie, we see now and again if there's a power fault. You see no other managers in here of a night.'

'What about your boss?'

'Kevan? You must be kidding. Not unless terrorists were storming the terminal and even then, he'd probably hide under the bed.'

'It wasn't terrorists, was it?' his colleague wondered. 'We ought to have called the police if it was terrorists. I had an email about it.'

Danny reassured them there were no suicide bombers in the terminal. Though somebody had been here. Unfortunately, he was in no fit state to go looking for them. He should be safe enough in sickbay. His minders weren't much of a deterrent, but if someone wanted to finish him off, they were unlikely to want any witnesses.

'How about I call Iain?' he suggested. The security twins were very much in favour of that idea.

'Go for it, pal. That covers our arses, without us putting them in the firing line, so to speak.'

Dany waited until six am before phoning the terminal manager. Iain Grant did not appreciate his thoughtfulness.

'What the hell time do you call this? It had better be important, lad.'

He explained about the explosion and his narrow escape.

'Are you serious? Jesus, Mary, and Joseph! You're saying someone from my staff intentionally blew up part of the terminal. Are you sure it wasn't an accident? I mean, that would be bad enough. If it's sabotage, that really ticks all the boxes. It probably wipes its arse in them and craps on the lid on the way out. I'll have the police, HSE and probably MI6 on my case before you know it.'

Danny left Iain to inform the relevant authorities while he tried to contact Gemma. She might be in danger again. Things were hotting up. She would want to stay and stoke the fire, but Danny thought she'd done enough of that already. It was time for her to leave.

Chapter
Fifty-Five

GEMMA REFUSED TO TAKE Danny's advice. He was not surprised. When had she ever listened to him? She appeared unconcerned about his latest near-death experience.

'I reckon it's about time I looked around that stinking terminal of yours, Danny-boy.'

'What the hell do you want to come here for? It's not a tourist attraction, you know. You can't just stroll in and ask for a guided tour.'

'Aye, I know. But I've got nothing to do here. Ruthie's locked up, the barn's a pile of ash and even the Balearic Shearwater has fucked off back to Ibiza.'

'The what?'

'It's a bird, pal. Critically endangered. If you were an experienced ornithologist like me, you'd know all this pish.'

'You do realise we have a murderer in the terminal?'

'Exactly. I want to be where the action is. I'm bored shitless here. So, who do you think did it? My money's on our new so-called investigator pal.'

Danny explained Marissa had left the island.

'So you say. Where's your proof? She might have been hiding. Or it might all have been done remotely. Have you thought of that?'

Danny had. He planned to find out where those wires went as soon as he regained full control of his legs. He was also keen to check out the whereabouts of all the suspects.

Gemma was right. Assuming the blast had not been triggered over the Wi-Fi, someone must have sneaked back into the terminal and flicked the switch. He had a nasty feeling he knew the culprit. He wasn't about to tell Gemma yet. Her way of getting a suspect to confess was probably in contravention of Scottish law, not to mention the Universal Declaration of Human Rights.

'Look, I can't get you into the terminal. It's a secure facility.' Not as secure as it should have been. 'How about I give you a list of names and addresses? You could try to find out if any of them had the opportunity to get back into the terminal last night.'

This was the sort of task that should appeal to Gemma. She was naturally nosey and never afraid of asking awkward questions. She seemed satisfied with her assignment. God knows how she was going to check on various terminal employees' whereabouts without attracting attention. He was past caring.

The police knew what they were up to. He had a feeling that the bomb-maker did too. If they were rumbled by anyone else, what was the worst that could happen? He might lose his job, but then he'd already pissed off half the workforce. And it was not as if this job was supposed to last, anyway. It was only a decoy for his investigation. His desk phone rang. Probably Grant calling to sack him.

'Mr Verity? It's Sergeant Campbell here. I had a disturbing call from Iain Grant. I'd like to discuss it with you face to face.'

Since Danny was still officially on call, Campbell agreed to catch the next ferry and meet him at Mallach pier. For once, the weather was appropriate for an outdoor chat. The weak sun was peeking through the clouds and the wind was little more than a gentle breeze. Campbell stepped off the ferry, and they strolled to a bench overlooking the bay.

'Perhaps you could start by telling me what happened yesterday. I've heard Mr Grant's version, but I'd like to hear it from you.'

Danny related the entire story to Campbell, including him breaking into the research building. It was the truth, but not necessarily the whole truth.

He omitted a few inconvenient details, such as his method of obtaining the keys and his use of covert surveillance cameras. At least he didn't embellish the story as much as Gemma, for which the sergeant seemed thankful.

'DI Gray is on his way with a specialist team. I've asked Mr Grant to seal off the research compound until they arrive.'

Danny reached into his pocket and handed over the only two spray bottles that had survived. Perhaps because he'd landed on his face rather than his hip. Every painful experience had a bright side if you looked hard enough.

'Thank you. I'll get these analysed and let you know what we find. I have something else to tell you. Good news, I suppose.'

He waved a printout of a DNA analysis under Danny's nose.

'This is from the teeth we found in Ruth Kerr's pig field. The one below was taken from Eileen MacLeod. It's not a match. Not even close.'

'That is good news. Have you told the MacLeods yet?'

'Mr and Mrs MacLeod have been informed. And before you ask, no, we don't have the DNA on our database. We are going through the missing persons' reports for Mallach and the other islands. There's a surprising number of people who disappear every year. Mostly youngsters, I'm afraid. However, I doubt it's one of them.'

'Because you already have an idea who those teeth belong to?'

'Ruth Kerr was brought up near Thurso. She moved here when she married a Mallach man named Greig Kerr. A nasty bastard, by all accounts. He's on our sex offenders' register.'

'So, what happened to Greig?'

'According to her, they fought. He upped and left. Took a ferry to Aberdeen and was never heard of again.'

'Sounds familiar.'

'Nobody reported him missing. Nobody missed him, I expect. So, Ruth took over the running of the farm, and the rest of the clan mucked in to help.'

'But you think he never got on that ferry? An accident with a farming implement, perhaps? Then his wife fed him to the pigs as a treat.'

'Something like that. We've never been able to prove it. No one cared to, most likely. Everyone seemed better off without him. But now...'

Now Ruth Kerr was in deep trouble. She'd already admitted to growing cannabis. Now the police had found the remains of a body on her farm. Maybe she could convince a jury that her husband had a nasty accident. But if they found another body, not even the slipperiest lawyer in Scotland could save her.

What about her mystery accomplice? Had they been responsible for any of her crimes? Would Ruth keep their identity secret even if it meant going to jail for the rest of her life? The police would do their best to persuade her to give them a name. In the meantime, Danny would continue his investigations. For the first time, he felt confident they would find the culprit. It was just a matter of time.

Chapter
Fifty-Six

NANCY WAS IN CUSTODY. Locked in a police cell without a window. She wouldn't like that. She was a farm girl born and bred. Doug felt sorry for her, even missed her. Unwelcome and unsettling emotions. If this was what love felt like, then it was best avoided.

She really ought to forget about Nancy. Despite Doug's best efforts, Ruth was never entirely ruthless. As Nancy, she might hold out under interrogation. As Ruth, she was bound to confess.

She might tell them the identities of her minions. They were young and stupid. A slap on the wrist and a suspended sentence, probably. Would she tell them about her lover? She hadn't so far, or he'd been in jail too. Doug had left it too late to end the relationship. The idea of breaking into the police station and slitting her throat had a certain macabre appeal. Too much of a risk, though. Better to gamble on loyal Nancy keeping her trap shut.

The word in the fields was that Gauld was leaving the island. Doug watched as a motorbike pulled up by the pier steps. The twitcher levered her ample frame out of Ellen's sidecar and waddled towards the ferry moorings. She was carrying a small rucksack. Not going for long, then. Was there some rare seagull perching on Muckle Skerry? Or did she have some more sinister purpose?

Ellen and her motorbike had left the scene. The tide was on its way out. Lots of jagged rocks under the pier. One push and that particular concern would be out of the way. Too late again. A Land Rover bumped along the road and discharged more passengers.

Nothing was going to plan anymore. Maybe it was time to leave Mallach for good. But that would mean that the lawmen had won. Not an acceptable outcome. Outsmarting authority was Doug's favourite pastime.

The explosion hadn't been a good idea. Too melodramatic by half. There was more than one way to skin a cat. And countless ways to cause havoc in a terminal full of highly combustible materials.

Chapter
Fifty-Seven

GEMMA PACKED HER WATERPROOFS, an extensive collection of snacks, and a flask. Then, as an afterthought, she stuffed the binoculars and the bird book into the rucksack. She was still undercover, after all. Heather reckoned the skuas often followed the ferries, diving for fish in the wake. That would be something to see.

The next boat wasn't due for an hour. Plenty of time to check out the local suspects first. Lorna Kerr was pretty much at the bottom of the list when it came to setting off an explosion. She was pleased to hear that Ellen could vouch for her whereabouts.

'Lately, she comes round here after work most afternoons. Trouble at home, I hear. I'm glad of the company anyhow. I made her omelette and chips. I don't know how she stays so thin. She ate half my shortbread while I was cooking and still wanted a second helping of crumble after.'

Despite his ban on terminal personnel, Stewart the barman, admitted to having served Alain and Anna, the dayshift security team, last night.

'There fae Mallach, you see. The both of them stayed in the bar till after nine. Then back to his place for a quickie, no doubt. And her married with a couple of bairns, ken. God knows what she sees in the auld loon.'

Be that as it may, they could never have got back to the terminal in time to lock Danny in the research building. So that left one more Mallach resident to check on: Dougie Warnock. He stayed in Quoy, at the opposite end of the island to the pier. Gemma had no choice but to accept Ellen's offer of a lift in her death-trap sidecar.

They made it to Quoy without incident, though Gemma was sure she'd shrunk a couple of centimetres. Dougie was at work. Gemma was trying to think of an excuse to allay his wife's suspicions, but she was too rattled to think of anything. Fortunately, Ellen started talking nineteen to the dozen. On the odd occasion she drew breath, Gemma chipped in with a few inoffensive remarks about the weather.

'Another lovely day, eh? Last night I was away up at the Loon watching the razorbills till it was dark nearly.'

'Aye, we see them off the Taing sometimes. I'll go for a stroll later if I'm feeling better. Just didn't feel up to it yesterday.'

Ellen was full of concern. It seemed that they were both martyrs to some ailment that could not be spoken of in male company.

'Oh, don't you fuss, I'm much better today. Poor auld Dougie was supposed to be helping our Angus with his chainsaw, but he stayed here with me instead. He's a real saint sometimes.'

Extracting the information on Dougie's whereabouts over the last few days was considerably easier than extracting Ellen from the house. After a few unsubtle comments and meaningful glances at her watch, she took the hint. They bounced along the road, back through Bron, arriving at the pier just as the ferry rounded Ruddy Gutter.

She waved cheerio to Ellen and prayed she never again had to get in that damn sidecar. Then, before clambering down onto the ferry, she rechecked her timetable.

Island-hopping sounded great when you were reading a holiday brochure. Unfortunately, it was not so much fun when you needed to get somewhere in a hurry. Ferries between Mallach and Sanday took half an hour but only ran at high tide. Kirkwall was a longer journey but more frequent. Getting to any other island involved complex maths, a tide table, and a map.

Fortunately, most of Danny's prime suspects stayed on Mallach, Mainland, or Eday. One was based on North Ronaldsay. She crossed him off the list. Unless he had his own powerboat, there was no way he could sneak back after hours. Surely it was impossible to sneak anywhere in a motorboat?

This particular ferry stopped at the nearby islands and then carried on up to the frozen north somewhere, presumably returning once the icebergs thawed out. She decided it would be easiest to hop her way to Eday, then return via Kirkwall and Westray.

Cara lived in Eday. Gemma was looking forward to hearing what her neighbours made of her. That plan fell apart as soon as she stepped off the boat. The island was sparsely inhabited and almost entirely lacking in road signs. The ferry was carrying a delivery of parcels, and luckily, she was able to ask the local part-time postie for directions.

'Cara, aye? Bonny lass. She don't wear much around the house, I'm telling you. The sights you see when you haven't got a gun, eh? No, I haven't seen her lately. She stays at the terminal when she's working late.'

Well, that was a lie for a start. The postie reckoned she hadn't been home all week. Was she really staying on Mallach? Certainly, she wasn't sleeping in the terminal, unless she was hot bunking it with Danny-boy. She wouldn't put it past Cara, but Danny wouldn't be so daft. Right? He was a man, though. A certain level of stupidity was to be expected.

She found the cottage easy enough, but apart from an elderly deaf woman half a mile away, the only neighbours were rabbits and sheep. If you were a psychotic murderer, paranoid about anyone tracking your movements, this was the ideal place. Or maybe Cara just wanted a quiet life. Gemma knew which theory she preferred.

There was nothing to see here and Eday was another island without even a pub to its name. Gemma walked back to the pier and sat on a bench to wait for the next ferry to Orkney Mainland.

After nearly a dozen days on Mallach, Kirkwall felt like a big city. She had four suspects to tick off the list here. Three of them lived in downtown Kirkwall and all three had cast-iron alibis. Or at least they had wives, girl-friends, or weird housemates prepared to swear they never left Mainland the previous evening.

After a heart-stopping deep-fried meal washed down by a refreshing pint, Gemma was ready to hunt down her final suspect. Kevan Knox lived outside town on a new housing estate. Gemma took a taxi from the harbour and asked the driver to wait. If this was anything like the last three, she would be back in the pub in five minutes flat.

The woman who came to the door had a face like a skelped arse. If anything, she looked even less cheery when Gemma mentioned Kevan's name.

'You another of his fancy women?'

'Wheest, woman. I wouldnae touch him with ma PPE on.'

'Aye, well. He'll need PPE if he shows his face around here. The dirty cradle-snatcher. I found her photo in his wallet. She must be half his age.'

Lorna Kerr, presumably. Gemma dared not mention her name in case it set Mrs Knox off again. Instead, she asked for a way to contact her husband and braced for impact.

'I don't know where he is and I don't care neither. I expect he's shacked up with that peedie hoore on Mallach somewhere.'

'I think she broke it off. The relationship, I mean. No one seems to know where he's staying. I'm just doing a favour for his boss, Iain Grant. He asked me to make enquiries.'

'Iain Grant? That pervert? Tried to feel me up at the Christmas party. He can stick his enquires up his hole, so he can. Good riddance to both of them.'

With that, she slammed the door. The taxi driver seemed to have enjoyed the exchange.

'I'm gonna upload the dashcam footage tonight. I've got a YouTube channel. It's called Oddball Orkney. If you subscribe, you get ten percent off your fare.'

Gemma was more interested in the reaction of the guy with the smirk on his face who was mowing his lawn two doors down. She marched over and unplugged him from the mains.

'Hey! Whatdya do that for?'

'You know where he is, don't you?'

'Kevan? Aye well, what if I do?'

'You either tell me where he is, or I'll plug this in and mow your back, crack, and sack. Free of charge, pal.'

The man didn't need asking twice. He typed an address into her phone, then scurried inside and locked the door.

'Nice one,' the taxi driver said. 'I zoomed right in on that one. The look on his face. Priceless. Where to next, hen?'

'The harbour, pal. Unless you've seen a posh Asian sow wandering about Kirkwall? Sounds like she's fae that Made in Chelsea show.'

'I ken the lassie you mean. I've no seen her for a while. But, if you're after a catfight, I ken the ideal bar for it.'

The taxi driver was very disappointed when Gemma directed him firmly back to the pier. A shame Marissa wasn't around. Gemma had been looking forward to making a citizen's arrest with a punch to her smug face.

Two more suspects and one more island to go. Iain Grant, the alleged sex pest, stayed in Pierowall, the main harbour and the largest settlement on Westray. So did Kevan Knox now. According to the ferryman, he was sleeping in the room over his boss' garage. That should make things simpler.

Grant's house was easy walking distance from the pier. It was late afternoon and one of the men could have returned from work early. Gemma needn't have worried. Mrs Grant was out in the garden playing with the kids. Her husband and her lodger were nowhere to be seen.

'Sorry to disturb you. I was hoping to have a private word with Kevan. I'm a friend of his from work. We've all been a bit concerned about him lately. I just wondered if he was ok.'

'Aye, he's fine right enough. It's me you should ask about. He's been dragging Iain away to the bar every night. Drowning his sorrows, he says. I'll be drowning him if they come back blootered one more time.'

'I take it they were out late last night, eh? I mean, Kevan didn't look too great this morning.'

'They were out late right enough, but I don't know where they'd been. Not the local bar. I checked. Probably round at his drunkard brother's place. I'm telling you, it's got to stop.'

Gemma promised to give Kevan a strong talking to. She didn't know what to make of it. Either Kevan and Iain were in the clear, or they were in it together.

She needed to find out where they'd been and if anyone had seen them. Those were questions better asked by the police or a private investigator with her hand around the suspect's throat. It was time to head back to Mallach and compare notes with her partner in crimefighting.

Chapter Fifty-Eight

DANNY SHOULDERED HIS WAY through the side door with a coffee in one hand and a sheaf of reports in the other. He could hear the sickbay phone ringing. He trotted as quickly as he could along the corridor and opened the door with an elbow and a sidekick. Coffee dregs sloshed onto his boots, but at least he reached the receiver before the ringing stopped. It was DI Gray. Another courtesy call. His opinion of the civvy police was improving.

'Forensics checked that bottle you gave me.'

'I don't suppose you found any fingerprints or DNA?'

'On a peedie glass bottle like that? No chance. They found a partial print, but I'm willing to bet it's yours.'

Gray could be right. Danny had been in a hurry and not very careful.

'So, what was in the bottle, then?'

'Nabiximols, or at least a close substitute.'

'Never heard of it,' admitted Danny.

'Not something you'd come across in an offshore sickbay. It's a cannabis oil. Licenced for reducing the symptoms of multiple sclerosis. It's only been legal for the last few years. Apparently, there's still some controversy about its effectiveness. A lot of doctors are shy about prescribing it for MS. There's quite an active black market for people who want to get it under the counter.'

'How difficult is it to manufacture? I mean, could an amateur do it?'

'I doubt it. The only guy we've bagged so far was a university lecturer. One of his students was supplying him with the raw ingredients. They were cooking it up together in the chemistry lab. He was making it for his daughter, so he got off lightly. His pal did a runner with the rest of the stock and we're still looking for him.'

'Does Ruth Kerr have MS?'

'Nope, we checked with her GP.'

'How about Lorna? Or someone else in the Kerr clan?'

'We're still waiting. It's not easy to get hold of medical records, especially for folks we haven't charged with anything.'

Fortunately, Danny did have access to medical records, for everyone who worked at the terminal. Not the complete NHS records, just the basic declarations that people made when they started employment. Some people might hide a medical condition, especially if it meant they might be declared unfit to work. Surely anyone who had MS would declare it, he thought. People needed to know in case of an emergency.

The only medical issues that Lorna listed were athlete's foot, constipation, and a painful wart, location unspecified. He worked steadily through the rest of the records. The terminal employees were not an especially healthy lot. Plenty of respiratory illnesses. Danny wondered if this was because of the terminal's atmosphere or the number of cigarette butts discarded by the bike sheds every day.

Only one MS sufferer was on site. There was no mention in their records of Nabiximols or any other medication. Not surprising if they were making it themselves. Danny stared at the file, head propped in his hands. How come he'd never made the connection before? This had to be Doug, Ruth's mysterious partner. It was so obvious now he spotted it.

He checked the datasheet for Nabiximols. It was supposed to be taken as an oral spray several times daily. That suggested Doug would need a ready supply on hand in the terminal. Before he called the police, Danny wanted to make sure he wasn't jumping to conclusions.

His previous attempts to search other people's offices had not been an unmitigated success. He would have liked to have waited until everyone went home, but there was no time to waste. There was a water cooler at the junction of the two main access routes. He hung around there for a suspiciously long time fiddling with his phone and making occasional small talk with passers-by.

This was getting ridiculous. Fiona MacAlpine had just hobbled past him for the second time and was giving him a funny look. He was about to give up and go back to sickbay when he saw his prime suspect walking towards the rear entrance. Danny followed and peered through the grease-smeared glass. The lone figure strode along the uneven paved path to the turbine hall, round the side of a large oil tank and disappeared from view.

He quickly scurried back down the corridor, passing Fiona for the third time. She stopped and turned towards him. There was a good chance she was about to ask him about her hip problem. With a fixed smile, Danny tapped his watch and marched on by. Around the corner, he stopped and checked the coast was clear. He pushed open the first door on the left and slipped inside.

There was a bag on the back of the door. He rifled through various compartments. Nothing suspicious apart from a large penknife and an unhealthy addiction to chocolate bars.

The desk drawers were locked, but the key was in the pocket of a work jacket hanging over the spare chair. Inside was the usual collection of snacks, notebooks, and computer paraphernalia. There was a wallet and more keys in the middle drawer. The bottom drawer was full of over-the-counter medicines, including several packets of senna tablets. Was everyone on the island constipated? Anyone would think it was contagious.

Among the painkillers and cough cures was a blister pack of steroid pills. Steroids were sometimes prescribed for MS but were also used for asthma and hives, among other conditions.

Danny was running out of ideas. In old films, addicts kept their stuff in hollowed-out books. Well, it was worth a try. There were only a dozen books and a row of lever arch files on the shelves. All the textbooks were reassuringly solid and incomprehensible to Danny. The files were covered in dust and looked like they had been long replaced by online research.

Lying on the top of the shelving unit were a couple of box files. The first was full of Orcadia Oil safety handouts. The second clinked when he moved it. Danny gingerly lowered it onto the desk. He opened the lid. Inside was a selection of Scotch whisky miniature bottles.

Someone was having a joke at his expense. He was tempted to taste the whisky, but that was one sure way to get the sack and lose any chance of finding out what happened to Ross. He stared at the bottles. Something was bothering him. It wasn't just the thought of all that alcohol coursing through his veins. Secret alcoholics don't generally drink out of miniature bottles, do they? And how come the box was more than half full of packing material?

Danny began removing some of the little golden bottles. Underneath was a sheet of foam. And underneath that, twenty or more little clear spray bottles. Bingo! The labels said they were a herbal cure for hay fever, but Danny knew what was inside.

Rather than stagger down the corridor with a box full of whisky, he picked up the phone on the desk and dialled DI Gray's mobile. There was no answer, so he left a message. He was about to call Sergeant Campbell when the door opened. Cara Douglas marched into the office and stood in front of her desk, arms folded.

'Hi Doug,' Danny said. 'It's good to meet you at last.'

Chapter Fifty-Nine

'How long do we have?' asked Cara.

'You mean before the police get here?'

Cara nodded.

'An hour maybe. Unless they decide to scramble a chopper.'

Cara checked her phone and then slipped it back into the breast pocket of her overalls.

'That works for me. They don't have a chopper, by the way. They have to call the coastguard and they won't come unless someone is in mortal danger.'

'And am I?'

'Not really. Doug would like to kill you, but I won't let him. Too noisy. Too messy.'

She removed her bag from the chair and sat down. Danny edged behind the desk and did the same.

'What should I call you?'

'Doug is fine. That's what they called me at school. Sometimes I'd turn up in my brother's uniform and use the little boy's room. Drove the teachers mad. And my parents. That was long before all this gender identity bullshit.'

'It must have been tough for you. Being a misfit. People constantly telling you there's something wrong with you.'

Cara shrugged.

'That's life, eh?.'

'And then you find out you have MS. When were you diagnosed?'

'On my twenty-fifth birthday. Nice present. Thank you, God. Of course, I'd done a lot of bad things by then. Maybe I deserved to be punished, but it was Cara who had to suffer. Hardly fair, is it? I've managed to keep the MS under control, thanks for asking.'

'So why do you need the Nabiximols?'

'Last year, my legs started spazzing so bad I could hardly walk sometimes. At first, the doctors wouldn't give me cannabis oil because it was illegal. Then, when it was legalised, they said it wasn't proven. Covering their overpaid arses, no doubt.'

'But you came up with another way to get hold of it?'

'Yeah. Cara would have just kept on whining to her GP. Doug found a supplier on the internet. The dosage was all over the place, though. You just can't rely on those illegal online suppliers. So, Cara started making it in the research lab. At first, Doug got the cannabis from a dealer in Aberdeen, but the dealer was also a user. He was also not very reliable. You know how junkies are.'

'And then you met Ruth?'

'Her name is Nancy. You'd do well to remember that. I told her she had to be Ruth-less. Like the little pirate girl in Swallows and Amazons. She thought I was being funny, but it was no joke.'

'Well, I never had you down as a comedian. What attracted you to Nancy?'

'A poor lonely widow. In denial. In need of some loving. In need of hard cash even more. We had a lot of fun setting up that underground farm. Especially since my esteemed employers were paying the bills.'

'But then Marissa arrived. She persuaded Ross to help her find out where all that spare power was going.'

'We're quite alike, Marissa and me. Doug ought to have pushed her over a cliff while he had a chance.'

'Instead, Doug killed Ross. A young lad who was just doing his job. Don't you feel any guilt?'

'So, you're a shrink now, as well as a medic? Jack of all trades. Haven't you been listening? Doug doesn't do guilt. You think you know all about me, but you really don't.'

'I think you're a psychopath.'

'Well, you're probably right. Half right, at least. Doug's never been tested, but he seems to have some characteristics, doesn't he? Psychopaths get such a bad name. They're not all killers. Some of the greatest leaders have been psychopaths. Take Gandhi, for example.'

'Very funny.'

'Well, Doug lies quite a lot. He knows his right from wrong. He just doesn't feel guilty when he does a bad thing. Not if he's done it for a good reason. For my good reason, that is. It really is all about me in the end.'

'But what about Ross? That wasn't an accident but murder.'

'Kevan thought so too, bless him. He's been following me around like a lost sheep. And then you started following him. Priceless! Neither of you can prove anything, can you?'

'I might if I can find Ross' body.'

'Nancy cut him up and fed it to her swine. That's what the pigs in blue think, anyway. I'm right, aren't I?'

'I think you led them there by the nose. I doubt you would take that kind of risk. You wouldn't trust anyone to get rid of all the evidence.'

'Why not? That's what Nancy did to her nasty old husband. Very appropriate, I thought. She got away with it for years. Would have probably got away with it forever if Doug hadn't come along. Poor Nancy.'

'What if Doug needed to get rid of a body? What would he do?'

'Something equally appropriate, I expect. Something senseless and coarse.'

Cara liked playing with words. Or perhaps that was Doug's weakness. Danny was tired of this game. Did Cara really have a split personality? He found it hard to believe. She enjoyed creating this impression of madness and chaos. All the while, her cold, calculating mind was figuring out the next move.

And then it struck him. He'd always assumed that most of the answers lay in the terminal. Where in the terminal would be most appropriate to dispose of a dead body? What if Iain had shown him the ideal place on his very first day?

Cara was becoming restless, crossing and uncrossing her legs and shifting in her seat.

'I think we're finished here, don't you, Danny? I had considered screwing you, by the way. To throw you off the scent, so to speak. You would have enjoyed that. So would Cara. Doug wasn't keen. Anyway, you managed to lose the trail all by yourself.'

'If you say so. You're a good-looking woman Cara, but you're a cold fish. You've as much sex appeal as a tailor's dummy. I agree with you. We're done here.'

Cara Douglas pulled on her jacket and emptied the box file into her bag, whisky, and Nabiximols bottles all clattering together. Danny made no attempt to stop her. He would rather the police found her with the evidence. That's if they could catch her. She gave him a pitying look and glanced down at her phone.

'Time and tide wait for no man. Or woman, for that matter. Give my love to everyone. It's been fun, but I won't miss them.'

She flounced out of the room. Danny waited until the clanking had receded and picked up the phone. Sergeant Campbell was not pleased to hear from him. He was even less happy when he listened to what he had to say.

'So where is Ms Douglas now?'

'On her way to the Calf Sound jetty, I imagine. She has a boat moored there. Green and white, with a cuddy cabin and an outboard. No name or markings, I'm afraid.'

'And you know this because...'

'A little birdie told me. Or a little birdwatcher, to be more precise.'

'Are you serious? I'll get the lads to run over to Mallach in the launch, but she could be halfway to Sweden before they arrive.'

'It's low tide, so she won't be able to get far just yet. Besides, she might be in for a surprise when she gets there. What about the terminal? How soon can you get here?'

Campbell promised to head straight over and drag DI Gray and the forensics team along with him.

Chapter Sixty

'Let me get this straight,' Campbell said when Danny met him and the rest of the team at the gate. 'You want us to search an operational area of the terminal. Based on a bad pun made by a disaffected employee.'

Put like that, it seemed a bit of a stretch.

'You came. I don't suppose you would have brought the whole gang unless you thought there was some merit in it.'

'Look, I agree that Ruth Kerr wasn't acting alone. She must have had an accomplice here in the terminal. Your information makes Cara Douglas our prime suspect. But we have no evidence. And we can't interview her because you let her run off to sea in a beautiful pea-green boat.'

'That's why you have to do this.'

Danny took Gray and Campbell to meet Iain Grant. The DI showed their search warrant to Grant.

'Can you show them the way, Danny? I have work to do. Talk to one of the operators if you need help. Try to stop them tripping any safety devices, will you? It's the devil's own job to get the process going again.'

Danny, Iain's sparsely labelled set of master keys in hand, led them through the plant. In theory, he could open every gate in the terminal. In practice, it took a dozen attempts to get through the first one. More by luck than judgement, he was able to get them to the tank farm without setting off any alarms.

'Here we are.'

'I still don't get it,' Campbell said.

'When I asked Cara where her crazy alter ego would have put a body, she said somewhere "appropriate", somewhere "senseless and coarse".'

'That certainly sounds crazy to me.'

'Senseless and coarse. These are the dead crude storage tanks.'

DI Gray nodded, but Campbell still looked uncertain.

'I always hated cryptic crosswords. So how did she transport the body?'

'She's highly qualified. I checked. As well as a degree in Chemical Engineering, she has a Level 2 NVQ in forklift truck operations.'

'That's handy. Let's suppose she managed to borrow a forklift and get the body here with no one noticing. How did she get it into the tank? I don't suppose it lifts like a teapot lid. Anyway, it's too high off the ground.'

It was a fair point. Danny walked around the nearest tank, scrutinising it. Above the sump valve was a man-sized plate held in place with a dozen bolts. On it was a label warning of dire consequences of opening it when the tank was full. That seemed obvious even to a non-expert like Danny.

'Here you go. This is the only practical way I can think of doing it. If you came alongside with the forklift, it wouldn't be too difficult to push the body through that inspection hatch.'

'And that could only be done when the tank was empty?' DI Gray said.

'Correct. The operations team gave me a copy of the daily logs for all the tanks on site. Of course, if they were filled and emptied on the same day, we'd be none the wiser. The ops guy I spoke to says that hardly ever happens.'

'So, all we have to do is to find one that was empty on or around the date Ross went missing.'

'Exactly. Look, there are two possibilities here: tanks three and five. Number five was only emptied the day before due to pipe leakage. That was an unscheduled repair. It should have been full. If Cara planned all this meticulously, then the body must be in tank three.'

'There's a lot of ifs in there. And I'm guessing tank three is now full, yes?'

'Half full. According to this schedule, they'll be offloading number six into a tanker today sometime. If I speak nicely to the team, they might change the schedule and empty number three instead. I'll tell them you think there may be evidence inside. They don't need to know any more than that.'

'Very wise. What's to stop the body, if there is one, being poured out into the tanker as well?'

'This diagram shows a couple of strainers on the inlet and outlet pipes. At least they are supposed to be there.'

'Let's hope so. Otherwise, that could seriously lower the price of oil. I might want extra body in my shampoo, but not in my fuel tank, thank you very much.'

The operators referred Danny back to Iain Grant, who reluctantly agreed to change the schedule. He wanted more details, but Danny persuaded him he was better off not knowing. It was going to take several hours before the tank was completely empty.

The police team traipsed back the way they came, following Danny through the maze of gates and turnstiles. When they reached the main entrance, half the team slunk off for a smoke, whilst the other half followed Danny to the canteen for a late lunch. The canteen staff seemed pleased to have the extra custom. Unfortunately, there wasn't much left by the time the smokers appeared. Just a few sausage rolls and the dregs of the salad bar.

By the time they'd finished eating, the canteen manager was ready to close for cleaning. There was nowhere else big enough to house the whole police team, so they sat in one corner drinking tepid coffee while the staff swept and wiped down around them.

Eventually, Dougie Warnock arrived with a work permit to be signed by the one in command. Danny waved him away and pointed to DI Gray.

'Alright. The tank is empty, the intake is isolated, and we've even opened the hatch for you. It's safe to go in. Just watch your step. If anyone passes out inside, don't go rushing in after them. I've got a lad on standby with breathing apparatus. And please don't let the medic go inside. You might need him.'

With those cheery words, he left them to follow Danny back to the tank farm. No one seemed keen to be the first to crawl into a dead crude tank, even if most of the oil had been drained out. Finally, Gray ordered the most junior SCO to get inside. She was wearing a white jumpsuit, which stayed white for about ten seconds. Danny hoped it was impervious to oil as well as blood.

It didn't take her long to find Ross. She called out and began taking photos. Danny peered through the hatch. Intermittent bursts of flash illuminated the outline of a body, stretched out on the tank floor by the outlet pipe.

More officers suited up and climbed in. The body was dragged towards the hatch. PVC gloves were handed out. Willing hands supported Ross as he was lowered into a body bag and lifted onto the waiting trolley.

'At least his folks will have something to bury,' Gray said.

It was closure of sorts. The smallest of consolations.

'I hope they don't want a cremation,' Campbell said. 'Not when he's been soaked in oil for a week. Whole place would go up like a torch.'

That was the police force for you. So considerate. Always looking out for the health and safety of the public.

There was still a formal identification to be done. Danny had no doubts about who it was. Ross's oil-painted face was perfectly preserved. Someone would be on their way to tell his parents. Danny was glad that this time, it wasn't him.

Chapter
Sixty-One

GEMMA WAS BORED. SHE'D started making up bird names just to piss off Heather and William.

'It that a bar-topped fuckwit?'

'No. It's not even a bar-tailed godwit,' Heather said. 'Sometimes Gemma, I do wonder if you're real birder at all.'

It occurred to Gemma that even though she'd told them about the investigation, she had left out the bit about the birds being a pretence. The urge to confess was strong, but Gemma preferred to maintain her cover for a while longer.

'Sorry. But there must be a hundred of them noisy bastard oyster-catchers out there. It's time they fucked off and gave some of the other birds a chance.'

'It was your idea to come here,' William said. 'There's not much going on in Calf Sound at this time of year.'

'Aye, well, I have my reasons. You might get a bit of entertainment soon if I'm right about a few things.'

'Does this have anything to do with all those police cars turning up at the terminal? I think you ought to be straight with us, Gem.'

Heather seemed to agree with him. She put down her binoculars and turned to face Gemma.

'Alright, alright. We're not here for the birds. We're keeping an eye on yon wee boat over there.'

She pointed to the jetty where the olive-green cuddy cruiser was still sitting in the mud with the tide just forming pools on either side. Through the binoculars, it looked in a sorry state. More rust than paint on this side. Not exactly seaworthy. Presumably, Cara wasn't planning a long voyage.

'How long before there's enough water to float it off?'

'About an hour, I'd guess,' William said. 'Maybe less. It's close to being a spring tide today.'

Danny-boy was cutting it fine. Cara must be on her way already. The polis should have been here by now, and where was the coastguard cutter?

'Any idea how you'd go about sabotaging a boat?'

'Perhaps you could pull the plug out?' Heather said.

'I'll take that as a no, then.'

She had expected little help from the bird nerds, but they lived on an island, for Christ's sake. You think they'd know about boats, at least. So, it was down to her. Again. She'd brought a few tools just in case things got messy.

'You landlubbers stay here and keep a lookout. I've got a boat to scupper.'

She slung her rucksack over one shoulder and trudged down the beach, following the line of the jetty. The top section was coarse white sand, more like ground-up shells. She crossed a small stream, stumbling through smooth round stones and slithering over seaweed-covered slabs. Finally, the rocks gave out, leaving nothing but thick, gloopy mud. By the time she reached the boat, she was up to her thighs in the stuff. It stank like a cesspit in summer.

Gemma pulled out the hook-ended wrecking bar that she called the Persuader from her backpack. She gave a mighty swing. It hit the boat with a satisfying clang, but the rebound threw her off balance and she sat down heftily in the mud. Fortunately, her boots were still stuck in the sludge and she couldn't fall far. By hooking one end of the Persuader around the anchor chain, she was able to haul herself upright again.

The hull had a small dent, but given the state of the metalwork, it was a feeble attempt. Brute force would not sink this tub. She would have to disable the engine. That meant climbing on board. Easier said than done. William was shouting something and pointing at the jetty.

'Aye, I know. I should have walked along the top and climbed down. I mucked up again. Thanks for letting me know, pal.'

A ladder hung a few slimy strides away. She pulled herself onto the bottom rung without losing her boots, which was a bonus. The incoming tide was straightening the boat, but it remained at a drunken angle. The only way of getting on board was to climb down the mooring line.

She carried on climbing until her head poked over the top of the walkway. She looked around just in time to see a ladies' size seven steel toe-capped boot heading towards her face. Ducking, she felt a rush of air as the kick missed by millimetres. So that was what sweet William had been shouting about.

The Persuader was tucked in her belt, but Cara was looming over her, carrying a baseball bat and a bowie knife. It was time for evasive manoeuvres. Gemma hooked the Persuader around the mooring line and swung away from the ladder. She had intended to wrap her legs around the thick rope to slow her descent, but she was already travelling too fast. At this rate, she would slam into the side of the boat and save Cara the trouble of beating her brains out.

She swung her feet up to the line and tried to slow herself down. It was partially successful, but the boat's bow was still approaching at an alarming rate. There was nothing for it but to throw away the Persuader and hug the rope like a long-lost friend. She hoped that Danny's fancy hiking gear was tougher than it looked.

By the time she reached deck level, there was a strong smell of burning plastic and her thighs felt like they belonged to an Orkney fried chicken. With as much aplomb as she could manage, Gemma swung her leg over the gunwale like a pirate boarding a stricken ship. By now, the boat was almost level. In her current state, even that was enough to throw her off balance and send her tumbling onto the sloping deck.

She lay there, staring up at Cara, standing on the jetty. Clearly, the bitch had a bit of a dilemma. She could scramble down the rope and beat the crap out of Gemma. However, the boat would still be tied up to the quay. Surely, the Orkney's finest were on their way by now. She also couldn't wait for the tide to bring the boat up to her. Finally, Cara unhitched the line and climbed down the steps with it in one hand.

Gemma staggered to her feet and prepared to repel boarders. At some point, Cara would either have to let go of the rope or the ladder. Instead, she accomplished both at once. Landing heavily on the wheelhouse roof, she slithered down into the cockpit. From here, she could gain control of the boat and leave Gemma as a helpless stowaway.

Gemma had to get to Cara before she could start the engine. She clambered around the wheelhouse and charged, fists flying and boots flailing. At least one blow hit home. Cara grunted and staggered backwards against the outboard motor. Then, before Gemma could apply the coup de grâce, Cara pulled out her knife.

Cara didn't look like an experienced knife fighter, but Gemma was taking no chances. She was ready to dive over the side, even though swimming in hiking boots in shallow, muddy water would be a bit of a challenge. She grabbed a buoyancy aid from off the back of the driver's seat and waved it in front of her as a makeshift shield.

'That will not help you. Doug's going to cut you and gut you and use you as shark bait.'

'You're completely barking. You realise that? I'll take my chances with the sharks, thank you very much.'

With that, she stepped up on the gunwale. Before she could jump, her foot slipped on the smooth steel rail and she tumbled back into the cockpit. Cara knelt on her stomach, pinning her to the floor. Gemma grabbed her wrist and held on for dear life as the knife came down.

Cara was surprisingly strong, but Gemma could bench-press her own bodyweight. She forced the knife well away from her body and used her free hand to ease herself out from under.

That was fine, but unless she could get on top of her crazed opponent, she would never get the knife off her. On the other hand, Gemma's grip was too strong for Cara to free her knife hand. It was stalemate. All they could do was wrestle until one of them tired or made a mistake.

She heard a clattering of running feet on the jetty above. Help was at hand. With a cry of 'Geronimo!', William landed on top of them, knocking Cara face down onto the deck. Heather scrambled on board and swung her precious binoculars at Cara's head. She stopped. Cara was not fighting back. A dark red pool was oozing out from underneath her torso. The rescuers stepped back, leaving bloody footprints on the rusting deck. Gemma got to her knees and looked around for the knife.

Cara was twitching feebly, making a revolting gurgling noise. Gemma stooped and rolled her over into the recovery position. It was a waste of time. This patient would not recover. There was a bowie knife stuck in her throat and an awful lot of blood on the deck. She stopped moving. For the sake of formalities, Gemma checked there was no pulse, then laid Danny's rope-burned jacket over her face.

Heather was consoling William, who was vomiting over the side.

'Oh, God! I killed her. I didn't mean to. I'm sorry. Oh, God!'

Gemma could hear the wail of sirens coming up the gravel track from the terminal. On the horizon, she could make out the polis launch cutting a swathe through the surf at the entrance to Calf Sound. The cavalry and the marines. They were a bit late, but at least they could clean up this mess.

The first car stopped at the jetty. Out jumped the big loon of a sergeant, closely followed by Danny and some other plain-clothes eejit. It was nice of them to run to her rescue, but she would fish them out of the sea if they didn't stop running soon. In any case, she didn't need rescuing. What she needed now was a hot bath, a bottle of scotch, and a generous helping of Ellen's home cooking.

Chapter
Sixty-Two

ALTHOUGH DI GRAY HAD witnessed most of the events leading up to Cara's death, for the sake of procedure, he insisted on interviewing Gemma, Heather, and William under caution at the police station in Kirkwall.

William blubbed his way through most of his interview. He blamed himself for Cara's death and suggested they lock him up immediately. DI Gray briefly considered that option, if only to shut him up.

Heather gave a rambling account of the incident, focussing more on the ecology of the intertidal mudflats than on actual events. She also blamed herself, local authority cutbacks, gender inequality, and climate change in that order.

Gemma offered a more robust defence of their actions.

'Did you see psycho Cara come at me with the big knife? About to stab me, she was. She's no one to blame but herself. Wee William should be suing her for post-traumatic stress, so he should. As for Heather, she wouldn't hurt a fly. I mean, seriously, she's probably a fellow of the Fly Conservation Trust or some such.'

'But you were waiting for her at the jetty,' countered Gray. 'And you were armed.'

'Armed? I had a wee crowbar, that's all. In case there was someone trapped in the boat, maybe. Luckily, we were there, I'm telling you. That lass would have got away scot-free if it weren't for us. Where were you boys? That's what I want to know. Out for a smoke break? Or stuffing your faces with doughnuts?'

'If you hadn't intervened, Cara Douglas would still be alive.'

'Aye, maybe. And I am sorry it ended that way. Truly. But I was just trying to smash up her wee boat, that's all. She jumped me, not the other way around. I had to defend myself. Unarmed and single-handed, I'll have you know. A pair of jessies like you couldn't have held her off, and that's a fact.'

All three of them were allowed to go. DI Gray told them not to leave Orkney for the time being.

On the way out, they passed Ruth Kerr, being led into the interview room they'd just vacated. Gemma asked for an opportunity to "interview" Ruth on her own, promising to go easy on the woman and to leave no visible marks. Sergeant Campbell appeared open to the idea, but Gray overruled him.

***

Once returned to Ellen's cottage, Gemma got another grilling from her comrades in arms.

'I knew you were bull-pooing me about being a birder,' Heather said. 'I just knew it. Why didn't you tell us you were trying to catch a murderer?'

'We trusted you,' William said. 'Why wouldn't you confide in us?'

'I'm undercover, see? It's not lying when you're undercover. It's essential concealment of facts. I didn't want to put you guys in danger.'

William nearly choked on his tea.

'Keeping us out of danger? Do I look like someone who gets into many knife fights? We were perfectly safe until you came along.'

'Nah, you just thought you were. Suppose it had been you that stumbled upon the cannabis farm. We'd have been fishing you out of the dead crude tanks instead of Ross.'

'What a horrible thought,' Ellen said. 'More tea, anyone? How about a slice of gingerbread loaf?'

It would take a while for them to come around, thought Gemma. Hopefully not too long. She had to leave soon for her next mobilisation to the Cuillin Alpha. It would be nice to come back sometime and be greeted as a friend. She would not bring any fecking binoculars next time. Heather could tell her all about the damn birds while she sat around eating cake and swigging tea.

Danny spent somewhat longer talking to the police when Gray and Campbell returned to Mallach. They hired a room at the memorial hall for a few days, displacing a disgruntled yoga group, a flower arranging class, and the Scottish country dancers.

Barman Stewart reluctantly allowed the off-island officers to order drinks at Wheelie's Bar. In return, DI Gray turned a blind eye to any infringements of the licencing laws and even bought a round for the whole bar. This did far more to improve the image of the police than any publicity campaign. Once they finished examining the various scenes of crime, they called Danny in for an informal interview.

'You're not under caution, you understand,' Gray said. 'But we expect full disclosure of your investigation.'

'The truth and nothing but the truth, eh?'

Danny saw no reason not to cooperate. The investigation was over. He'd even been paid. Twice. The loss adjusters had included a generous bonus. The cheque that Mr MacLeod gave him, on behalf of the Mallach community, was less substantial, but much appreciated all the same. He considered refusing it, but his current financial position was too insecure, and he still had Gemma to pay. He compromised by donating half of it to the memorial hall roof fund.

He was less confident about Orcadia Oil paying his contractor's invoice. Iain Grant had been less than impressed to find out his replacement medic was also an undercover investigator. He'd wanted to send him home early, but the terminal couldn't operate for any length of time without an on-site medic. Gordon Breck refused point-blank to cut short his holiday.

Grant threatened to dock his pay instead, claiming he'd been carrying out his investigations in work's time. This was undoubtedly true, but as Danny pointed out, he wasn't the only employee not to be completely focused on their day job. There was Lorna and Kevan's romantic rendezvous, not to mention Cara's cannabis production. He hoped that the oil company would find it too difficult to work out how much money to hold back and just pay up.

In light of his contribution to the hall and DI Gray's generosity at the bar, Danny found he was now allowed to buy a drink and even sit inside and drink it.

'Oh well, you'll be leaving soon and I doubt you'll be back,' Stewart said. 'We get outsiders here from time to time, but they never return.'

'You ought to use that as a slogan for the tourist board website,' Danny suggested.

Word had got out that Ruth Kerr had been arrested and charged with two counts of murder.

'Not my idea,' DI Gray said. 'She'll get manslaughter with diminished responsibility for the husband and conspiracy to murder for the MacLeod lad. That's only my opinion, of course, and the prosecutor never listens to the likes of me.'

He implied he might give them an update later after his evening meal. Ellen had offered to cook up something for the police team and he was eager not to miss out on the Orkney patties.

Word got around and the bar was packed by the time he returned. Heather and William appeared to be back on speaking terms with Gemma. They joined Danny at his corner table. Ellen was cosying up to PC Angus Flett under the dartboard. Rumour had it that Flett's marriage was in difficulties.

'Jesus Christ!' Gray said as he walked into the bar. 'This is not a bastard press conference, you know. If there are any bastard journalists in here, you can feck off right now.'

Nobody moved. Journalists weren't required. The bush telegraph would do the job much better. By the end of the evening, everyone on the island would know what he'd said with a few embellishments and just a hint of conjecture.

'Right then. Ruth Kerr has been arrested, as you well know. Though how you know beats me, since I haven't even told my commanding officer yet. We've also arrested three of her charming nephews for drug offences and assaulting a police officer. That was me, by the way, so they're not getting off with a caution, I assure you.'

Gray took another sip of his pint and glanced around as if considering how much he was prepared to tell this crowd.

'I expect most of you guessed that Ruth Kerr killed her husband. She confessed to chopping him up and feeding his body to the pigs. He was a nasty bastard. I've seen photos of her scars. No jury's going to call that murder. Once we told her Cara Douglas was dead, she tried to claim the drugs and the killing of Ross MacLeod were all down to her. That might be true, but that's for a jury to decide. She's been confessing to other stuff we didn't even know about. Just a word to the wise. If any of you have been buying herbal remedies off the Kerrs, I suggest you dispose of them sharpish. That's all I'm saying.'

Several regulars downed their drinks and slunk out of the door. Those who remained began firing questions at him, which he waved away with his non-drinking hand.

'All right. Give it a rest. I've no idea what will happen to the farm and what's left of the warehouse. If the liquidators are called in, they might go at a knockdown price, if that's what you're wondering. But if you're hoping to blag a free electricity supply, forget it. That lassie from the revenue just arrived, and she means business. I wouldn't try anything with her around if I were you.'

Danny pricked up his ears. So Marissa was back? Gemma glanced over at him, so he took a gulp of beer and feigned disinterest.

'We've released Ross MacLeod's body to his family. Funeral's on Tuesday, I'm told.'

Danny's spell as the terminal's medic was coming to an end in a couple of days. He considered staying on for the funeral, but not having even met the lad, thought better of it. He'd better leave those who knew him to mourn in peace.

Chapter
Sixty-Three

DANNY WAS ENJOYING THE novelty of being able to purchase guilt-free alcohol. It was like being eighteen again. He offered to buy another round, but even Gemma seemed reluctant to stay long.

'I'm due back on the Alpha, have to get back home tomorrow. I've my packing to do and I'm down to my last pair of knickers.'

'Got any plans for tonight?'

'Not really. I'm gonna finish this wee glass and then have an early night, I reckon.'

'Sorry, we have to be going too,' Heather said. 'Rona will wonder where I've got to. And William promised to help Ellen with her Wi-Fi.'

William mumbled something about hoping to see them again soon and followed Heather out of Wheelie's Bar. Danny was disappointed and ordered a solitary pint. His phone rang. It was Marissa.

'Hello, Danny darling. How are you? I hear you've been awfully busy. Congratulations on cracking the case. We ought to celebrate. Open a bottle of bubbly. It's on me. Shall we say eight at the Grand? I doubt there's anywhere else in Kirkwall that has a decent Bollinger.'

When he could get a word in edgeways, he agreed to head over on the next ferry. Spending his last night in Orkney listening to Marissa talk about herself wasn't that appealing, but it didn't look like he would get any better offers.

'I might be able to set you up with a few contacts. Friends in high places in the oil business. The Far East, the States, Nigeria, you name it. You scratch my back and who knows what I might do. I'll let you use your imagination. See ya later.'

'Sounds like you've got a date,' Gemma said, who was unashamedly earwigging his conversation.

'Business meeting. Marissa says she can get me some work abroad.'

'Oh, aye? And what does she want in return? You'd be safer staying on Mallach with me, even if it is the murder capital of Orkney just now.'

'I thought you were having an early night.'

'I only said that so as not to upset wee William. He's got a bit of a crush on me, see.'

'Well, I can always cancel the date. I mean the meeting. Marissa would understand.'

'Nah, dinna fesh yersel'. You've your career to think of. Amongst other things. And don't forget the safe word, mind. She's the sort that might not untie you otherwise.'

Gemma got up to go and gave him a friendly punch on the arm. The bruising would probably go down in a few days.

'Anyway, I reckon I owe wee William one. He did try to save my life, even if it nearly killed me. Don't worry, I'll break him in gently.'

Danny didn't think she was serious, but you never knew with Gemma. He tried to thank her for everything she'd done, but she was having none of it.

'Aye well, it's no good blowing smoke up my arse, Danny-boy. You do realise that if it wasn't for your polis pals, we would never have been in this mess. I mean, what's wrong with growing a bit of skunk? It's no worse than smoking cigs. The only bother is when yer organised crime gets involved. It's about time our eejit government exercised a wee bit of common sense for once.'

'Which one?' asked Danny. 'Westminster or Edinburgh?'

'All the same to me. Bunch of wankers, every last one of them. This whole sorry business would never have happened if cannabis was legal.'

'I've a feeling Cara would still have been up to something dodgy.'

'Well aye, but no one would have died. You'd rock up here and find Ruthie handling stolen goods. Your pal Marissa would catch Cara thieving power from the terminal. You'd hand them over to the polis and they'd end up sharing a cell in Cornton Vale nick. That's it. End of story.'

'Not exactly a bestseller.'

'I read a few bestsellers, but I'd hate to be in one,' Gemma said, polishing off the remains of Heather's discarded gin and tonic. 'I'd rather be in one of them old classics where nothing ever happens. I like it when you get to the end and nobody died.'

'I'll drink to that.' Danny raised his glass. Gemma had already turned away. He leaned back in his chair and watched as she walked out of the bar without a backward glance.

Acknowledgements

I'd like to thank my wife, Chris, the Blackwater girl, for her support, her medical knowledge, and for lending me her name.

Havant Writers have provided me with years of help and encouragement. Special thanks and to my beta-speed-reader, Lesley Talbot. Dunford Novelists, marshalled by Della Galton, encouraged, critiqued, and honed the first chapters. Thanks to Loree Westron and Portsmouth Author Collective for help with marketing and sales and to Caroline Cole for her professional expertise and assistance.

Finally, I'd like to thank you, the reader, for making it all worthwhile. Extra thanks if you've left a nice review on Amazon, Goodreads, etc. It makes a huge difference. And if you haven't done it yet — go on. You know you want to...

About the Author

Chris Blackwater is a writer and chartered engineer from Leeds, England. His first novel *Emergency Drill*, set on a North Sea oil platform, was shortlisted for the 2020 CWA Debut Dagger Award when it first came out. His short stories have appeared in a variety of magazines and anthologies, including contributions to the much-missed *Mad Scientist Journal*.

Chris began writing to entertain himself whilst working on offshore oil platforms and remote power stations. His career has taken him all over the world to unusual locations and introduced him to some remarkable characters.

In recent years, Chris has gradually drifted down to the south coast of England, where he spends his spare time learning to sail and play the flute, though not at the same time.

Connect with Chris Blackwater on social media:
Website: chrisblackwater.co.uk
Facebook: @ChrisBlackwaterAuthor
Twitter: @BlackwaterChris
Instagram: @BlackwaterAuthor

Printed in Great Britain
by Amazon